## "YOU MEAN MOS[...]

"Moscow's not the only government in what used to be the Soviet Union," Kurtzman stated.

"The Russian Mafia?" Brognola looked puzzled. "But we haven't run into any Russians in this so far."

"Yes, we have. The Budapest hit. That was a huge shipment of heroin by anyone's standards. And as we all know, the Russian Mafia has the Afghan franchise locked up. But we knocked over the processed product. That means it was processed somewhere east of Hungary, i.e., Romania. Then to cap it off, the Iron Guard troops brought it to Hungary to hand off to their Russian buddies, and we run into those scumbags in Bucharest. The Russian Mob is doing something at that cultural site, and I can tell you for sure it's not archaeology."

Brognola could be a hard sell, but he bought it. "How soon can Striker recon up there?"

"The guys are ready to move out now. You'd better square it with the Man, because it's not going to be a walk in the park to get to that place. Then there's the virus...."

DON PENDLETON'S

# STONY

AMERICA'S ULTRA-COVERT INTELLIGENCE AGENCY

# MAN®

## OUTBREAK

## A GOLD EAGLE BOOK FROM
# W🌐RLDWIDE®

TORONTO • NEW YORK • LONDON
AMSTERDAM • PARIS • SYDNEY • HAMBURG
STOCKHOLM • ATHENS • TOKYO • MILAN
MADRID • WARSAW • BUDAPEST • AUCKLAND

First edition December 2003

ISBN 0-373-61952-9

OUTBREAK

Special thanks and acknowledgment to
Michael Kasner for his contribution to this work.

**Printed in U.S.A.**

# OUTBREAK

# CHAPTER ONE

*Outside Paris, France*

One didn't have to get too far outside the greater Paris area before the urban bustle was left behind and returned to the picturesque small-town France of the forties and fifties. The little suburb of Le Baran was just beyond the end of the longest suburban métro line, but from the antique, subdued feel of the place, it could have been miles, and decades, away from the City of Light.

Beyond the garages and small shops servicing the locals, the only sign of a real commercial enterprise in the village was a single-story cut-stone building in the center of town. The sign on the front of the building read Doumer Laboratory. The sign was modest in keeping with the nature of the building, and the neighborhood itself, as if not to draw too much attention to itself.

As an old family business dating back to the twenties, the facility didn't need to be audacious.

Everyone in town knew that the building housed a medical lab. As far as what went on inside the walls, the townspeople knew only that it was something scientific and the French had revered science since the days of Napoleon.

As in most of small-town Europe, the lights in Le Baran went out early. Only the streetlights on the main streets showed that anyone was alive in the town past ten. That and a single lighted window in the Doumer Lab building.

A black Mercedes sedan pulled into the cone of darkness between two lamp posts a block down from the lab. Leaving the engine running, the driver took a pair of powerful night-vision glasses from the seat beside him and studied the building. As expected, the only light showing was from the window in what was the lab's night crew's break room.

The driver picked up a handheld radio. "You are go for insertion," he said in French.

"Acknowledged," a voice with a heavy accent answered.

A Renault van driving with its parking lights on pulled into the darkened alley beside the lab and stopped at a side door. The security light over the door was out, but it burned out often and the bulb was rarely replaced.

Six black-clad figures, weapons slung over their backs, exited the vehicle. Two of the men guarded the front and back of the alley while the other four quickly went through the door. A seventh man stayed behind the wheel.

The Mercedes driver didn't have to have an open mike to tell him what was happening inside the lab. Nor could he hear anything, but he didn't need to. His instructions to the men from the van had been specific, and they had practiced the operation until they had it down perfectly. There could be no mishaps this night.

AFTER SLIPPING THROUGH the side door into the building, the gunmen split up into pairs. They had memorized the layout of the rooms, and each team had its own route to take. The lead team stopped at the break room first, their crepe-soled boots silent on the floor tiles. The only occupant in the room, a man wearing a white lab coat, looked puzzled when he saw the black-clad intruders. Before he could say anything, though, a burst of silenced slugs from a 9 mm Beretta Model 12 subgun tore into him.

The gunmen turned and made for their next stop on their tour, the records room. It was empty, but they got a bonus on their next destination, the microscope room. Two men and a woman sat at their benches, going through a series of microscope slides and making notes. So intent were they on their work, they didn't even look up. But that saved them seeing their deaths.

From there, the pair headed to the containment room in the basement of the lab to meet up with the team that had cleared the other half of the ground floor. The second pair had already taken care of the staff in the basement, three more bullet-ridden bodies littering the floor, so phase one was complete.

One of the gunmen stepped up to the biosecurity door of the containment room and punched in the code for the electronic lock. When the door swung open, he saw the two metal boxes they had come for where he had been told that they would be. They were still closed by their complicated security locking systems, and the digital panel on each box showed that the contents were as they should be.

"They are here," he said into his radio.

With two men on a box, the gunmen carried them back up the stairs to the ground floor and headed for the side door.

SEVERAL MINUTES LATER, the Mercedes driver saw the men who had entered the lab exit the side door carrying the two metal boxes. As soon as the boxes were secured inside their van, two of the gunmen pulled a body wearing a white lab coat from the truck and carried it inside the lab. Two more picked up twenty-liter cans of diesel fuel and took them inside as well.

After another short interval, the four men returned to the dark alley, closing and locking the side door behind them before getting back into their van.

"We are clear," the Mercedes driver heard the accented voice on his radio announce in French.

*"Très bien,"* the driver replied.

The van pulled out of the alley and turned its parking lights back on as it drove toward Paris.

The Mercedes driver continued to watch the lab building until he saw the flicker of flames through the darkened windows. As soon as the fire burst through the first window, he, too, left his parking spot and drove off at a normal speed. The characteristic warble of European sirens could be heard in the distance.

THE NEXT MORNING, the fire investigators were just beginning their search of the smoldering ruins of the lab when a small fleet of black Citroën four-door sedans pulled up in front. The driver of the lead vehicle quickly got out and opened the rear door. The man who stepped out had that unmistakable polished, well-tailored look of high-level French bureaucracy. Le Baran was in the sticks, but it was close enough to the capital for the man to be instantly recognized for what he was.

The head fire investigator walked up to him and automatically saluted. "I'm Inspector Roen," he said.

The bureaucrat nodded to return the salute and glanced over at the building. "Your men did a good job of containing the fire, Inspector Roen. Thank you. And—" he paused "—you are dismissed now. My people will take over the investigation from here."

"But, sir!"

The bureaucrat pulled out his ID folder, flipped it open and let the fireman glance at it.

"Yes, sir," the fireman said.

As soon as the locals had cleared the area, the bureaucrat ordered the local police to throw a cordon around the lab and the eight-man team from Bureau Two, the French version of the CIA, went to work inside.

Though it had operated under the cover of being a civilian facility, the Doumer Laboratory had been under contract to the French government for clandestine research. Had it not been for that contract, the company would have long since gone bankrupt. Ten minutes after the cleanup team entered the building, a man came out and drew the bureaucrat aside to whisper in his ear.

"Damn!" the bureaucrat swore as he turned to return to his car to use the phone.

An hour later, two trucks full of troops and forensic investigators drove up.

THOUGH THE FRENCH had supposedly been America's ally since the days of the Revolutionary War, the relationship hadn't always been cordial. Sometimes it had been downright nasty on the French side. The alliance further degenerated after WWII when the French ended up a third-rate power at best. The subsequent losses of Indochina and Algeria only fed the raging postwar French envy of the new superpower on the block, the U.S.

Not all Frenchmen, however, loathed the United States. There were still those few who hadn't fallen prey to the nostalgic mythology of inherent French superiority in all things. Henri Colbert was one such Frenchman. As an astute student of world history, he knew full well that France's time of glory had passed and she would never again be a major player on the world scene. At best, La Belle France could only hope to be a favored little brother to the powers that were. But to do that, they had to start acting the part.

Colbert had become a CIA source. Since he worked in Bureau Two, the French intelligence agency, he was a source that CIA station chiefs usually could only dream of, particularly since he worked in classified records and his job was to log in classified reports before routing them to their destinations. This could have been an endlessly mind-numbing job had it not been for the information he gleaned from reading them as they went through his hands.

It was, though, a very dangerous pastime to be engaged in. The French mounted so many intelligence operations against their neighbors and the United States that they were very professionally paranoid.

Knowing that the counterintelligence section of Bureau Two ran routine, random checks on their own people just like the KGB had done with theirs, it wasn't easy for Colbert to pass any intel he had gleaned on to his CIA handler. He had to use a difficult dead drop delivery system as if he were operating inside an enemy nation, which in a way he was.

When the report on the investigation of the fire at the Doumer Lab crossed Colbert's desk, he realized it was the most explosive document he'd seen in the past ten years. It had the highest possible classification and had an "eyes only" reading list of only four names. Only in the deeply entrenched, archaic bureaucracy of the French government would such a document have been transmitted through his office. It should have been hand couriered to each of the names on the reading list. He made his copy and quickly routed this potential bomb on to its first destination.

On his way to the métro station that evening after work, Colbert stopped at a corner to light a cigarette. Taking a drag of the strong tobacco, he brushed off his hand against the green, cast-iron lamp post he was standing by and left a yellow grease pencil mark on it at waist height before walking on. Later that evening, a CIA Paris station walker would check the lamp post and know that he would be leaving a dead drop that night. The angle of the mark said that it would be at drop site three.

That drop was in a little park a block from Colbert's apartment, and he would load it when he walked his dog after dinner. This item was so hot, he couldn't risk having it in his possession any longer than absolutely necessarily. He used site three only for items like this, so he knew the catcher would retrieve it well before morning.

Walking one's dog in the evening was a common Parisian pastime, so no one paid any attention to Colbert as he strolled through the small park. The drop itself was a hollowed out block on the side of a sculpture of a long-dead mayor of the city. It was simple, but effective. Standing by it while his dog relieved itself, he loaded the drop before cleaning up after his animal.

Once back in his apartment, Colbert poured himself a Campari aperatif and read a little of the latest spy thriller before going to bed.

ONE OF BUREAU TWO'S better counterintelligence efforts were the people they had planted in the CIA's Paris station's staff over the years. Most of them were in menial positions, but one French-born U.S. citizen, Roger Laval, was an actual CIA officer and a member of the Threat Committee. Since French was his first language, he also reviewed the take from the Company's few native French agents. When Henri Colbert's report crossed his desk, Laval damned near blew a fuse. Knowing of the lab's connections and the fire that had destroyed it, he immediately left his office. At the corner tobacco shop, he quickly contacted his own handler in Bureau Two and alerted him to the spy in their own classified reports office.

Being French, the Bureau reacted to this information in its usual manner. Colbert was snatched out of his office as soon as he arrived the next day. Two days later, the lifeless body of the Frenchman who had wanted to make a difference in the relations of his two favorite countries took a late-night dive into the dank waters of the Seine.

Colbert's dreams of French accommodation with the world's sole superpower floated down the river with his body.

# CHAPTER TWO

*Stony Man Farm, Virginia*

The Shenandoah Valley of Virginia was a many storied place. Once its fertile fields had been churned to bloody mud by the boots of clashing armies and its forests splintered by artillery shell fire. It had been at peace long enough now that almost all the scars of that great conflict had faded. Eroded white marble cemetery markers and the odd statue in a village square flanked by antique cannon were about all that remained of its bellicose past. That and spectral visions of marching troops that many reported seeing on moonless nights.

The Shenandoah was now a peaceful, rural area much loved by Yankee tourists drawn to the lush scenery and picturesque environs. Thoughts of war were far from the valley, except at one little farm nestled on the flank of Stony Man Mountain.

Named after the mountain looming over it, this little farm looked as peaceful as its neighbors. It also looked to be prosperous, more so than many of the farms around it, and it had a sizeable labor force. Visits to the farm were discouraged. But, that was ill advised. The farm hands were polite, but firm, when unexpected visitors came to call. No one visited the farm uninvited.

The fifty-acre patch to the north of the farm had been planted in fast-growing poplar trees for the rapidly expanding Southern wood pulp industry, and they were growing well. In anticipation of their reaching harvesting size in another year, a wood pulp mill had been built in the middle of the plantation. Again, this wasn't out of place in a rural South that was forging ahead to meet the economic realities of the twenty-first century.

It was the clandestine operations center hidden deep under the pulp mill that would have seemed a little odd had the neighbors known about it. Known as the Annex, this was the heart of the Sensitive Operations Group that was the reason for Stony Man Farm's existence.

IN THE COMPUTER ROOM under the pulp mill, Aaron Kurtzman looked as out of place in his wheelchair as a grizzly bear teetering on a bar stool. The bullet that had severed his spine had stuck low enough that it had only cost him his legs. He'd been a big man when he'd been hit, but now his upper body would have made a Turkish wrestler nervous. That, and a temperament that didn't brook being messed with, had given him his nickname of The Bear. This day though, the bear in Kurtzman was napping. It was a slow day at work in the Annex.

After rolling his chair across the room to retrieve the day's intel take, on the way back to his work station, he stopped at the much abused coffee maker that was as much a characteristic accessory as was his chair. The metamorphosis that had occurred after his shooting seemed to have converted his metabolism to burn caffeine instead of what the rest of humanity lived on. If you wanted to shut The Bear down, you cut off his coffee. If, of course, you wanted to be charitable and call it coffee.

The rest of the Stony Man Annex crew had other names for it, some of them even utterable, but *coffee* wasn't one of them. Sheep dip was one of the kindest. *Carbon remover, gun cleaner* and simply *battery acid* were a few others.

Once topped off, he rolled back to go through his pile of paperwork. Even though Kurtzman could keep track of streaming data on five computer screens at the same time, he still liked the feel of hard copy in his hands. The biweekly download from Langley could get lengthy, but it made for good reading. Most of it, though, was trivia. A self-proclaimed Ruwandan colonel had come face-to-face with a land mine. The Tamil Tigers had destroyed five percent of Sri Lanka's tea crop, but the government troops had knocked over a major cache of Red Chinese weapons. A sandstorm in Kurgastan had knocked out most of the nation's power grid.

Kurtzman's trivia tolerance level was rapidly approaching meltdown when he came across the report on the lab incident passed on to Paris station by Henri Colbert. Since the source was who he was, his report had been judged A-1 without outside confirmation. That the French had been screwing around trying to make a smallpox bio-war agent was news, but it wasn't unexpected. The bastards were always trying to pull something like that. That their unauthorized sample had gone missing, though, was the real shocker.

When Kurtzman finished the report, he ran it through the scanner to add to the bio-war threat file and noted that it followed a recent disclosure that the Soviets had also worked on mutated smallpox as a war agent. A third recent report stated that the world's smallpox vaccines were few, old and failing, particularly in the United States, leaving millions vulnerable to viral terrorism.

Stony Man Farm was the American government's premier counterterrorist arm, albeit extralegal, and protecting the nation was more than a full-time job. That didn't mean, though, that every threat, no matter how well authenticated, was acted on. For Stony Man to stay off the radar both in Washington as well as foreign capitals, they had to pick and choose their missions carefully. Most often, they were sent into action on orders from the Oval Office. Having the Man cranked up about something was a good way to get it taken care of. Other times, though, the targets were developed within the Farm. And that's why Kurtzman's file system existed and bioweapons were a hot-button item with him.

Bioterrorism was an easy, invisible way to kill large numbers of people, and the Farm had taken care of a number of bioweapons threats, usually of the anthrax and Ebola variety. They were always difficult missions, but fortunately, they didn't come up often. The threat, though, was always present and the file grew almost every week.

Dropping the hard copy in the Out pile on the floor beside his desk, Kurtzman went back to his cyber project for the week, trying to figure out what the North Koreans were building at the port of Inchon. Calling up the real-time feed from one an NRO satellite parked in the area, he nudged it a little to give him a better look. Once he was on target, he had the satellite fire a laser pulse. When it bounced back up to the satellite's sensors, they would tell him the density and composition of the concrete structure he'd been keeping an eye on.

He'd had no idea that concrete could be such fascinating stuff, but he was quickly becoming an expert on it. If this sample turned out to be extra dense, he'd have a better idea of what they were doing there.

THE EX-SERBIAN PROVINCE of Kosovo had gained its independence in all but name. Under the watchful protection of U.S. and UN forces, the Kosovar Albanians were more or less the guardians of their own destinies. It would be some time before the international legalities caught up with the realities, but at least for now they were free. Free, that was, to starve or freeze to death.

The predations of Slobodan Milosevic's Serbian forces had ravaged the small Muslim region with an even greater savagery than they had unleashed on Bosnia. This time, though, the UN had tried to help, but the minute the U.S.-led bombing campaign of 1999 started, the Serbs kicked their ethnic cleansing program into overdrive. What they couldn't kill, and that included farm animals as well as the farmers and their families, they burned. Wells were poisoned, fields contaminated, farm machinery destroyed and anything of value looted.

In the thirty days it had taken the bombing campaign to force the Serbs to pull their forces out of the region, Kosovo had gone from a medieval existence all the way back to the Stone Age.

With the Serbs back in their cages, the UN, NATO and the EU had all moved in relief agencies to try to salvage something from the ruins. The World Health Organization had been one of the first UN organizations to arrive in the ravaged region. Though the Kosovars had no food and nowhere to live, the greatest danger to the survivors was the outbreaks of disease inevitable in such circumstances. Modern medicine and UN food supplies took the immediate edge off the crisis, but it would be a long time before the Kosovars would be self supporting again.

Though it had been several years since Kosovo had been freed of Serbian domination, it was far from being back to what passed for normal in that part of the world. It was true that their tormentor, Slobodan Milosevic, had been ousted as dictator of Serbia and was on his way to a lifelong vacation in a prison cell for war crimes. While that was heartening for the Kosovars, it wasn't a substitute for normalcy. Small steps had been taken to rebuild, but it would be a long time before the people could get their lives back to anything like what they had been before the onslaught.

The WHO was still running clinics throughout Kosovo until such time as the local hospitals could be rebuilt and staffed. Since the country was one of scattered villages, these were usually sited within easy walking distance of two or more communities. Patient care ran the gambit from the mundane to the serious, and many cases were related to the semi-starvation most Kosovars lived with.

One day, the medics at WHO Clinic 34 Bravo saw a small convoy of farm trailers pulled by a wheezing old farm tractor approach. In a land where almost every motor vehicle had been stolen or burned by the Serbs, seeing even a tractor was a rarity. When the motorcade arrived, the medics discovered that the trailers were loaded with sick people and started to help them off.

The younger medics on the team hadn't seen smallpox in action before, but the doctor who led the team recognized it immediately. He had done his early work in Africa and knew it well.

"See the shape of the pustules," Dr. Lauran Dix pointed out as he examined a child. "It's smallpox."

"But that's impossible," a young American female doctor assisting him said emphatically. "Smallpox has been completely eradicated."

Dix glared at her. "Nothing's impossible in infectious medicine, my dear," he snapped. "I don't care what they taught you at UCLA medical school, and I don't care what the UN says. These people have smallpox."

The American reddened, but wisely held her

tongue. Dr. Dix was an old sexist pig, but he knew medicine and he didn't like to be contradicted.

"We have to set up a quarantine ward immediately," Dix ordered. "And anyone who presents with even a single pox goes in there. We'll have to take strict precautions for the staff as well until we can get help here."

The report of smallpox at Clinic 34 Bravo put the WHO in a panic. Vaccines were immediately flown in, but because of their age and the patients' weakened condition, they weren't effective. Several dozen Kosovars, most of the village's population, died and those very few who survived were hospitalized for a long time.

The source of the infection hadn't been identified when another smallpox outbreak occurred in a Muslim village in Bosnia. Again it was difficult to contain the disease, which only increased the concern about its origin.

Smallpox had once been a major killer, but most people in the modern world hardly knew of the disease. Like the Black Death, it had been relegated to the long list of things that had plagued humankind before modern science had eradicated them. In fact, in 1993, the samples of the virus held by the United States and Russia were supposed to be only cultures of the highly infectious disease left in the world. The last outbreak of smallpox had occurred in Somalia in 1977, and the once deadly scourge was officially considered to have been completely eradicated.

That year, though, the UN's World Health Organization made a decision not to destroy these last two samples as had been previously agreed to in 1990. The decision to retain them was reached after heated debate about losing their genetic material to future research. The opponents argued that since the virus had been DNA mapped, the samples should be destroyed to prevent them from being used to create biological weapons. In the end, scientific caution won out and the samples were retained for future study.

Now, the killer had appeared again.

When samples of the virus from both the Kosovo and Bosnia outbreaks were sent to the Centers for Disease Control in Atlanta, their DNA analysis showed them both to be identical, nonstandard strains. Due to the isolation of the two sites, the infection couldn't have been innocently carried from one to the other. A worldwide UN bioterrorist alert went out, just the latest in a long list of such alerts, but no other outbreaks occurred.

THE MAN IN CHARGE of the Stony Man operation liked to fly down from Washington, D.C., at least once a week for a face-to-face with his people. Exercising his oversight of the Special Operations

Group was a good excuse to get away from his desk in Wonderland.

With nothing on the threat board lit up past DEFCON TWO, Brognola convened the briefing in the Annex break room. Open, airy and well lit, it didn't have the crisis atmosphere of the War Room in the farmhouse. Since this wasn't a crisis briefing, more than half the chairs around the table were not occupied.

Barbara Price led off with the usual weekly laundry list of routine matters. She was Stony Man's mission controller and the general of her small armies. When they were in the wait mode, though, she took care of the chores of running a facility as large as the farm. The in-house staff wasn't all that large, but it had to be fed and supplied, which wasn't a small task.

"That all sounds right." Brognola approved her actions as he always did. The more work she took care of, the less there was for him to do.

He turned to Aaron Kurtzman for the intelligence update. Since this was just a weekly briefing, Kurtzman represented the Computer Room crew and let the others waste their time as they wanted to. He had only one thing to bring up of any importance and so far, he was the action guy on it.

"Remember that CIA report from that French source we got about a mysterious fire in a medical lab right outside of Paris?" he asked.

Brognola nodded. "Did we ever get a confirmation on that?"

"Hardly." Kurtzman laughed. "The smallpox samples they were reportedly working with were completely off the record. In fact, their existence was in violation of UN Bio-War treaty, and the French would be in deep shit if they admitted that they'd had them. That's about the only thing the UN's real serious about."

"So it's a dead issue."

"Not quite," Kurtzman replied. "If you'll remember, the French Bureau Two report indicated that the samples were missing from the fire debris. And the staff had all been gunned down. There's no doubt in my mind that the missing virus is in hostile hands, and I think whoever took them used them to attack those two Kosovo villages. Even the CDC says there's simply no way that those were accidental infections."

The UN bioweapon alert had been headline news for a couple of days. But, after so many false alarms on the subject, no one took them too seriously.

Brognola frowned. "Has a positive ID been made linking the French material to the outbreaks?"

Kurtzman shook his head. "Since no one DNA mapped the French virus, we have no hard evidence. But the samples collected in Kosovo and

Bosnia were mutated, rather than being the standard variety of smallpox. If it's not the French material, it's Russian. But we have UN confirmation that the Russians got out of that business right after Gorby took a nosedive.''

"What do you want me to do?"

"Give the President a heads-up on the French thing,'' Kurtzman said, "and get his permission for us to start looking into the Kosovo outbreak.''

"I'll pass it on to him,'' Brognola promised. "But I can tell you that he's focused on North Korea and the Middle East right now. As well as Colombia, Algeria, sub-Saharan Africa and, let me see, any other hellhole on Earth except Kosovo. The Balkan states aren't going to be on his plate any time soon, and he's not anxious to move them up in the batting order. We've not had good results in that region recently.''

"If this was an intentionally mutated virus,'' Kurtzman said, hammering his point home, "and if it was purposefully used on those poor bastards, he'll have to deal with it sooner or later. Hopefully, he'll take the time to look into it before someplace like D.C. gets wasted.''

"Actually, that doesn't sound like a bad idea. Just let me know when it's going down so I can get out of town.''

Brognola glanced down at his watch. "Oops, how time flies. Gotta run.''

Stuffing his papers back into his briefcase, Brognola snapped it shut, got up and left the table.

Kurtzman and Price exchanged glances and stared after him. There had been a time that a report like that would have sent him charging up to D.C. to fight for a mission. Maybe he was slowing down.

# CHAPTER THREE

*Stony Man Farm, Virginia*

"What in the hell's gotten into Hal?" Aaron Kurtzman asked as Barbara Price walked with him back to his work station. "I expected him to at least pay some attention to something like that."

"You know him," she replied. "He's got to have the sharp end of the stick an inch away from his eye before he blinks. I'm sure he'll pass your heads-up on to the Man, but you know how that goes most of the time, too. The president yawns and checks his watch to see when his next photo op is scheduled."

"Jeez!" Kurtzman shook his head. "Who's your guy at CDC? I'll pull my Dr. Kurtzman drill on him again and see what they're coming up with."

She pulled her Palm Pilot out of the holster and tapped in her query. "That's Dr. Jim Davenport at 202-555-2836, extension 384."

"Let me start working the edges of this thing and see what shakes out," Kurtzman said as he slid in front of his keyboard and entered the name and number. "This has the earmarks of being a classic 'jump through your ass' scenario when we finally get the go-ahead."

Trusting to Kurtzman's sense of the inevitable, she nodded. "While you're doing that, I'll go back to redlining Cowboy's latest dream list." John "Cowboy" Kissinger was the Farm's armorer.

"What's he drooling over this time?"

"It's some new kind of super 40 mm round, something called Dragon's Breath."

"Different strokes."

"And when I'm done with his list, I'm going to go over yours, too."

"Wait a minute! You know I only ask you for things we really need."

"Right." She laughed.

"Dammit, we really need that phase shift monitor."

"We'll see."

"Come on, Barbara!"

THE AMERICAN MILITARY presence in Germany was a far cry from what it had been in the glory days of the Cold War when determined G.I.s had stood eyeball to eyeball with the Red Bear, fingers poised on their triggers. No longer did thousands of U.S. mechanized Infantrymen and tankers sit in their EDPs, waiting for the Russians to jump the fence to ring in Armageddon and the end of civilization. Peace with the Russians had broken out, and the old ways had faded quickly.

There was still a fairly large American military commitment in Europe, but it was more in the supporting services and command and control arena linked with NATO and UN peacekeeping operations. There were still two U.S. combat divisions in Germany, but the battles being planned for, and fought, were in places like Bosnia and Kosovo rather than the Fulda Gap. Although there was no creditable enemy on the horizon, the primary defense of Germany was in the capable hands of the German army.

One of these American support units, the 63d Maintenance Battalion (Direct Support) stationed in Hanau wanted to celebrate the anniversary of the unit's founding with a formal dining-in. The battalion commander had decided to cater the affair with a local company rather than burden his own mess facilities. This was smart, because his mess hall hadn't scored very high on its most recent health Inspection. It was rapidly improving, thanks to a new mess chief, but wasn't up to supporting a party of that size yet.

As was the military custom with this kind of celebration, the unit's officers ate in one dining room while the NCOs and troops partied in another. That way everyone could enjoy themselves without the officers keeping a critical eye on the men and the men not witnessing the officers getting just as drunk and as stupid as they did.

The first of a long line of sick soldiers started reporting to sick call at the battalion's dispensary by the end of the day after the celebration. Most of them presented with flulike symptoms, but a couple of the troops were showing the pustules characteristic of smallpox. They were immediately medevaced by chopper to the army hospital at Frankfort where their illness was immediately diagnosed.

That first medevac flight was quickly followed by many others as the dispensary started filling up. Choppers were flown in from other units to handle the overflow, and a triage station was set up in the quarantined battalion. When the last medevac had cleared the chopper pad, eighty-five percent of the officers and men of the 63rd had been admitted to the hospital. Only the fact that most of the troops had their vaccinations up-to-date prevented a major loss of life. As it was, some forty men and women died of the worst outbreak of smallpox in American troops since the end of WWII.

THERE WAS NO DOUBT in anyone's mind that the smallpox outbreak in Germany hadn't been an accident. Following as it did on the two incidents in the Balkans, it had to have been a bioterrorist attack. The initial investigators on the scene were U.S. Army medical personnel and they quickly traced the virus to the small local company that had catered the celebration. When a U.S. military medical team went to inspect the company, they were gunned down.

Gunfire in a European town wasn't a usual event, and it drew an immediate response. And, the Germans being who they were, responded professionally with heavy firepower of their own. When the German SWAT team arrived in their armored cars, however, they found the catering company's offices abandoned and cleaned out down to the walls.

Even the skeptics now realized what they were facing.

As ALWAYS, BARBARA PRICE was waiting when Hal Brognola stepped out of his black helicopter on the Stony Man helipad. She didn't have to be a mind reader to know that he was carrying marching orders for the Stony Man action teams again. Reading the squint of his eyes, the set of his jaw and even the condition of his clothing was as good as reading his mind. She'd given warning orders to both Phoenix Force and the Able Team, so they would be ready to launch as soon as she got back in contact with them.

She hadn't been able to get in contact with Mack Bolan yet, but she expected to hear back from him before long as well. The Executioner wasn't an official part of the Stony Man operation, but things always seemed to run smoother when he was in the field with his old comrades.

She updated Brognola as they walked to the house.

THE WAR ROOM in the farmhouse had been activated for this mission briefing, and the operational Farm staff was on hand. David McCarter and Carl Lyons, though, were off-site in mission prep with their teams and would be briefed later when they checked into the Farm.

"Aaron," Brognola started out, "the President wanted me to tell you that he appreciated the heads-up you had me pass on. Unfortunately, it couldn't be acted on before the incident in Germany. Anyway, the Man has asked us to get involved in this as soon as possible."

"Better late than never," Kurtzman muttered.

"As you can imagine," Brognola said, "this is being taken very seriously. Damn near every agency in Europe and the United States is onboard. Task forces are being organized, position papers are being prepared, lists are being drawn up, press conferences are being held, blame is being assessed and impassioned speeches are being made with all the usual trappings of an international dog-and-pony show.''

He smiled grimly. ''In short, if anything is going to be done about this anytime soon, we're going to have to be the ones to do it.''

''What's new?'' Kurtzman asked softly.

''Simply put,'' Brognola said, ''our mission is to find the people responsible for this and recover or destroy the virus as well as them.''

''No sweat,'' Kurtzman said. ''We'll just give everyone an electron scanning microscope and tell them to use it on everything they see. Or don't see as the case might be. You can never tell with one of those pesky viruses'.''

Brognola let Kurtzman's jab pass without commenting.

''You'll have full cover and the authority to call upon the full resources of the government this time. Nothing will be spared to keep you from doing whatever is necessary to complete this mission.''

''So—'' he looked up from his briefing paper ''—what are your thoughts on how we can deal with this?''

Even with as little as they had to go on at that point, a bare bones plan had been hammered out. ''Simply put,'' Kurtzman began, ''this is an almost impossible task we're being asking to do. Since there's no way to detect a virus except under a microscope, we're going to have to determine who's behind this and then ferret out where they're growing the virus. With no hard targets to go against yet and not even a clue as to who's doing this, you're going to have to tell the President not to hold his breath on this one."

There were no shortage of groups who would eagerly use a bioterror weapon if they could get their hands on one. Every whacked-out group of malcontents knew that a few cc's of a mutated virus could devastate a major city, and they'd be more than glad to do it in the name of whatever they were revolting against.

"With the push being put on this, I'm sure that everyone else will be looking at the usual suspects. But that approach is only going to be good for daily status reports, not results. If we're going to do our thing, it's going to take time because we're going to have to do it the right way."

"And that is…?" Brognola queried.

"The problem with the threat of bioweapons is that while acres of rain forests have been sacrificed to writing about them, they simply can't be whipped up in the kitchen sink. Culturing a virus, even a standard strain, takes skills well beyond the reach of most of those who have an inbred, cultural urge to kill those they did not agree with. Applied science isn't high on the list of skill sets needed to join a terrorist group. The trick is going to be finding the right group and find them quickly."

Brognola could only agree with that. "And when do you see that happening?"

"Not as quickly as you'd like," Kurtzman admitted. "We have damn near nothing to work with at this point. But my recommendation is that we get started anyway. Able Team should go to Paris, set up a mobile command post and start working the lab-fire angle. I think it might be key."

Brognola nodded.

"Phoenix Force can go straight to Germany and see what they can come up with there."

"Where do I fit into this plan?" Mack Bolan asked as he walked into the War Room.

"Glad you could make it, Striker." Brognola smiled.

The Executioner took a seat at the table and turned to Kurtzman. "Did I hear you say Paris?"

"Want to go along?"

"Sure."

*Paris, France*

AN OLD ACQUAINTANCE of Bolan's gave him their real lead by revealing that the French authorities were convinced that the lab arson had been done by a Serbian gang. No mention was made of the missing smallpox samples, but that was to be expected. Bolan knew his informant wouldn't have had any knowledge of what had really been taking place in the small town.

To have Serb criminals involved came as no surprise to him, either. Europe in the twenty-first century was awash with gangsters like America had been in the early decades of the twentieth. Since dictatorships were little more than criminal gangs operating on a national scale, the fall of the Soviet's "Evil Empire" had been like opening the doors of the largest prison in Europe and flushing out the inmates. The first wave of post-Cold War criminals to inundate Western Europe in the waning days of the twentieth century had been Russians.

The Russian *mafiya* had quickly established itself to the detriment of the local gangs. One advantage the Russians had over the homegrown Mobs was that they were heavily armed and not unwilling to use their firepower to settle disputes. Once the Russian mobsters were doing quite well for themselves, they were joined by enough petty criminals from other ex-Soviet republics to have created a small army. Until a couple of years ago, the Russian Mob had dominated this new European underground as they had dominated the old Soviet Union. That dominance, though, was now being challenged by a new group of players.

The long war in the former Yugoslavia had flooded Europe with new waves of refugees over the past decade. Recently, though, the ethnicity had changed from primarily Bosnians and Croats to Serbs. The NATO action against Serbia had severely damaged what was left of its economy and, since that also cut into crime profits, many of Serbia's gangsters had moved their business to Europe. The Russian Mob had earned a reputation for brutality in its dealings, but even the *mafiya* had to back away from the Serbians. The training of ten years of ethnic cleansing against the Bosnians and Croats had given them an attitude no one wanted to mess with.

Killing a dozen French lab workers, stealing a deadly virus and setting a fire to cover their tracks would have been nothing to them.

EVEN IN PARIS, one day's inactivity had started wearing on Carl Lyons, and he approached Bolan when he returned from one of his neighborhood recon walks.

"How 'bout you and I go out there and rattle a few cages, Mack?" Lyons said. "We're going to have to get started on it sooner or later, so why not now?"

Bolan looked up from the map he had been studying, "Thought you'd never ask. What'd you have in mind?"

"The Serbs were supposed to be tied into this," Lyons replied. "Let's see what's on the targeting list for Serb operations. It doesn't have to be a major event, just a probe."

"Let's do it."

# CHAPTER FOUR

*Paris, France*

"Let's check to see what my contact listed in truck stops," Bolan said. White slavery and forced prostitution were Serb specialties, and they ran many of their bordellos out of truck stops. Mobsters usually liked to primp, wave their guns and flex their muscles in front of women and what better place to find a subservient audience than in a whorehouse?

"There's one at Beauchemire." Bolan flipped through a sheaf of papers. "That's a few miles out of Paris and it might be worth looking into. The French think it's some kind of combination Mob R and R center and hospitality suite."

"Do they service trucks and drivers as well?"

"It says they do."

Lyons picked up the map from the table. "What's the name of that place again?"

"Beauchemire."

Lyons found it. "I was thinking of a quick in, quick out type of deal," he said. "Rosario goes in as a trucker needing to get his ashes hauled. If he can develop good targets once he's inside, you and I'll do a sweep and clean the place out. We may not develop anything from it, but it'll put them off balance."

"Works for me."

Lyons turned to Rosario Blancanales, who'd joined them. "How'd you like to be a Spanish truck driver? Stop off for gas and a lube job on your way north."

"Sure." Blancanales grinned.

"Can I be his relief driver?" Gadgets Schwarz asked.

"We'll need you to monitor his gear while he's surveilling that place," Bolan said.

"I'll handle it solo, Gadgets, no sweat," Blancanales said.

"I wasn't worried about that." Schwarz grinned. "Euro truck stops have become quite popular lately. Don't you guys watch cable?"

Bolan shook his head.

"How about doing it tonight?" Lyons asked.

"Saddle up," Bolan told him.

THE SUN HAD BARELY gone down over rural France north of Paris, but the Stony Man commandos saw the lights from the Beauchemire truck stop a full two klicks before they reached it. Neon signs were certainly not unknown in Europe, but this gaudy display looked completely out of place on the edge of a small village.

"Jeez," Gadgets Schwarz said. "That looks like it was transplanted directly from Vegas."

"If the French had the bad taste to build a Disneyland here," Carl Lyons said, "can Reno and Vegas look-alikes be far behind? They've got the Mobs to finance it now and it fits with their mentality."

"It's gaudy, but it looks like it's working," Bolan noted. "There's a lot of trucks parked there."

"Speaking of trucks," Rosario Blancanales cut in on the com link. "I'm coming up on kilometer stone 114, so I'm right behind you."

"Keep it coming, good buddy," Schwarz replied, slipping into his Burt Reynolds Bandit imitation. "We got your back door."

THE TRUCK STOP'S parking lot looked like a United Nations truck drivers' convention was going on inside. It was crammed with rigs ranging from semis to vans from every corner of Europe and even a few from the Middle East. Blancanales's two-ton Mercedes was emblazoned with the logo of a Spanish furniture company from Madrid so it would fit right in. Finding a open spot on the edge of the lot, he parked, locked up and stepped out.

"I'm on the ground," he said.

"Got you Lima Charlie," Schwarz sent back. "Show me the parking lot."

Blancanales did a slow turn from left to right as if he were panning a camera, which he was. Two of them in fact. One was in the frame of the flat lens glasses he was wearing and the other in the embroidered company logo on the breast of his driving suit. "How's that?"

"Got good coverage," Schwarz sent back. "Just make sure to look straight into the faces of the people you meet. We need the mug shots."

"Been there, done that."

Blancanales's first stop was at the Euro-style, fast-food cafeteria right inside the main entrance. Going through the stainless-steel serving line, he grabbed a plate of blood sausage, hard cheese and olives and added a small loaf of bread and a bottle of beer to his dinner. Standard fare for a Spanish truck driver.

Finding a table alone, he ate his meal, finished his beer and headed for the minicasino next door. Being free of the odd cultural attitudes about "sins" that bedeviled so many otherwise sane Americans, Europeans were free to drink and gamble as they wished. They were also free to pay to have sex, but that was in a different section of the truck stop. Before Blancanales went there, though, he had to stop off and drop a few Euros in the casino to maintain his cover. He wasn't unaware of the Vegas-style surveillance cameras silently keeping track of the customers.

The casino wasn't jammed, but it was busy. Most of the players were plainly truckers like himself. While road weary, they were relaxing at cards, roulette and the slots. Grabbing a beer from a wandering waitress, he sat in front of a slot machine and started dropping Euro coins in the one-armed bandit.

Since the casino was only a come-on for the bordello, the slots were set to pay off fairly regularly, and he soon had a small pile of Euros in the tray in front of him. When the machine hit big, Blancanales let out a war whoop and started stuffing the coins into his pocket. With his loot secured, he grabbed another beer, overtipped the waitress, nodded at the goon standing guard by the cashier's cage as he cashed out and headed for the cathouse on the second floor.

Another goon by the stairwell eyed him severely as he started up the stairs to the "club," as did another surveillance camera. Whoever was running this place was making sure that their customers behaved themselves.

Even though the truck stop was in France, the bordello was run with almost German efficiency. There was an entry room where he paid a sizable cover charge before being let through the security door to the waiting room. It was plush, dimly lit and well supervised: no fewer than four goons were in residence here and they couldn't be missed. They weren't showing iron, but there was no doubt that they were packing, the posture was there.

Blancanales went straight to the bar for the one drink owed him for his cover charge and picked up a half-liter bottle of red wine and a glass. Finding a seat, he poured himself a glass of wine and checked out the circulating bodies for hire.

The girls in attendance had several things in common: they all were young, they all had the high cheekbones of Slavic beauties and they were all a little drugged out. Not stoned enough to be sloppy, but they had that glazed look to their eyes. He caught them speaking several different languages, and they all spoke French with an accent. There didn't seem to be a native French speaker in the room and that went with the house being stocked by white slavers.

He had time for only a solitary sip of his wine before a pair of beauties descended on him. One was a rangy blonde and the other a stockier redhead. Both of them, however, were fine, as Hawkins would have put it, very fine. They seemed comfortable in their "business suits," which made for good viewing. The blonde had on a filmy negligee and the redhead, a black bra and thong set. Both were wearing spike heels.

"*Hola,*" he said in Spanish, patting the couch beside him.

"I'm sorry," the blonde said in accented French. "I do not know your language."

Since neither of the girls spoke Spanish, after stumbling around in broken French, they settled on conducting their business in English. He made sure, though, to put a heavy Hispanic accent on his.

WHILE BLANCANALES was getting acquainted with his new friends, Bolan and Lyons reconned the grounds around the back of the building.

"What do you have out there?" Schwarz's voice came in over Bolan's com link.

"The second story doesn't have any windows," Bolan reported. "And there's only one access to that level, a stairway on the north end. Beyond the main entrance, the ground level has a door leading to the cafeteria from the back and another one into the casino."

"Doesn't sound like they're in compliance with OSHA fire code for a business establishment."

"I don't think they have OSHA in Serbia."

"Oh, yeah, I forgot."

"How's Pol doing?" Lyons asked.

"Quite nicely, actually." Schwarz was monitoring his teammate in a parked van. "He's got a couple of real cuties cornered in there. Or they have him, it's kinda hard to tell with those mini-cams. Anyway, there are four hardguys on the second floor so far, and that's just in the waiting room."

"What did he see on the ground floor?" Bolan asked.

"There's another two or three in the casino and one by the stairs. There's also surveillance cameras all over the place."

"Cute."

SINCE BLANCANALES'S girls were on the clock, it didn't take them long to separate him from the waiting room couch and start the long walk back to their bed of paradise. The hallway leading out of the waiting room had a series of numbered doors on either side marking the cribs. Blancanales noted, though, that the length of the hall didn't account for the length of that wing of the building.

"What's down there?" he asked, pointing.

"A private club," the blonde said. "We cannot go."

"I got it," Schwarz said in his ear. "That's the part we want to look at."

"I got that covered," Lyons sent back. "The outside stairs leads right up to it."

"Let's do a diversion in the parking lot," Bolan

suggested. "To clear the place out a little. I don't want to inflict any collateral damage."

"Good idea," Schwarz replied. "What do you want?"

"I'm thinking a minicharge in a gas tank or two. That should get the drivers' attention. No one wants to see his ride explode."

"You need any help out there?"

"That's a negative. Plant the charges and then watch Carl's six when he goes up the stairs. That looks like the danger point."

"If I pick up a souvenir in there," Schwarz asked, "can I keep it?"

"Only if it's a gun."

"Bummer."

RETURNING TO THE VAN, it took Bolan only a minute or two to review the tapes Schwarz had made of Blancanales's movements through the truck stop. The miniature cameras gave a distorted view, but the images were good enough to clearly show what he was up against. It also allowed him to spot the surveillance cameras watching the place.

"Gadgets?" he sent over the com link. "You ready?"

"Gotcha covered, two on the stove."

"I'm on the way now," Bolan replied. "Pop one."

A second later a semi and trailer in the middle

of the lot experienced a small explosion in its fuel tank. An instant later, a larger explosion sounded as its fuel went off. When the first couple of alarmed drivers appeared, Schwarz triggered the charge in the second truck to show them that it wasn't an accident.

Bolan held his silenced Beretta 93-R close to his thigh as he quickly walked toward the truck stop.

The explosions had cleared out the cafeteria and most of the gamblers. The drivers were running into one another in the race to save their trucks. It had also drawn two of the thugs to the entrance to see what was going on. They had given up all pretense at innocence and had their iron openly in their hands, Czech-made Skorpion machine pistols.

One of the hardmen spotted Bolan right off the bat because he was the only guy heading into the truck stop instead of racing for his rig. As he swung his Skorpion around, Bolan came up with the Beretta and triggered a single silenced shot to the thug's head.

The second gunner was slow bringing his piece into play and took a shot in the head, as well.

"Two down," Bolan said into his mike. "Heading in now."

"We're in place at the top of the stairs," Lyons whispered.

Stepping over the bodies, Bolan moved into the casino. Finding it empty, he quickly crossed the floor to the stairwell leading up to the cathouse. The thug stationed there was speaking into a radio when he came into Bolan's view. Rather than create a panic by giving the goon a chance to start a firefight, the soldier loosed another head shot.

"That's three."

The surveillance camera's light wasn't on, but Bolan look the time to shut it off permanently before bounding up the stairs.

The gatekeeper in the entry was watching the chaos of the parking lot on his monitor and turned away only to catch a 9 mm slug in the head.

"Four down," Bolan sent. "And I'm right outside the waiting room, Ironman."

"Roger, I'm going in now."

BLANCANALES HAD BEEN monitoring the com link chatter between the commandos while the two girls did a striptease to warm him up. Hearing that Lyons was about to make his entrance in the back was his cue. Reaching behind his back, he came up with a Glock pistol.

The girls stopped dead in their tracks when they saw the piece, but he put his finger to his lips. "Stay here," he said in English, "and you won't get hurt."

Going to the door, he opened it a crack and peered down the hall. Other than a girl dragging a drunken truck driver into her room, it was empty.

He didn't expect it would stay that way very long, though. Not with Striker coming in from one side and the Ironman from the other.

He waited behind the door for the action to get under way.

# CHAPTER FIVE

*Beauchemire, France*

Gadgets Schwarz was standing by when Carl Lyons put the muzzle of his semi-auto 12-gauge to the door lock and triggered it. It wasn't a very subtle entry technique, but it was effective.

The door flew open to reveal a small kitchen with two hardmen who had been sitting at the table desperately trying to bring their weapons into play. Lyons gave them both a blast to the chest before they could succeed.

Schwarz stepped past his teammate, his MP-5 subgun ready. Someone on the other side of the door leading into the rest of the wing drilled a long burst of fire through the door, sending splinters flying.

Schwarz answered with a burst of his own and was rewarded by hearing a heavy thud in the hallway.

Lyons paused just long enough to stuff three

fresh 12-gauge double aught rounds in his magazine before seeing what else was on the other side of the door.

THE ABLE TEAM leader's unique doorbell was Bolan's cue to get back to work. This time, he chose his Desert Eagle as his tool of choice. The 93-R was fine for general overall work, but the big .44 was best for specialized jobs like this that called for a one-round kill.

Opening the door to the waiting room, he stepped in. Two of the four thugs Blancanales had spotted were gone, probably reinforcing against Lyons's attack. The other two were looking down the hall rather than watching their backs. Most of the girls were cowering for cover behind the overstuffed furniture, but one stood by the Serbs and also looked down the hallway.

Since only one of the gunmen had his iron in his hand, Bolan targeted him first.

The sound of his shot was almost lost in the barrage of gunfire that erupted from the end of the hallway. Over the sharp clatter of 9 mm rounds, Bolan could hear the authoritative blasts of Lyons's shotgun and knew who was getting the worst of it in there.

The second Serb gunman spun when his buddy's head exploded and grabbed the girl standing beside him. Holding her as a shield, a Makarov pistol jammed against the side of her head, he shouted something Bolan didn't understand.

Bolan didn't waste time trying to figure out what the thug was trying to say. Swinging around his Desert Eagle in one smooth move, he got a sight lock and stroked the trigger. The .44 round took the gunman above the right eye and blew out the back of his head. The Makarov fell from his nerveless fingers as he slumped to the floor.

Striding over to the hysterical girl, he extended a hand to help her back to her feet.

"Go now," he said. "I won't hurt you."

The girl kissed his hand before fleeing.

"I'm clear out here," he sent over the com link.

"I've got the office secured," Lyons sent back. "Come on back."

Bolan counted half a dozen bodies in the office suite and party room at the end of the hall. Schwarz had out his Polaroid camera and was taking the mug shots while Lyons ripped open the drawers of the huge wood desk to rifle through the contents. Bolan was disappointed that there was no computer, but went to what looked like a shelf of account books and started there. Twelve minutes later the team was back in the van and heading back to Paris.

PARIS'S MORNING PAPERS led with the story of the gang slayings at the Beauchemire truck stop. The attack was characterized as having been gang related because it had been such a professional job. The explosive diversion in the parking lot was reported as well as the looting of the paperwork and surveillance camera tapes from the office. The fact that the casino hadn't been robbed, though, was taken as further evidence of it being a turf war hit. The National Police were rounding up the usual suspects, but so far, no leads had been reported.

The second front page story was about the two dozen white slave prostitutes who had been freed in the truck-stop attack. The editorial writers screamed that the EU needed to increase its efforts to halt this vile flesh trade. The girls had been taken into custody for safekeeping until they could be returned to their native countries. But several of them from EU member nations were protesting being sent back and demanded to be allowed to remain in Europe as free workers. The EU Immigration and Labor Commissions both promised to look into their cases.

"It would help if this stuff was in a language we could read," Lyons growled as the Stony Man warriors went over the paperwork they'd taken in the raid.

"I faxed most of it to the Farm," Schwarz said, "and Aaron's running it through the translation program."

"The tapes are plain enough," Bolan said as he

fast forwarded through a stack of tapes. "They liked to film their parties."

Blancanales glanced over to see that Bolan had freeze-framed on the smiling faces of two men lashing a pair of young women. "Didn't you get those two?" he asked.

"I did," Bolan replied.

By nightfall that day, the word on the French truck-stop hit had spread throughout Europe. Mobsters of all nationalities tightened security at their establishments and wondered what in the hell was going on. They'd had no clue that a war was in the offing.

NOW THAT THE OPENING round had been successfully concluded, Aaron Kurtzman had the time to work his cyberspace magic on the photos of the dead mobsters from the truck-stop brothel. When nothing came up, he contacted a cyber-acquaintance at Interpol. A computer made the transfer of the information both easy and instantaneous. His contact, a French police official named Maurice Favre, got back to him in a little over an hour.

"Aaron, I really have to meet your photographer some day. He takes pictures of very interesting people."

"How interesting, Maurice?"

"Well—" the Frenchman sounded almost gleeful "—I ran them through our ID comparison program and one of them, your file number 01-394, turns out to be a well-documented Russian Mafia crime figure Gregor Gregoravitch. He has a high-level KGB background and once was second in command of their infamous terrorist training school.''

''That is interesting.''

''Do you mind if I mark his file closed?''

''I'd rather you kept that on hold for a while. It's an operational necessity thing.''

''I understand,'' he said.

''How about the others?'' Kurtzman pressed.

''There's only one other notable, number 01-399, a Josip Gornic. He's ex-Serbian Secret Police and he's wanted for war crimes committed in Bosnia. A rather nasty piece of work, that one.''

''You'll send me the files on them, right?''

''Of course, Aaron. We in the intel field must stick together. And when I come calling looking for a favor...''

Kurtzman snorted. ''Maurice, I know how to keep my friends happy.''

''Good luck.'' Favre broke the connection.

With these two solid connections to proven bad actors, Kurtzman knew they were on the right track. It wasn't a confirmation that Serb mobsters had made the lab hit, but it was getting them closer to it. Finding a Russian mobster involved with them wasn't too surprising. He'd have been more surprised if someone like Gregoravitch hadn't been connected with it. His background, though, was a concern. So was having a wanted Serb war criminal as a sidekick. That put this as a yet unidentified Serbian gang outside of "normal" for Euro mobsters and more in the terrorist category. But, using bioweapons was a terrorist activity.

THE DAY AFTER Bolan and the Able Team had made their opening play, Phoenix Force arrived in Oberhausen, Germany, to start its investigation of the smallpox attack on the U.S. base. As Brognola had promised, along with the U.S. military and German investigators, everyone from the UN Commission for the Protection of Endangered Microscopic Life to the European Food Service Workers Union were stumbling over one another in the name of solving this crime against humanity. In short, except for twice daily press conferences and photo ops, very little was being done to actually discover who had been responsible for the attack.

With that cast of characters in play, it was easy enough for the Phoenix Force commandos to blend right into the background. They weren't, though, holding press conferences or mugging for the cameras.

T. J. Hawkins and Calvin James teamed up as an American news team, Gary Manning and David

McCarter used a British based WHO cover and Rafael Encizo went solo for their initial probe.

Taking a tip from the Able Team's successful truck-stop raid in France, Encizo decided to try his luck with the area's service industry. His first stop on the outskirts of Oberhausen turned out to be a small, but well-equipped, establishment. Girls, high-stakes gambling and whatever you liked to snort, smoke or shoot was available at reasonable prices. So was dropping off your laundry, getting a tank of gas, a kilo of sausage or a bottle.

For a neighborhood Mob establishment, though, there were older women and kids hanging around. Except for some of the merchandise, it looked more like an honest family business rather than a Mob operation. But he decided to try his luck anyway.

Pulling in his Fiat rental car for a tank of gas, Encizo played a Spanish laborer new to Northern Europe looking for work. Along with the gas, he bought a lid of grass, turned down the offer of a romp with a teenaged hooker and got a job tip. Not bad for an hour's work.

WHEN THE TEAM reassembled at the end of the day, Encizo was the only one who had much to show for his efforts.

"I think I've got a hot one." He laid out his map to point out the target. "It's one of those mom-and-pop, gas station-minimart joints with their living quarters in the back. But they sell drugs and quickies on the side.''

"What makes you think it's a Serb operation?" McCarter asked.

"The Orthodox icons." Encizo grinned. "There was even one in the men's room."

"That works for me." McCarter checked the location on the map. "You say it's a family operation?"

"I spotted two older women, a handful of little kids, two teenaged hookers and half a dozen adult men and women."

"Okay, then," McCarter said. "Let's try not to whack anyone then unless we have to. I'll play the out-of-town drug boss who's pissed, so a gun butt to the head and plastic restraints should be enough to get what we want. And we'll go black suit rather than full assault kit."

THE SIGN ON THE DOOR of the gas station-minimart read that it closed at nine, so Phoenix Force made its call at five after. Since they were making a soft hit, they didn't go in shooting. In fact, Encizo went to the door alone and knocked hoping he'd be recognized and let in. After banging for a while, the teenaged girl who had propositioned him that afternoon answered.

"You come back for me?" She winked as she spoke through the closed door.

"Yes." He smiled. "I found work today and want to spend my money."

The girl laughed as she unlocked the door. "Come..."

The instant the door opened a crack, Encizo ripped it all the way open, pulling the girl off her feet with it. He had her in a lock hold with his hand over her mouth before she could scream.

"Be quiet," he said as he pulled his silenced Beretta 92 from behind his back.

The girl's eyes went wide, but she didn't struggle.

Manning, McCarter and James were through the door in an instant. Manning watched the entrance back to the family living quarters while McCarter slapped a piece of tape over the girl's mouth and cuffed her hands behind her back with plastic restraints.

"We're in," he whispered over the com link to Hawkins who was watching the rear of the building.

"I'm clear back here," Hawkins replied.

"Watch the door, because we're going for the living quarters."

It was child's play to take down the rest of the building. One of the men put up a bit of a fight, but was hammered to the floor with a gun butt.

The rest were so surprised to see black-clad men with guns that they did the smart thing—they surrendered.

Surprisingly enough, none of the men had weapons on them or within easy reach. Nonetheless, the commandos cuffed all of them and brought them into the largest room of the living quarters.

The oldest man in the group looked like the guy in charge, so McCarter sat him in a chair in the center of the room.

"Your countrymen have made a big mistake," the Briton said. "I deal to the Americans, and killing my customers makes me unhappy. It makes me so unhappy that all I can think to do is to kill Serbs until I feel better. I'm sure you understand."

"But I didn't have anything to do with that," the Serb answered. "I do most of my business with the American soldiers, too."

"Who did this, then?"

"I do not know," the Serb replied, trying to keep up a front.

"Oh, I'm sure you do." McCarter pressed the cold muzzle of his silencer sound suppressor into the Serb's forehead. "And, if I get the names I want so I can talk to them, you can live. If not..." He shrugged expressively.

Even though McCarter could be nothing other than a Brit, the meaning of his shrug wasn't lost on the gangster. In his homeland it was usually the last thing a man saw before he was shot in the head.

"There were some new men around Oberhausen recently," he started out. "They were Serbs, yes. But they were not part of my family or my operation, I swear by the Holy Mother. My people are all from my family, and I don't let outsiders in. It's not good business."

"Who did those other Serbs work for?"

"That I do not know," the man replied. "But," he hastened to add when McCarter tweaked the muzzle against his head, "I know they came from Berlin."

"How do you know that?"

The man shrugged as best he could with a pistol jammed against his head. "They bragged about it. They were from Berlin, a big city, while we were stuck out here like villagers back home. When they came by, they bragged about how much money they were making."

McCarter knew that Berlin had been a major clearing house for the Russian Mafia from the beginning. And he wouldn't be surprised if the Serbs were now big there, too. The two groups often worked together. It wasn't much of a lead, but anything helped at this point in time.

"You're a lucky man." McCarter pulled his pistol back and lowered the hammer. "You get to live."

He glanced around the room. "And so does the rest of your family. But," he cautioned, "if I hear that you are selling drugs again—" he looked over at the two young women with their hands tied behind their backs "—or your young girls, I'll be back and I won't be happy. Find another way for your family to make a living because doing this is only going to get all of you killed."

The Serb had enough decency left to look both ashamed and grateful. "I promise."

"I will hold you to it," McCarter said.

# CHAPTER SIX

*Oberhausen, Germany*

Back in their hotel, David McCarter briefed Kurtzman on the results of the raid in Germany. "He didn't have any reason to lie," the Briton said of the Serb patriarch. "And he was sincere as hell. He knew he was walking on the edge of his grave and, if he fell, he'd take the rest of his family down with him. So, if you don't have anything else for us, I'm thinking of taking off in the morning for Berlin. This town's crawling with official investigators and the guys we're looking for are long gone. Maybe we can shake something loose in Berlin."

"I'll see what I can get from Interpol for you," Kurtzman said. "They might be able to scare up some intel."

"That'll help." McCarter sounded disgusted. "At this point we don't have Sweet Fannie Adams, so anything we can get is more than we have."

WHILE THE ACTION TEAMS were doing what they did so well in Europe, the Stony Man computer crew was sorting through both their terrorist files and the records of virus researchers. To make bioweapons from the missing smallpox samples, the specialized knowledge of a scientist was essential to grow the virus. And, if that scientist could be found, the terrorists would be close by.

Thanks to their Cray mainframes, the search was going quickly, but it wasn't coming up with the answers Aaron Kurtzman wanted. Not finding any known bioweapon researchers who were unaccounted for put him at a virtual standstill.

Rather than just stew in his own juices, he picked up the secure phone and called Bolan in Paris. "Something reeks here," Kurtzman growled. "And it's not a Parisian urinal. For the stuff that went missing from that lab to be of any use to anyone, they have to have someone who can use it to make more viruses. This isn't one of those 'destroy the research project to protect the Earth' crap the Eco-Nazis do over here to research centers. If that'd been the case, they wouldn't have executed the staff."

"How's the search going?" Bolan knew the answer, but he had to ask anyway.

"It's not," Kurtzman replied. "I can't find a single researcher who could culture those samples who's out of pocket. There's a couple of shady characters in the viral research business who'd do it for the right price, that's for damned sure. But they're all under some kind of close supervision, even the Russians. So, I want to go way off the reservation to look for our guy.''

''What do you have in mind?''

''I want to check out that Dr. André Germaine, late of the Doumer Lab,'' Kurtzman said. ''And I need your help to get it going.''

''Why him?'' Bolan asked. ''The French say he's dead and they buried him.''

''They buried someone who had half of his face blown off from a couple of shots to the back of the head before being burned to a crisp. Since he was wearing the good doctor's lab jacket with his metal name tag, they made an assumption.''

Bolan was well aware of the nature of assumptions. ''Don't assume anything'' was one of the cardinal principals of war. ''What do you need?'' he asked.

''I'm going to contact my friend in Interpol to see if he can get me the photos of the bodies, Germaine's in particular. And another shot of him in life. We're dead in the water here until we have something to work with. I'll keep you in the loop.'' Kurtzman signed off.

IN A LITTLE OVER AN HOUR, the full French police report on the lab arson, complete with the mug shots of the casualties came into the Farm over the fax. It confirmed that the right number of bodies had been pulled from the ruins and most of them bore bullet wounds in their torsos. The body that had been identified as Germaine, however, had taken multiple shots to the rear of the head with the exits in the face.

"I knew it," Kurtzman said as he looked at the faxed photo of the shattered visage of the corpse.

"Akira," he roared, "come over here. I need some help."

"What'd ya need, boss?" Akira Tokaido asked, his ever present headphones pushed to the back of his head.

Kurtzman handed over the two photos, one supposedly of Germaine dead, and the second a copy of the doctor's most recent passport photo.

"Run a comparison on these will you?"

"I'll get right on it."

One of Tokaido's better achievements was the program he had cooked up that allowed him to take almost any photo of a person and compare it to any other. What made his system work better then those in use by other agencies was that he was able to make a comparison with less than perfect full-face shots.

In this case, he had two photos that were only a couple of degrees off ninety-degree obliquity. Even with the one face so heavily damaged, it still should be a piece of cake to work them. Slipping his headphones back down over his ears, he clicked on his CD player as he slid the first photo into the scanner.

WHILE TOKAIDO was running the two photos through analysis, Hunt Wethers got deep into André Germaine's background. Fortunately, the doctor had lived pretty much out in the open and he could access his academic and medical history without much digging. It didn't take long to find out that he'd been a well-respected virus researcher before he'd gone to work at the Doumer lab. He had also been very well paid for his clandestine work and, working his bank account, he discovered that he'd had a Serbian mistress.

"She's Marina Stombolic," he told Kurtzman. "Forty-one, late of Belgrade. She was a leading actress in Yugoslavian films, but moved to France when Tito died. She met Germaine when she was in a Paris theater production and he started paying her bills. As of last week, he was still paying them."

"Is she political?" Kurtzman asked.

"Not that we know at this time," Wethers said. "But her father was a minor functionary in the Tito regime. He died a year before his boss. How that played into her decision to bail out when she did, we don't know at this time."

"Try to find out," Kurtzman said. "Serbian women have a habit of doing the behind-the-scenes-number to good effect. And forget all about the traditional, Eastern European weaker sex. Look at Slobodan's wife, she was a real Dragon Lady. Since we still don't have a motive for this, I want to work all the angles."

"We'll get on it."

KURTZMAN CALLED BOLAN to announce that the guy in the French police photographs with the destroyed face couldn't possibly have been Dr. André Germaine.

"I can see how this one slipped past them, Aaron. For starters, they had no reason to suspect that the body wasn't Germaine's. Plus, since his work was being done well under the table, Bureau Two wanted to conclude the investigation as quickly as possible so nothing would leak about what the good doctor was really up to. Having that CIA source pass the initial report to Paris Station would have spooked them."

"That could be," Kurtzman conceded. "But they still dropped the ball big time. God knows where the bastard is by now."

"We can start trying to trace him easily enough," Bolan said. "We'll start by taking a drive to the country and take a look at the doctor's house."

"You don't really expect to find him there do you?"

"No, but we can take a look at what he might have left behind."

DR. GERMAINE'S country house was one of those places you knew you'd seen before in a movie staring Grace Kelly and Cary Grant or Sean Connery. It had that unmistakable French country estate look that was more its setting than its architecture. The stone building with the slate roof could have been found several places in Northern Europe, but the pastoral setting could only have been French. The only thing the place lacked to be a movie set was an old guy in a battered beret peddling an ancient bicycle past the hedge in front.

"Nice place," Gadgets Schwarz commented as he pulled off the road at an observation point overlooking the valley.

"No lights, no smoke from the chimney, no one moving around inside," Carl Lyons stated as he lowered his field glasses.

"Well, he *is* supposed to be dead," Schwarz pointed out. "And according to Aaron, he has no family to take over and his will's still in probate."

"We won't have to knock, then." Lyons grinned.

"We will, though," Blancanales cautioned. "Have to keep an eye out for his neighbors. Country people can be as nosy as hell, so I'll do all the talking.''

"I don't *parler* worth a damn anyway.''

"I'll tell them that you're all British EU observers.''

"Right.''

Not only did they not have to knock, the door to Germaine's house wasn't locked. "It's been a long time since I've seen an open door like that,'' Lyons observed.

At first glance, the house looked as if the presumed late Dr. Germaine had just stepped out for a glass of wine at the local bistro. Or he had gone to work not expecting to be shot six times in the back of the head. But since he hadn't been shot, it was worth a closer look, one of Lyons's many specialties.

"Most of what should be here is,'' Lyons stated at the conclusion of his inspection. "But enough's missing that this isn't the house of a man who was suddenly killed. He might have fooled the French cops, but not me. He traveled light, though, as if he expected to have a house waiting for him at the end of his trip. Now let's take a look at his girlfriend's place.''

ONCE BACK IN PARIS, Lyons and Blancanales slipped past the concierge and entered Marina Stombolic's apartment building. On the off chance that Germaine was holed up there, Schwarz broke off to go around the back to cover the building's exit.

A plastic credit card bypassed the apartment's door lock. The kitchen looked untouched, but all of the dishes were clean and in their proper places. A glance into the refrigerator showed that it was clean, and empty. Very little food was stocked in the cupboards. The living room was neat and tidy. Even the magazines were piled neatly. The bathroom, though, as would be expected in a woman's apartment, told the tale Lyons was looking for.

The tub, sink and toilet were clean and the linens neatly folded. Opening the medicine cabinet, though, showed serious gaps on the otherwise well ordered shelves. This woman was obsessive about neatness, but she had failed to rearrange her medicine cabinet when she pulled out a few necessities to take with her.

A look in the lingerie drawers confirmed Lyons suspicions when he saw what was missing. "She's booked," he stated. "She just left the place cleaned up so the old woman downstairs wouldn't talk about her behind her back."

Back in their car, Lyons put in a quick call to the Farm. "The woman's gone, too," he told Kurtzman. "She took more of her personal belongings with her, but not enough to look like the apartment had been cleaned out. Since this confirms your photo analysis, see if your Interpol contact can put out an alert on the woman. If we can find her, I think we'll find him, too.''

''Works for me.''

''That means, though, that we're done here,'' Lyons said. ''I think we'll join Phoenix Force in Berlin and work their lead together.''

''I'll tell Barbara.''

HAL BROGNOLA HAD his mission-induced, harassed face on when he came storming out of the annex elevator into the Computer Room. Aaron Kurtzman, Barbara Price and Hunt Wethers were waiting at the break table for him.

''Needless to say,'' he started out, ''the President is anxious to see some progress on this. But so far no one has come up with anything useful, so I'm hoping you have some good news I can take back.''

''We know that the man who was in charge of that clandestine lab is in the wind,'' Kurtzman said as he handed over the two photographs supposedly of Germaine and Tokaido's analysis for Brognola's perusal.

''Enough of the damaged face was left intact that Akira had no difficulty getting his reference points for comparison on it. But when lined up against the passport photo, it's obvious that someone else's head took those shots.''

"I'd have thought that Bureau Two would have picked up on this themselves," Brognola said as he examined the photos. "All jokes aside, the French're usually not quite this slack."

"They wanted Germaine to be dead because they were in a big fat hurry to cover up the missing smallpox," Kurtzman suggested. "That's big league stuff and they know it."

Brognola shook his head. How many times did a situation become a crisis because someone wanted to cover something up? "Any leads?"

"Nothing yet," Price said as she reported the negative results of the search of Germaine's house. "Phoenix's raid in Oberhausen did come up with a link to the Serb Mob in Berlin, though, and they're on-site to check it out. Carl thinks it's the best thing they have so far, and he's moving to Berlin to link up with David. But we're still in the recon phase because we don't have a name or even a motive. As soon as we get either one, we'll have something hard to work with."

This wasn't what Brognola wanted to take back to the Oval Office, but he knew that realistically this was going to be a long process. If he could just convince the President of that inconvenient fact, his life would be a lot less stressful.

# CHAPTER SEVEN

*Berlin*

It had been years since Berlin had been reunited, but the new capital of post-Cold War Germany was still being built, or rebuilt as the case might be. The building cranes that could be seen from almost any vantage point was called the Berlin Forest in the local media. Though the eastern side of the city needed it the most, most of the construction was taking place in what had been West Berlin.

It was true that the core of the once Communist half of the city around the Brandenburg Gate down along Unter den Linden to Alexander Platz and Museum Island had been spruced up a little. Trendy boutiques, upscale shops, and small exclusive restaurants catered to the ''Wessies'' with money who had followed the seat of government to Berlin. Money followed power, and there was money to be made in the new Berlin.

Most of rest of old East Berlin, though, still

showed the ravages of decades of Communist planning and construction. With a city full of architecture that few Westerners would willingly live in, it had become mostly a city of the elderly, refugees and other foreigners looking to live on the cheap.

Even before the fall of the Berlin Wall, Germany had been a Mecca for refugees. Turks, Algerians, Greeks and other Eastern Europeans had settled in droves in West Germany. Many had come in under the Gast Arbiter, Guest Worker, programs instituted in the sixties and seventies to provide entry level laborers for rapidly expanding German industry. Others had smuggled themselves in and worked without documentation in the small ethnic enclaves.

East Germany had also imported tens of thousands of workers for the same reason. But their ''guests'' had been Vietnamese, North Koreans, Africans and Islamic peoples chosen more for their ''socialist'' leanings as for anything else. The reunification, though, had sent most of the Third World socialists packing to be replaced by the next wave of refugees.

The long drawn-out process of disintegration of what had once been Yugoslavia had flooded all of Europe with hundreds of thousands of Serbs, Croats and Bosnians with a sprinkling of Albanians, Bulgarians and Romanians thrown in for flavor. This greatest mass migration in Europe since the end of WW II meant that the united Berlin hadn't turned out the way the West Germans had expected. Not only were the "Ossies," the ex-Communists, not making the transition to free market capitalism and working for a living, the old East Berlin held the largest collection of Eastern European refugees in Europe.

As was always the case when a metropolitan center was turned into a refugee camp, the various ethnic groups didn't want to "live together" as liberal, democratic mythology expects them to. It was against human nature for a people thrown into a strange setting not to want to be with their own kind, hear their native language, eat familiar food and pretend that they were "at home."

So it was in the refugee communities of Berlin.

KURTZMAN'S INTERPOL contact had been glad to provide him with a copy of their file on Serb Mob operations in Berlin, which was forwarded to McCarter. Included in the data pack was a map showing Serb refugee concentrations in the city. The main Little Serbia was a several square block area in the old East Berlin neighborhood of Friedrichshain. Filled with crumbling, multistory, Stalinist Era apartments built for the socialist workers, these boxey, ugly buildings were considered palaces by their current inhabitants.

For a Serb family to live in one of these "palaces," though, required that they swear allegiance to one or another of a number of "patriotic" organizations that informally oversaw the area. In more plain terms, this was simply a home base for the Serbian Mafia and the gangs drew their manpower from these instant homeboy villages.

"Damn!" Calvin James said as Phoenix made a drive by of their target area, "that looks as bad as public housing in Chicago. Nasty."

"It's the Communist East German version of it," David McCarter replied.

"No wonder the East Germans were pissed," T. J. Hawkins said. "That's like living in Alcatraz after it was abandoned."

"It's a hell of a lot better than what the people living there now left behind," McCarter pointed out. "At least there's no bombs falling on their heads and the police aren't political."

Since Gary Manning wanted to get the surveillance going, he scanned the area for a likely place in the neighborhood to go to work.

"How 'bout setting up across the street?" He pointed to a derelict apartment building. "We should get real good coverage from there."

McCarter nodded. "We should be able to handle any squatters we find there without too much trouble."

"In this town, just flashing a piece should be about all it'll take," Rafael Encizo stated.

"Let's get to flashing then," Hawkins agreed.

WHEN ABLE TEAM ARRIVED in Berlin the next day, Manning had his surveillance station up and running nicely. "Man, do those guys like their cell phones," Manning said to Lyons. "We've been getting everything they say in the clear. The problem is that none of us understand the language. I've been sending it back to the Farm and Aaron has been running it through his programs and sending it back to us in English."

"Anything interesting yet?"

"Not really." Manning handed Lyons a stack of faxes. "We might as well have me listening in on routine Family business in Cleveland or something like that."

"Mob is Mob."

SINCE IT WAS LIKELY to be some time before the surveillance developed anything worth acting on, Bolan decided to go out on the town that night and find his own target. And he didn't expect to have a difficult time finding one.

With a dramatically increasing population, the criminal opportunities in Berlin were boundless. Though the Russian Mafia had much of this trade staked out as its own turf, there were still enough opportunities to keep the Serb Mob bosses in nice apartments, fancy cars and their pick of young playmates. And, as in France, the specialty of the Berlin Serbs, and their biggest moneymaker, was white slavery.

The new nations of Eastern Europe held few opportunities for unattached young women. Jobs in their own countries were still in such short supply that they went to men with families. Dreams of Western luxury seen on TV and a naiveté born from having lived in a closed society made these women easy prey for Mob recruiters. Offers of modeling jobs, au pair situations, hotel staff positions and other traditional women's work in the West had no lack of eager respondents.

The fact that the young women never seemed to make it through the first interview wasn't seen as a problem. Eastern Europe was known for its beautiful women. A preference also seemed to be given to women who did not have much family. And, of course, the recruiters didn't ask for confirmations of birth dates on the job applications. If the girls were old enough to have breasts, they made the cut.

Since white slavery was abhorrent to Bolan he decided he'd start there.

Berlin's sex-for-sale business wasn't as blatant as it was in Amsterdam or Hamburg, but it wasn't hidden either. Except for the Strassen Kommandos, streetwalkers, though, it was discrete. Gentlemen's Clubs weren't hard to find and they were usually very civilized establishments. It was the Mob-run places, though, particularly the Serb establishments, that Bolan wanted to look into.

"Rafe," he asked Encizo, "you feel like taking in a little of the local nightlife?"

"Sure, Striker." Encizo grinned. "I've got a well-developed taste for the lowlife. What'd you have in mind?"

"I thought we'd wander around and see if we can find something useful to do."

"Oh, I'm sure we will."

THE PART OF BERLIN Bolan started out in had none of the trendy gloss of the Ku'damm or Unter den Linden. During the divided city days, Wedding had been a working class area in West Berlin. More and more now, it catered to foreigners with enough money to avoid living in the Stalinist cubicals of the old East Berlin. It was also a popular destination for Wessies looking for cheap and dirty thrills.

Places that offered cheap thrills were the same all over the world. Encizo didn't have to speak the language to know what was going on around them as he and Bolan made their way down the street. The hookers, the junkies and the dealers were the same no matter what language they spoke. So were their needs and the goods they were selling.

He and Bolan were both wearing what would pass for Euro worker's clothing to better blend in with the sidewalk traffic. Their first stop was a bar where Encizo ordered beer in accented English. Even before the waiter could return with their drinks, a pair of hookers sauntered up to their table and tried their luck.

"Sorry," Encizo said in English when one of the girls spoke to him in German. "I no have German."

"Are you lonely?" the girl replied in English.

"No." Encizo shook his head.

"Maybe your handsome friend?"

Encizo turned to Bolan and spoke in Spanish. "She wants to know if you wanna get laid."

Bolan shrugged and replied in English. "No. They're too old."

On his way back to their table the waiter had overheard the conversation and delivered his pitch with the beer. "If you want a younger girl, I know a place."

"Yes, please." Encizo smiled.

The waiter's recommendation turned out to be a bar around the corner. Walking in, Bolan instantly recognized both the decor and clientele. It was a dive and not a particularly clean one at that. The Serbian flag over the bar announced the nationality of the patrons and the macho swagger IDed their profession. Ordering a couple of beers at the bar got them a further recommendation to visit the club upstairs.

After downing their beer, Bolan and Encizo took the stairs to the second floor and knocked on a door bearing a Serbian inscription above a rather well-done painting of a nude blonde. A thug answered their knock and motioned for them to enter. This club wasn't as well decorated as the French truck-stop brothel had been, nor was it as genteel. This was a sexual production line, and the girls showed it. Since this was Berlin, though, the "managers" weren't packing iron. Big-city Germans could get seriously offended when it came to urban gunplay.

The Stony Man warriors hadn't been in the room for sixty seconds before two girls rushed up to them. Both of them looked like they'd been through a month of unending bad days, but they pretended that the two Stony Man warriors were their new best friends.

While Bolan and Encizo were being molested in a friendly manner, one of the resident thugs walked up to two other girls and started yelling at them. Bolan didn't have to speak Serbo-Croatian to know that he wasn't inquiring about their welfare. When the goon delivered a stunning blow to one of the girl's head, he moved in.

The thug turned and snarled something at Bolan before going back to his work. But, when he drew his arm back to hit the girl again, he found his arm in a lock. Before he could react, the Executioner effortlessly broke his arm.

The Serb screamed and fell to the floor writhing in pain.

The other three men in the room went for Bolan, but found Enciso in the way. The largest of the three, an unpleasant-looking man with a shaved head, drew back a meaty fist. The little Cuban stepped into him, grabbed his fist and levered it around into a dislocation hold. A sharp shove completed the job, and the man went down to join his comrade in pain.

The other two hesitated. Had they been armed they would have gone for their weapons, so Bolan and Enciso cornered them. After a rather brief encounter, they too had their right arms out of action with clean breaks.

The bald man on the floor with what should have been a dislocated shoulder arm dug into his pants and came up with a small caliber pistol.

"Rafe!" Bolan called out.

Enciso stepped up and delivered a snap kick to the point of the gunman's jaw. Being in a bit of a rush, he didn't gauge the kick properly and snapped his neck. Oh, well, he'd try to do better next time.

With their masters dead or disabled, the seven girls huddled in tearful confusion. Bolan walked up to them. "Do any of you speak German?" he asked in that language.

"I do," a blonde replied in kind.

"Good. When the police come here, tell them you were being held prisoner by these men. They will give you medical care and send you back to your families."

One of the girls grabbed Encizo in a bear hug. "Thank you, thank you," she sobbed in English.

"It's okay," he said as he unwound her arms from around his neck. "It's okay."

Their fun over for the evening, the two Stony Man warriors took a cab back to their hotel.

WITH TWO DAYS' WORTH of surveillance material to work with, Aaron Kurtzman called to give the Stony Man team report on the intercepts.

"I think you've tapped into some kind of head-quarters for that bunch," he said. "And, they are Serbs. That guy, Radom, you've been listening to seems to be the local kingpin. He's been ordering people around, threatening others and generally having a good time. The only thing of real interest is that he's expecting a 'shipment' in sometime tomorrow morning."

"What kind of goods?" McCarter asked.

"I'm not sure," Kurtzman replied, "but I'd say women or drugs."

"Either one works for me."

"And he ordered it be sent up to his office."

"We think we have that area plotted."

"Good," Kurtzman replied. "Because I haven't

been able to get a layout of the building from the Berlin city's database. It was built before computers, and the Berlin city planners weren't about to waste bytes adding something to their database that they're going to tear down as soon as they can get around to it.''

"No sweat," McCarter said. "David has located the phones we've been monitoring on the top floor, the penthouse as it were, so that has to be their offices. Rosario and Rafe also made a foot recon of ground floor shops and entrances and we can wing it from there.''

"Good luck, Hal's counting on big things from this.''

"I don't know about that, but we'll sure as hell put a little pressure on them.''

MCCARTER, MANNING and Bolan sketched out what they knew of the target so far and called the others in for a briefing.

"Okay," Bolan said as he looked at the sketches, "let's walk through this. We're looking at hitting the fifth floor and we can't depend on the elevators. The problem with taking the stairs is that we don't know who's living on the other floors. If he's got his troops billeted there, we might have a problem with people coming in behind us.''

"We can secure the doors to the stairwell on the way up with assault wedges," McCarter suggested.

"And cut the power to the elevator," Schwarz added. "We should be able to access it from the basement."

"I'll go with David's team once you're inside," Bolan stated. "Ironman, you and your guys are the security team."

Lyons nodded.

"I figure you can get a clean entry, but from there it's going to get dicey."

McCarter yawned. "We can handle it, Striker."

# CHAPTER EIGHT

*Berlin*

Berlin was too well policed for the Stony Man commandos to parade across the street in full combat gear in broad daylight. So, they waited and went for an after-dark assault. Parking their Mercedes sedans on the unlit back street a hundred yards away, they made it to the building's rear stairwell unseen.

Once inside the vestibule, the commandos paused while Gadgets Schwarz and Carl Lyons slipped into the basement to disable the elevator. Being an archaic lift, that was as simple as pulling a fuse.

With that avenue of escape or reinforcement blocked, the team started up the stairs. There had been no surveillance cameras in the vestibule and there were none on the first-floor landing. Schwarz paused long enough to slide an assault wedge under the door, preventing anyone from opening it behind them. The second-floor landing had a dim bulb over the door, which Schwarz unscrewed before wedging that door as well.

Bolan paused on the fourth-floor landing. A light was showing from the landing above, which could mean a guard had been posted. Motioning Lyons over to him, he signaled the two of them going up together. Lyons nodded, and David McCarter signaled that he would back them up.

Drawing his silenced 93-R, Bolan hugged the left side of the stairs with Lyons on the right. Even with the light on, it was so dim the stairwell was in semi-shadow. A goon standing in the light would have trouble spotting men in black combat suits and face paint against those shadows. Five steps from the landing, Bolan clicked his com link and Lyons moved ahead of him, his hands empty.

The guard was startled when this man in black suddenly appeared and grabbed for the AK slung over his shoulder. He had it halfway up to firing position when a luminous red dot appeared over his right ear. That was quickly followed by a 9 mm round drilling into his skull.

Lyons snatched the AK from his dead hands to keep it from clanging off the concrete. "We're clear," he sent over the com link.

When the rest of the assault team joined them on the landing, Lyons stepped up to boot the door. After all these years, it was still his favorite way to warm up for a bullet fest. He had his leg cocked when Schwarz reached past him and tried the door handle. It opened, and the Able Team leader had to catch himself to keep from falling on his face. Bolan passed him and made the entry.

The corridor inside was dimly lit, revealing three apartment doors on each side of the hall and what looked like a larger suite at the end. Music was playing on a couple of different radios, and muffled men's voices could be heard. It sounded like someone was partying.

The door to the second room on the left opened and a man stepped out buttoning his shirt. When he saw Bolan, he looked puzzled. But, before his recognition circuits could kick in, he collected a 9 mm slug in the head and collapsed to the floor with a thud.

With the first kill, the rest of the team quickly joined the Executioner. Deciding to clear each room as they went, Bolan signaled Lyons to take care of it. The first two rooms were empty. The one the man had come out of had two girls still in it, both of them dead drunk or drugged.

Something was going on in the room opposite. Loud voices could be heard through the door, and a radio. Lyons listened at the door and held up five fingers. The commandos took up positions and Bolan nodded.

Rearing back, Lyons booted the door and spun

out of the line of fire. The five men inside the smoke-filled room were drinking and playing cards at a table while a girl was passed out on a couch against one wall.

After a stunned moment's hesitation, instead of doing the smart thing when faced by heavily armed, black-clad commandos the men scattered for their weapons. Only one of them reached his AK, but he got off one burst before he soaked up a 9 mm triburst to the chest. The other Serbs died in a barrage of silenced fire.

With unsilenced shots echoing in the hall, the doors of the last two apartments opened and heads poked out. The guy with the pistol in his hand went down to a short burst of 5.56 mm rounds from Schwarz's silenced M-4. The other guy wisely slammed his door.

That left the door at the end of the hall. The radio that had been playing in there had been turned off.

Rather than risk losing a leg this time, Lyons used his shotgun to take the door down with a double blast to the lock. No sooner had it crashed open than a fusillade of automatic fire erupted from the suite. The characteristic clatter told them the auto-weapons were AKs.

Only the fact that the Communist Germans had built the interior walls of their buildings with concrete kept the Stony Man commandos from eating bullets.

Snatching a flash-bang grenade from his assault harness, McCarter sidearmed it through the open door.

Lyons pulled a frag, jerked out the pin and gave a three count before lobbing the bomb. The grenade detonated before it had time to hit the floor, sending razor-sharp frag flying.

"Damn," Lyons muttered as he pulled his other frag. "These bastards have short fuses."

This time, he held the frag for a two count before tossing it, and heard it hit the floor.

The instant the second grenade detonated, he put the muzzle of his shotgun around the edge of the door and emptied it in blind fire. The roar of the 12-gauge was as effective at keeping the enemies' heads down as the double-aught buck.

Lyons's final shot was the signal for the other commandos to get in on the act. Rather than rushing in through the single door, they lined up along both sides of the door and blasted the room. A couple of gunmen were still in the game, but after the commandos each dumped a magazine on full-auto, all was quiet.

Encizo swapped his empty mag for a full one before going into the room low and sweeping it from side to side on one burst. Manning followed to cover him, but there was no one left for him.

All targets were down.

The office body count was nine and, when added with the cleanup they'd done on their way down the hall, that meant this branch of Berlin's Serb Mob was going to have to reorganize big time before they'd be too much bother to anyone.

ON THEIR SWEEP through the Serb's office suite, the Stony Man warriors had grabbed up every paper in sight. Again, though, there had been no computers. Back at their hotel, they started going through the evening's take to see if anything important popped out.

"There's a couple of interesting things here," Bolan said. "We've got a discussion of how to get into the NATO headquarters in Italy and the headquarters of the U.S. forces in Kosovo."

"Is it an attack plan?" McCarter asked.

"Doesn't seem to be. But, I'll fax it to the Farm and have them run it through translation."

Hawkins didn't read a word of Serbo-Croatian, but the last thing in his pile, a copy of a flyer or poster, caught his eye. It looked a lot like a garage-band flier from the eighties. It was, however, partially in English and apparently was promoting a concert to be held in Prague in a couple of days.

He passed it to Bolan. "How about this?"

"Interesting," the soldier said as he scanned the

poster. "The concert's going to be at an Army R and R Center in Prague."

McCarter took a look as well and shook his head. "I can't believe that the only thing of interest we've found in there is a bloody rock concert poster."

"What in the hell are Serb gangsters doing mixed up with rock bands?" Lyons asked.

"Other than making a bucket of money?" Hawkins said. "How about the audience, American G.I.s out for a good time? A lot of G.I.s packed into one place makes a good target for whoever these guys are."

"That's a stretch," Lyons said. "Too much of one for my tastes."

"What else do we have?" McCarter pointed out.

Lyons shrugged.

"Get packed," Bolan stated. "We're moving out."

HAL BROGNOLA WAS PLEASED with how the Berlin operation had gone down. Once more the Stony Man warriors had brought havoc to another Serb Mob operation and gotten away clean. It was only when Aaron Kurtzman went over the results of the take from the sweep of the office that he was disappointed. Once more, they hadn't found what he most desperately needed.

"What's Striker planning next?" he asked.

Kurtzman handed him a faxed copy of the concert poster. "They're going to a rock concert in Prague."

"A rock concert?" Brognola arched a skeptical brow. "How am I supposed to tell the President that America's most potent covert action team is at a rock concert?"

"Well," Kurtzman said, "you can tell him that they're a real good band. Their first CD went platinum in less than a month."

Tokaido spoke up from across the room. "And you can tell the Man that their lead singer and manager are both Serbs. The backup singers and the band are a mix of Serbs and ex-East Germans."

"And the road crew are Serbs, too," Kurtzman added. "Striker thinks they're up to some kind of no good."

Brognola fumbled with his antacid tabs. "That raid got the biggest headlines in Europe since the days of the Baader-Meinhoff Gang, and I can't believe that all they got out of it is a rock concert."

The big Fed sighed heavily in frustration. "Don't we have anything else to work with?"

"You wanted us to go proactive, instead of just reacting, and this is *pro* instead of *re*," Barbara Price pointed out. "If another attack is in the offing and our guys can shut it down beforehand, they might be able to finally get a firm lead to who's behind this.''

"Okay." Brognola capitulated. "But I'll keep this one quiet unless we get some solid results out of it. I don't think the President's going to want to hear it."

"Don't trust a man who doesn't appreciate good rock and roll," Kurtzman warned.

"If they're that good—" Brognola looked puzzled "—why the hell're they playing in Prague?"

"The audience," Kurtzman pointed out. "It's a major R and R center for NATO and U.S. forces in Bosnia and Kosovo. We pay well to keep our men and women in uniform entertained when they're on leave. There'll be a thousand U.S. and NATO troops cheering them on when they play...."

He turned to Tokaido. "What's that current number one of theirs?"

"'Trash Baby.'" Tokaido grinned. "It's called 'Trash Baby.'"

Brognola shook his head. "Whatever."

WATCHING A ROAD CREW set up the stage for a rock and roll concert wasn't all that exciting. At least not for the Stony Man commandos. The fact that it was being done in the largest city park in Prague, the capital of the Czech Republic only made it worse. With open access to the city, curious onlookers were making their job more difficult.

They'd had to split up into three teams to try to cover it all, but not much was missing their surveillance. There was also no missing the woman walking toward David McCarter, Gadgets Schwarz and T. J. Hawkins.

She was somewhere over twenty, but less than forty, and could only have been an American. No European could have had that overinflated Barbie doll look, it just wasn't in the gene pool.

She came to a stop in front of them a moment before her breasts did. "Hi," she said. "I'm Trixie."

"I'm sure you are," McCarter said gallantly.

"Are you guys with the band?" she asked as her china-blue eyes zeroed in on each man in turn, making an appraisal before moving on. "I just love musicians."

"I played drums once for Cold Road Kill," Hawkins said, stepping forward with a smile. "Maybe you remember them?"

Not to be outdone, Schwarz took his shot. "I was in charge of security for the Eagles reunion at Monterey."

"Security?"

"That's right." He nodded. "And, man, I can tell you that wasn't an easy job. Those girls were something else, they were all over us."

When McCarter just shook his head, Trixie looked from Schwarz back to Hawkins. "Well, I guess I have to screw you then, don't I?"

When Hawkins froze for a second, she hung a lip lock on him. "See you later, big boy," she said as she broke contact and sauntered off.

McCarter watched the woman walk away, and there was a lot of movement to catch the eye. "I hope your flea collar's up-to-date, T.J."

Schwarz broke up laughing.

"I'll use a biohazard suit." Hawkins grinned.

"The things we're called upon to do for our countries."

"Come on, guys," Hawkins protested. "I'm sure she's a good kid who's just lonesome for the sound of down-home American English."

"Is that what you speak?" McCarter asked. "I've wondered about that for some time now."

"At least I'm not going to offer her a warm beer."

"Vodka, neat, is more her drink, I'd wager."

"David," Bolan's voice came in over the com link. "We've got the pyrotechnic unit coming in. Check them out real thoroughly."

"Will do," McCarter replied. "Which gate?"

"The one to your left."

McCarter, Hawkins and Schwarz drifted over to the fireworks area to see what was going down.

The pyro van stopped and three men got out.

They looked harmless enough as they opened the back of the van and started off-loading their equipment. Then Hawkins went up to get a closer look and changed his mind.

"I don't like the looks of this," he muttered over his com link. "They've got a lot of artillery with them."

"Rafe and I are closing the back door on them," Calvin James announced.

"Bring it on."

"Do you need Pol and me?" Lyons asked from the other side of the park.

"We can handle it," McCarter sent back.

When James and Encizo were close enough to support if it went down, McCarter and Schwarz moved up behind Hawkins. One of the pyro guys spoke English and recognized guns as well and stood stock-still. When McCarter told him to have his men stand aside while their goodies were inspected, he had no argument.

McCarter patted the men down while Manning and Hawkins started going over the pyrotechnics charge by charge. With nothing for them to do, Schwarz and Encizo left them to it and continued to make the rounds of the rest of their sector of the area.

# CHAPTER NINE

*Prague*

At the concert stage in the center of the park, a small crew was erecting a tall framework of pipes on each side. They looked like speaker towers until Gadgets Schwarz saw a man connecting a steel canister to the base of the framework. There was something about the steel canister the man was working with that hit Schwarz as strange. Even stranger were the glances the man kept shooting at them. His partner working on the other framework didn't look too happy at seeing him, either.

Rafael Encizo caught the same vibes and keyed his com link. "How're you guys doing with the fireworks?" he asked.

"Nothing so far," Gary Manning came back. "And we're almost done."

"When you get finished up there, come over to the stage, I think we've got a hot one here. We've got a guy rigging steel canisters, like small welding tanks, to a system of pipes that look a lot like a sprayer of some kind.''

"Could it be a smoke dispenser?'' Hawkins asked. "Or maybe $CO_2$? They're used a lot at rock concerts.''

"It could be,'' Encizo replied. "But it could also be a smallpox sprayer.''

"I'm on it,'' Lyons sent. "We're coming in from the east.''

"Make it fast.''

THE GUY WORKING with the canister was starting to sweat bullets under the unblinking gaze of the two Stony Man warriors. He finished connecting it, though, and called out to his comrade on the other tower as he reached for a second one. That man joined him, and three more came from the back of the stage with nylon sports bags in their left hands.

Encizo keyed his com link again. "Carl, we got four more here who look like they want to play. And, I think they're packin'.''

"We're here,'' Lyons announced as he and Rosario Blancanales closed in on the other side of the stage.

With Lyons and Blancanales coming up on one side and Schwarz and Encizo on the other, the five stage hands panicked. When they started reaching for their hardware, Encizo whipped back his windbreaker and had his H&K in his hands.

Schwarz went wide to give the opposition more targets to have to track.

The firefight was brief, but selective. Of the three men moving in from the rear of the stage, two of them managed to clear their pistols while the third fired through the side of his bag to signal the opening of the fair.

Considering where they were, the commandos' had to let the other side show their weapons first. But now that the genie was out of the bottle, they wasted no time wasting the stage hands with guns in their hands.

Lyons took one down with his Python, Encizo got the second and Schwarz and Blancanales shared the third.

At the first shot, the man with the canister and his partner had gone face first on the stage with their open hands held out to their sides.

THE BRIEF CLASH BROUGHT an instant response from the Army R and R Center personnel. A squad of armed American MPs led by a young captain were the first to show up. His eyes went from the Stony Man commandos who had grounded their weapons to the three bodies littering the stage and the two stage hands standing with their arms as high in the air as they could get them.

Bolan stepped up to the officer and flipped open his ID card folder. "Major Don Fontaine," he said. "Get those people out of here and don't turn them over to the Czechs until we've had a chance to interrogate them."

Seeing the rank on Bolan's ID card, the captain had no trouble saying, "Right away, sir."

"And," Bolan added, pointing to the canisters, "cordon this place off and get a HAZMAT out here ASAP to collect those damned things. Tell them they might contain smallpox virus."

The captain paled. Every U.S. serviceman and -woman in Europe knew of the attack against the army unit in Germany.

"Make sure the bodies are photoed and printed before you turn them over as well. I want to know who those people were."

"Yes, sir."

"Hey!" Schwarz shouted when he saw one of the MPs reach for one of the loose canisters. "Don't mess with that! It's a biotoxin."

That warning sent the curious scrambling to get clear of the area.

Three of the stage hands were dead. Two others had had brains enough to know not to mess with people who were packing. They stood, unmoving, as the MPs took them into custody and cuffed them.

THE NEWS OF THE PRAGUE takedown sent Hal Brognola hurrying down to the Farm to get the details to take back to the Oval Office. The Man already knew that Stony Man had been involved by the way the "security team" that had intervened had evaporated immediately after stopping the attack. The R and R center had reported that they had been led by an army colonel and that could only have been Bolan.

"Damned good work, guys," Brognola said as he slid into his seat at the Annex briefing table.

"We didn't do anything," Barbara Price said. "That was Striker's call. And, if I remember correctly, you were more than a little dubious about them going to a rock concert."

"Sorry about that," he had the honesty to say.

"The bad news," Aaron Kurtzman said, "or good depending on your viewpoint, is that the rock and roll canisters didn't have smallpox virus in them. It was just garden variety homemade sarin nerve gas. It's not very effective, but there was a hell of a lot of it."

Brognola shuddered. Even sarin would have killed half of the men and women at the concert and left the rest crippled for life. The only good thing that could be said about sarin was that it wasn't contagious.

"How does this tie into the smallpox attacks then?" he asked.

"We don't think it does." Kurtzman shrugged. "I don't see why anyone would want to stop using a proved winner like smallpox, which is relatively easy to dispense and switch over to using something like sarin. The gas is much more dangerous to handle, and you have to use a lot of it."

"I was afraid of that," Brognola said. The lack of progress on the smallpox issue was costing him sleep as well as stomach lining.

"What's the deal then?" he asked. "Who were those people and what did they think they were doing?"

"Well," Kurtzman said, "it turns out that the two bozos we bagged alive have rap sheets showing they're members of an anti-American-anti-NATO group. They style themselves the Anti Capitalist Coalition and want NATO disbanded and the U.S. out of Europe."

"Sounds like the old Red Brigades."

"Basically the same old crap," Kurtzman agreed. "But they aren't waving the Red banner. They're more in line with the antiglobalization freaks who've been acting out at the WTO meetings."

"But some of them were Serbs, right?"

"Right." Kurtzman nodded. "Two out of the three dead and one of the others."

Brognola looked thoughtful. "We keep coming up with Serbs in this every time we turn around.

The initial tip in France, the Berlin tip and then the lead to the concert. Why do we keep running into these guys, but we can't tie them directly into the attacks?''

"Well," Hunt Wethers cut into the conversation, "there are a lot of Serbs in Western Europe and not many of them have much good to say about NATO or United States actions in their homelands. Actually, I'm surprised that there aren't more Serb terrorist groups bothering us right now. We gutted their country and they're angry.''

"Most of the bastards are too busy selling drugs and girls to build bombs,'' Kurtzman pointed out.

"Don't forget that the Serbs are the original bomb throwers,'' Wethers said. "They practically invented political terrorism back at the turn of the twentieth century in the days of the old Austro-Hungarian Empire. We even had a couple of cases here in the States. New York, if I remember.''

"Enough of the history lecture,'' Brognola stated. "What do we know about this anti-U.S.A. group?''

"We don't have anything,'' Wethers admitted. "They're brand-new. But I'll get on it.''

"Quickly.''

Brognola turned to Barbara Price. "Can I tell the Man about this without queering the rest of the operation?''

"Sure. He'll tell his press guy, who'll pass it on,

but that might actually help us. Whoever Germaine's working for might think that we're completely off his track if we're chasing after the nerve gas guys."

Brognola smiled. "You're getting to be as sneaky as the rest of this bunch."

She shrugged. "There's a lot of that going around, some of it must have rubbed off."

He glanced at his watch. "Give Striker and the guys a way to go for me, will you? I need to get back, so I can get this to him today."

FOR A PLACE WHOSE name meant "New City" in Greek, Naples, Italy, had been around for a long time. Back when it had been a "new city," its population had been Greek. In the twenty-five hundred years since then, Naples had been populated by many peoples, ranging from Romans to Moors as the Italian Peninsula had enjoyed an interesting history. The fact that Naples was the premier port of the western Italian coastline was the reason it had lasted so long. It was still a major port and a welcome stopover for NATO naval forces in the Mediterranean. In particular, the U.S. Navy enjoyed a close relationship with the Italian city dating back to WWII.

The USS *Bunker Hill* was the current American cruiser on duty in the Med. Unlike the hulking, long-range gun-carrying cruisers of WWII fame, the *Bunker Hill* wasn't that much larger than a modern destroyer. Rather than slugging it out in ship-to-ship battles or bombarding shore targets with heavy guns as in days of old, a modern cruiser was a floating missile launch site. Its primary mission was to protect the skies over a carrier battle group. It could still raise hell with offshore land targets, but with Tomahawk cruise missiles.

Since too much time at sea wasn't good for the morale of the crew, the cruiser's itinerary included visiting several ports of call. One of those ports was Naples. The *Bunker Hill*'s crew was particularly looking forward to shore leave in Naples.

On the second day of the ship's scheduled five-day visit, the crew had been invited to a Navy Appreciation Day event hosted by the town's business community. An elaborate lunch buffet had been set out in one of the town's parks to show that the Italians hadn't forgotten the contribution America had made to freeing the country during WWII. The feed had been well publicized, and the crew flocked to it.

The *Bunker Hill*'s skipper, Captain Lewis Clark, had always had a soft spot in his heart for Naples. As a young ensign on his first cruise, he'd been invited to a high society party that had been a stunning introduction to the power of a uniform and the cultural wonders of Europe. He'd never forgotten it. He had declined several invitations this time, though, including the buffet. He was getting too old for that kind of life.

The next morning, he was in his cabin taking care of routine paperwork when his private line rang. "Clark," he answered.

"This is Molston in sick bay, Skipper. We have a problem."

Since the ship's surgeon wasn't prone to getting excited, Clark was immediately concerned. "What is it?"

"I believe that we've been hit with a biological attack, sir. I've got a sick bay filling up with people."

"What's wrong with them?"

"Believe it or not, Captain," the doctor answered, "they have smallpox."

"I thought we were vaccinated against that?" Clark replied.

"We are, but whatever strain they've caught doesn't seem to be affected by the vaccinations. If I can't get a handle on this real quick, I'd estimate that we're going to start having deaths as early as tomorrow."

With the attack on that army unit in Germany, bioterrorism had gone from science fiction to grim reality, but he'd never expected it to hit his ship.

"What's your recommended course of action, Doctor?" Clark asked formally.

"We need to put to sea as soon as possible to

try to keep from spreading this any further," Molston replied.

"A quarantine?"

"Yes, sir," the doctor answered. "Right now we're a plague ship."

"ATTENTION ON DECK," one of the enlisted men on the watch crew called out as Captain Clark entered the bridge.

"Officer of the deck," Clark said, "what's our fuel status?"

"We're at twenty-eight thousand gallons, sir."

"Secure from refueling, sound general quarters and issue an immediate emergency recall of all crew."

"Aye, sir."

Clark went to his intercom. "Engine room, this is the captain. Who's on watch down there?"

"Lieutenant J. G. De Palma speaking, sir."

"Fire off the burners and prepare to get underway immediately."

"Aye-aye, sir."

Clark stayed on the bridge as the XO monitored the personnel reports as each division reported each time one of their crew returned. "We have enough crew to put to sea now, Captain," the XO reported up to the bridge.

Clark looked down on the pier and saw another

half dozen sailors running for the gangplank. "How many are still unaccounted for?"

"I have fifty-three crew still ashore, including four officers."

"Prepare to get underway immediately," Clark commanded the bridge officer. "Alert the helo crews to lift off and land on the pier after we're clear of the dock. They're to ferry the remaining crew out to us as they show up."

"What's the plot, sir?" the officer of the deck asked.

"Make for the first patch of unoccupied water you can find that's at least fifty miles off shore."

"Aye, sir."

As the *Bunker Hill* made for open waters, Clark went down to his CIC and reported his situation to CINCMED.

AN HOUR AFTER REACHING the open waters of the Med, a medical team was choppered in to the *Bunker Hill* from the carrier USS *Nimitz*. Having been warned of the situation, the chopper went into a hover a foot off the deck and the team jumped down wearing full biohazard suits.

In the sick bay, the team took photos of the stricken sailors to be sent over the Internet and samples that would be physically sent back in a special container. That done, they remained behind. The biohazard suits protected them from the contagion, but the exteriors of their protective gear themselves were now contaminated. They would stay in their suits as long as they could and assist the *Bunker Hill*'s medical staff. When the suit's filters failed, they could take them off and take their chances with the rest of the crew.

And, from what they'd seen so far, those chances weren't that good. The first death, a young woman, occurred right after they arrived.

WHEN THE WORD CAME from the medical lab on the *Nimitz,* Captain Clark took it on his private line in his cabin. After speaking with the carrier's chief surgeon and the admiral, he clicked on the *Bunker Hill*'s intercom.

"Now hear this, now hear this." His voice went out to the entire crew over the intercom. "This is the captain speaking. As I am certain most of you know, the *Bunker Hill* is under a medical emergency. Until further notice we will be relocating to the Atlantic for the duration of the emergency. Further information will be made available to you by your division officers. Good luck, and I'll keep you informed of developments as they occur."

Captain Clark didn't tell his crew what was awaiting them in the mid-Atlantic. Until such time as an effective vaccine could be found to defeat this virus, they would steam in a big circle escorted by a small supporting flotilla. If the virus couldn't be defeated, however, he had received classified orders as to his ship's ultimate fate. Rather than letting the multimillion dollar warship become derelict with all hands aboard dead, a firestorm of bombs would be detonated over the Bunker Hill to hopefully incinerate the contagion and send the ship and crew to the bottom.

That solution gave a new meaning to the captain going down with his ship. In this case he would be going up with it and it was a damned shame. The *Bunker Hill* was a good ship, but the loss of the crew was the real waste.

# CHAPTER TEN

*Stony Man Farm, Virginia*

"Tell him nothing's changed," Aaron Kurtzman growled when he saw Hal Brognola charging across the floor of the Annex at full steam.

"I've got to give the President an update, Aaron," Brognola replied. "You know that."

"How about giving him a clue instead?" Kurtzman asked. "And that is to dig his head out of his rear end the next time I send him a heads-up and pay attention to it. If he'd done something with that first report we got on the lab fire, we'd've had a couple of weeks' head start on this and might not be in the situation we're in now."

"Put a lid on it." Brognola was in no mood to take crap from anyone. An hour earlier, the President had off-loaded on him, and he had to take something back to get him off his case.

The computer wizard spun his wheelchair around. "I'll tell you what, Hal. If the Man isn't satisfied with my work, he can replace me any time he wants. He knows that and you know that, so how about clearing the area so I can go back to work?''

''Or—'' he gestured to his keyboard ''—anytime you want to slide on in here and try to do my job, have at it.''

With that, Kurtzman backed out, maneuvered past Brognola and headed for the elevator leading down to the tram connecting the Annex to the farmhouse.

Brognola let him go and turned to Hunt Wethers. ''Do you have anything, Hunt?''

''Like Aaron said,'' Wethers said calmly, ''nothing substantial has changed. And until the CDC finishes working on the samples they got from the *Bunker Hill* or the field teams develop new information we can work with, that's going to be the only answer we can give you.''

Hearing the bad news from the unflappable Wethers wasn't any better, but it went down a little easier.

''Why the hell didn't he just say that?''

Wethers didn't dance. ''He did.''

''Okay, okay, reload.'' Brognola held both hands up. ''At least can you tell me why we're at this impasse. I have to tell the Man something other than he screwed up by not letting us get going on this earlier. U.S. sailors have died a horrible

death, and a multimillion dollar warship is scheduled to be incinerated and he wants to know why.''

''No,'' Wethers said bluntly. ''He knows why.
What he really wants to know is first off, who he
can blame it on and, only secondly, how he can
keep it from happening again.''

''Okay.'' Brognola's hand snaked into the
pocket of his sport coat for his roll of antacid tabs.
''You're right, but he's in a real bind.''

He popped two tabs and tried again. ''Look,
Hunt, half the population of the planet is in a blind
panic right now over a disease most of them have
barely even heard about. American ships are being
denied entry to foreign ports, tourists aren't being
let out of planes, underground labs are marketing
'vaccines' that are killing the people who pay
thousands of dollars for a single injection. The
president has to get this panic under control, but
he doesn't have anything to tell the public.''

''And, even if he did,'' Wethers said evenly,
''he should keep his mouth shut.''

''Dammit, Hunt, I didn't need to hear that.''

''Oh, yes, you did.'' Barbara Price took that as
her cue to get into the conversation. Hunt could
fight his own battles well enough, but this was
turning into a donnybrook and that wasn't going
to be helpful for anyone.

''And, you need to pass that on to the President,
Hal. That's what you're paid to do. Whoever's be-

hind this isn't doing it from a locked basement room somewhere. They know enough to watch CNN and log onto the Drudge Report at least once a day to find out where the investigation's at. You tell the Man anything about what we're doing, and he's going to blab it to anyone who'll listen. Our people, both in Europe and here in the Computer Room are working their asses off. But, a vial of mutated virus isn't something we can pick up on a satellite run or a electronic intercept, and it doesn't show up on radar."

She took a deep breath. "We're screwed, Hal, totally dead in the water until the guys can turn over the right rock."

She paused. "And that's the name of that tune."

Brognola didn't want to go three for three by taking on Price. It just wasn't in the cards.

"Can I at least tell him where we've been?"

"Why?" Price asked. "So he can have his press guy release it? Get real."

"And, what in the hell are you doing spending your time up there anyway? We've got a mission going on, and we need you here."

"But, he—"

"The Man can talk to you on the phone anytime he wants. He has our number."

"I don't know what I can do here," Brognola honestly admitted. "I'm just the face man for this circus."

"Hal—" Price took his arm. "Yeah, you're our front guy. You take the political shots for us. You throw your body into the steady stream of shit rolling down from Capitol Hill and try to stem the flow. But you're a hell of a lot better than that. Any moron can throw himself in front of a bullet—"

"Thanks a lot."

"—but you're a wily old bastard, and you've got moves you haven't used yet."

"You're not getting a raise," he growled.

"They pay me too much as it is now," she said. "I've already started sending my paychecks to the old folk's home I plan to retire to."

"I didn't know that they had retirement communities for people like us."

"They don't," she said. "That's why I'm making payments on a room right now. I want it to be there for me when I get run out of here or go completely nuts."

"Can you check and see if they have room for me, too?" he asked. "I may be needing it before you do. I have to go back up there today. He's expecting me."

"And while you're doing that," she said. "I'll try to get Aaron back on line. He's really been busting his butt, but we're just not developing the kind of information we're used to working with."

"Just keep on it," Brognola pleaded. "And call

me as soon as you get anything at all. I'll give the Man my lecture on the need for him to keep his trap shut to the press, but I've got to have something to tell him.''

PRICE FOUND KURTZMAN on the porch of the farmhouse. "You wanna go for a stroll?" she asked as she walked out the front door.

He shook his head. "I need to get back to work."

"Screw work." She took the handles on the back of his wheelchair. "You need to take a mental health break."

"Barb!"

"Don't Barb me, dammit! I'm the mission controller around here, and your mission right now is to take a walk with me."

"I'll push myself."

She shrugged. "Suit yourself."

Kurtzman wheeled himself down the ramp onto the pathway leading into the orchard. Even though the path was gavelled, his powerful arms made easy work of it. Barbara walked beside him silently. He'd talk when he wanted to, but she wasn't letting him back inside the Annex until he did.

"I shouldn't have off-loaded on Hal like that," he started out. "Even if the President had turned us loose earlier, we'd still be where we are. Until the bastards make a mistake and go on CNN bragging about what they're doing or the guys can grab someone and make him say the right things we're screwed. Other than that, I don't know what we can do from here, and it's really biting my ass.''

"You'll figure out something sooner or later, Aaron. But you know you can't force it. That's not the way your mind works.''

"It's not my mind I'm worried about,'' he said. "I want to get into the mind of the bastard behind this.''

"You will.''

VIKTOR BLADISLAV firmly believed that his family had been Serbian nobility back in the legendary days when the Turks had been forced out of the Balkans. He had no historic proof of this lineage, but that didn't stop him from believing it. Until recently he had been an ambitious general in the army of Slobodan Milosevic's Serbian republic. Being a fervent and vocal Serbian nationalist, his rise through the ranks of Milosevic's army had been swift. He had become a brigade commander at thirty and a general four years later. Then came the war with Bosnia and Croatia.

He earned more honors from Milosevic for carrying out his duties in that protracted conflict. But he had also earned an UN indictment as a war criminal for crimes against humanity. His troops, a shock unit known as the Iron Guard, had conducted particularly brutal purges against both the Bosnians and the Croats on his orders.

When NATO had gotten involved in the Bosnian war, Bladislav had foreseen the only way the situation was going to resolve itself. Milosevic had gambled big on his Greater Serbia plan, but he had not been man enough to carry it out successfully. He had set himself up to fall, and Bladislav was too good of a military man to stick around and go down with him. A move to Europe had made more sense.

To see Bladislav today, most indications of his military background were gone. There was still a trace of it in his bearing, but his iron-gray hair flowed long, and he wore a close-cropped beard in the style of his ancestors. He favored Armani suits in gray or dark blue and expensive shoes and, had it not been for the beard, he would have looked like the well-to-do European Mob boss that he was.

His office in Milan, one of three he maintained in the West, while plush and a bit gaudy in the Euro Mob-style, gave a hint of his military career. A large map of Europe covered most of one wall and map pins decorated much of it showing his areas of interest.

The large-screen TV in the corner of the room was tuned to CNN and, even with the sound off, he knew what the reporter was talking about. The long-range shot of the American warship in the distance told him everything he needed to know. The pending destruction of the ship in a cleansing fireball was the top of the news at every hour.

"It seems that the doctor has finally found the right mutation," he said.

The other man in the room, Zoran Dinkic, had once been Bladislav's operations officer. When Bladislav left Serbia, he had taken Dinkic and a small cadre of his old Iron Guard officers and men with him to set himself up in his family's old business. While publicly proclaiming their heroic ancestry, in more modern times his family had enriched themselves by operating in the shadow world of supply and demand. Outsiders called it smuggling and drug dealing.

Dinkic smiled. "It is working exactly as you planned it, General."

"It is taking time." Bladislav smiled. "But the wait has been well worth it. The tests in the provinces and that American unit in Germany showed that we weren't ready yet. The ship, though, that's the results I wanted. The reports are saying that almost all of the crew are dead, and the Americans are afraid to even try to take their bodies home."

"It is too bad," Dinkic said, "that we do not have enough of the virus right now to go into full operation."

"I do not mind waiting," the ex-general said. "We have enough to do as it is to prepare the way for us. Our people will have to suffer just a little more, but we Serbs are good at suffering. We have done it for centuries, but it will be over soon enough."

The operations officer had heard his general launch into this topic more than once, so he decided to bring him back to the matter at hand. "I still do not know who hit our establishment in Berlin," he said. "While it was a loss, it is not going to affect us in the long run. I expect that we can get back in operation within a month."

"Good," Bladislav replied. "We are going to need a lot of money when we reestablish our nation."

"We should have what we need by a large margin," Dinkic said. "Even with the raids, our receipts are growing every month as our investments. Best of all, our operational expenses have leveled off."

"Good."

Bladislav hadn't had to create his empire from scratch when he fled his homeland. Other Serb gangsters before him had established the operations and he had simply inherited them. After, of course, eliminating the current operators and naming himself their heir. It was an old Serbian custom, and he was Serb to the core.

What he did differently when he had taken over, though, was to bring military-style planning and discipline to his criminal enterprise. At first, he had tried to absorb the existing Serbian mobsters into his organization and retrain them to his methods. But when that proved unsuccessful, he replaced them with handpicked ex-soldiers. The bodies of the hoods they replaced had been discretely buried.

Knowing the value of allies, Bladislav quickly extended peace feelers to the major players of the European underground. The old Italian Mafia families rebuffed him without a second thought. To them, the Serbians were crude, classless thugs with no sense of honor. More than that, though, they were cutting into the established Families' business. The French also snubbed them.

The Russians, though, hadn't been so judgmental, nor had been the Ukrainian, Rumanian and Bulgarian bit players. With them, a strong element working in Bladislav's favor was that the Serbs were of the Eastern Orthodox faith as they were. It was true that during the days of the Communist Soviet Union, strong religious affiliations hadn't been a good thing to have. But, the Slavic people had been Orthodox far longer than they had been Communists. Once the statues of Lenin and Marx had been toppled, the once outlawed Orthodox Church quickly regained a role in the former Soviet republics.

"What is the status on our talks with the Russians?" Bladislav asked.

"Well, they are still waiting to see how successful we are going to be before they commit to us completely. I was able to work out the last few problems with the Russian Mafia leaders, but the military and the political people are being more cautious. We have a certain amount of Kremlin support now, but they're holding back because they're afraid of NATO stepping in at the last moment.

Bladislav stared at his map for a long moment. "We have to do whatever it takes to get them behind us now, Zoran. We need to get the military equipment lined up so it will be ready when we need it."

With the Russians no longer sponsoring terrorism as a policy of their new style of international relations, someone had to step in to sign up for the excess military equipment and Bladislav was glad to do it. Unlike in the old days, though, he would have to pay for it with hard cash, not vague promises of imposing communism when he was victorious.

"That may take more bribes than we have already paid," Dinkic warned. "For socialists, they have all fallen ill to greed. Even getting an appointment costs money now."

"Pay what you must," the ex-general said. "Particularly for the antiaircraft weaponry and the armor. Along with the tactical missiles, they are our top priority.''

Dinkic grimaced. ''It's not right that we have to spend money on bribes that could be spent freeing our people.''

Fortunately for Bladislav's plan, money wasn't a problem for him. Business was good and, taking a page from Wall Street, he was doing very well with his investments. He had a treasury and much of it had been earmarked for military hardware to replace that which had been destroyed by NATO in its operations against Serbia.

''It is a fact of life, so live with it.'' Bladislav smiled. ''We can afford it.''

''I would have thought that as brothers, the Russians wouldn't treat us this way.''

''We are their younger brothers right now,'' Bladislav said. ''And we are untested. We have yet to prove our manhood. When that is done, they will willingly support us as will all the other Slavic peoples.''

Dinkic knew better than to get into this part of Bladislav's plans. He was as good a Serb as the next, but he didn't have the general's blind faith in pan-Slavic Brotherhood. He wouldn't mind seeing it come about, but he also was too pragmatic to count on it. Until it happened, he had to plan as if Bladislav was standing alone against the Western world.

# CHAPTER ELEVEN

*Prague*

In the aftermath of the successful Prague action, Aaron Kurtzman phoned his Interpol friend to see if there was any information available on Germaine's mistress. After another genial conversation, Maurice Favre wrote up the request for a search of recent reports and put it into the pipeline.

The man who processed the information request instantly recognized the name. Ratic Mitrovic was serving as an Eastern European expert for Interpol, as he had once been a Serbian police official. But since he had left Serbia well before the fall of the Milosevic government, the International Tribunal considered him untainted by the war crimes scandal.

What his current bosses didn't know was that he had been part of a Milosevic security unit specializing in suppressing internal dissent against the regime. He had been good at his job and as soon as

Bladislav took over Greater Serbia, he was to be the new head of the national police the general would form. His job would be the same as it had been for Milosevic—to crush the enemies of the state.

Now, though, his job was to keep watch for anyone who might want to stop the creation of Greater Serbia. Whoever was looking for Marina Stombolic fell into that category.

Mitrovic knew that Marina Stombolic was a top-level operative in General Bladislav's organization. He also knew that she had been ordered to become the mistress of the French scientist the general had recruited. The fact that someone was looking for her had to be passed on to Bladislav as soon as possible.

Telling his supervisor that he wasn't feeling well, Mitrovic left work early. Stopping off at a métro station, he bought a one-time phone card and used it to place a call to Dinkic in Milan.

WHEN THE REPORT from CDC on the *Bunker Hill* attack came in, Hal Brognola flew down from Washington for a briefing on the results and walked into the Annex with a smile on his face for a change.

"I understand they nailed this one down," he said to Aaron Kurtzman.

"They did a good job on this one," the computer expert agreed. "Someone you're close to was biting their butts."

"Let's have it."

"The contagion was focused by the method of primary transmission," Kurtzman stated. "There was a mister installed over the salad bar and, since shrimp-and-lobster salad was featured, most of the crew ate some. The Italians were chowing down at the pasta table, and few of them were infected because they were too far away.

"The Italians," Kurtzman continued. "Seem to have contained the outbreak among the locals, but the death toll among those few who were infected was still pretty high, well over eighty percent. Interestingly enough, though, the virus used against the *Bunker Hill* isn't the same as the one from those two Kosovar villages or the German base. It's a related strain, but not the same."

Brognola frowned. "Does that mean we have two groups working on the same virus?"

Kurtzman shook his head. "CDC thinks that this new one is a modification of the original mutation. The basic DNA pattern is the pretty much the same, but it's had something added to it. It's that extra something that's causing the increased lethality this time."

Brognola shook his head. "The son of Frankenstein."

"Something like that."

"And they haven't identified what the extra thing is?"

Kurtzman shook his head. "Not yet. But they're working overtime on it."

"Is there anything we can do that we're not doing yet?" Brognola asked.

"Nothing," Barbara Price said, entering the conversation. "Since we still don't have a motive or a lead actor, we're running around in circles reacting to events as they unfold."

Brognola didn't have to be told that reacting wasn't going to make this situation any better. Stony Man needed to go proactive. But to do that, they needed what they didn't have—a target.

He turned to Price. "Tell Striker to start rattling cages over there. Tell him to go to war and see what falls out in the debris."

"Against whom?"

Brognola's eyes turned cold. "Against anyone he thinks might have any kind of connection to this entire mess. Tell them to kick ass, take names and I'll see that the Man is on board to back them up and bail them out with the Euro cops if they get caught."

"That's going to get dicey," she reminded them. "The EU has some strong opinions about us interfering in what they see as their internal affairs."

"I'll get the Man to invoke the UN counterterrorist statutes if I have to," Brognola growled. "But I want them stomping on someone and stomping hard."

She smiled. "I don't think Striker and the guys will have any problem with that. Any particular place you want them to go for starters?" she asked.

"You're the mission controller, you pick it."

"Got ya covered, Hal," Price smiled.

"You'd better 'cause I'm covering you."

THE STONY MAN warriors were still in Prague when the call came in from Barbara Price. "Hal wants you guys to go even more proactive over there," she said, "and he wants you to start doing it yesterday."

Bolan asked the question on everyone's mind. "Any particular place he wants us to start?"

"He left that up to me and I'm passing the ball to you. What looks good?"

"We keep running into Serbs. I know that Aaron's team hasn't been able to put together a direct link yet, but as far as I'm concerned, we have enough right now to pin it on them. What's their motive? It's probably the some old tired story in that part of the world. They want the U.S. out of their affairs so they can butcher whoever they want, whenever they want. Slobo's history, but the problems in the Balkans didn't end with him."

"Who do you see behind this scenario?"

"That's the problem," Bolan told her. "So many Serbs have bailed out since this thing started back in Bosnia, it's had to tell the players without a score card. We know that they're working the Mob number all over Europe. But the noncriminal, if you want to call them that, nationalist groups aren't showing up on the radar. There could be an entire Serb government-in-exile in Europe without anyone knowing about it."

"Well, I guess you'll just have to wing it then," Price told him. "You've done pretty well so far. Hal did say that he'd get the President on-line to get you guys out of jail in case you come up against the authorities."

"I won't hold my breath."

"Good hunting."

THE STONY MAN team had no problem lining up behind the idea of being allowed off their leashes to start getting serious.

"I'm getting tired of crashing the party at whorehouses," Carl Lyons growled. "All we've been doing is taking out the low level dirtbags. I want to score some real hits." He looked over at McCarter. "You game?"

"Why not?" the Briton replied. "The guys we want to lean on aren't going to be worried about a few cathouses going off-line for a couple of days. We need to hurt them and hurt them badly. Did

Aaron send any intel on major drug depots or something like that? Hit them where their money is, that always works for me.''

"None as hard targets," Bolan replied. "But his contact did have rumors of a major shipment coming into Budapest for transshipment.''

"How good are they?''

"They came from Interpol, so that can be either good or bad. In many ways, they're as hopeless as the FBI. But, in this case, the lead came from some high-level Russian Mob goon the Germans grabbed.

"According to what Aaron got from Interpol," Bolan continued, "most of the year's Afghan heroin output is being brought into Hungary on a freight train. The train will pull off onto a siding at the border and the contraband will be off-loaded and replaced with something else to keep the manifest straight. A couple of trucks will bring it to a warehouse in Budapest where it will be distributed.''

"That's a decent ops plan," McCarter said. "Who's behind it?''

"That's where is gets a bit confusing," Bolan told him. "The informant said that the Russian Mob was going to take control of the shipment once it reached the warehouse. Who was bringing it in was unclear.''

"It might very well be our Serbian playmates,''

the Briton said. "It has to come from somewhere to the East and Serbia is right along the rail lines from most points east." He whipped open a map and did a quick recon.

"The most likely avenue of approach," he said, "is from Romania. They're long believed to be one of the major refiners of Afghan opium. You'll notice that the rail line goes close to the Serbian Republic right before it crosses into southern Hungry. That would be a good place to hijack it, transfer the goods and smuggle the trucks into Hungary. From there, it's a straight shot up to Budapest."

"Where would you take them down?"

"There's three good places. At the rail siding as it's being transferred, en route to Budapest or at the warehouse. For max effect, I'd say we do it at the warehouse. That way we can get the blokes bringing it in and the people picking it up as well and do max damage to both organizations."

"The warehouse will be well secured, though," Bolan pointed out. "They'll be expecting trouble there."

"Jolly good." McCarter smiled slowly. "All the more for us to bag,"

"I like it," Lyons said. "If we're going to piss someone off, we might as well do it big time."

"It works for me," Bolan added.

"I'll get with Aaron and see what they can give us in deep space overwatch."

VIKTOR BLADISLAV was disquieted by the report from his agent in Interpol that someone was checking on Marina Stombolic. The man hadn't known why the request for information had come in, merely that it had. While knowing the reason would help him, the fact that someone was looking for her was bad enough for him to act on. This also help him understand why his establishments in Europe had been hit.

At first, he had considered the attacks turf wars, the cost of doing business in a field that was so competitive. But when he had inquired about who might have been trying to put him out of business, he had drawn a complete blank. He knew it wasn't his Russian allies, and the Italians knew better than to cross him as did the Union Corse. He had thought that the IRA might have been trying to move some of their UK based operations over, but that, too, hadn't panned out.

Now, he knew why he hadn't been able to find a European crime family connection to the raids. If someone was looking for Marina through Interpol, that someone had to be official and they were probably behind the attacks. More than likely, they had somehow connected her with Germaine and were actually looking for the "dead" doctor. And that made this inquiry even more dangerous to him. The best defense was always a strong offense and he had just the man to put on it.

Reaching out, he keyed his intercom. "Zoran," he said, "I need to talk to you."

Dinkic was in his office a minute later. "What is it, General?"

Bladislav quickly told of the report from his agent in Interpol. "That bothers me, General," the operations officer said.

"It bothers me, too," Bladislav said. "But I am not going to sit and wait to gather more information before I do something about it. I want you to send Iron Guard detachments to all of our major operations. Not major units, but at least four-man security teams."

"We just got a large shipment of the Russian AKSU submachineguns in," Dinkic said. "I'd like to send them out with those detachments."

"Good idea." The general nodded. "Side arms work well enough with the local thugs, but if we are being targeted by some kind of strike force, they'll need better firepower."

"And grenades?"

"And body armor, too," Bladislav said. "Let's do this right."

Dinkic grinned broadly. Operating in Europe had been extremely frustrating for him. Obeying the unwritten rules limiting allowable firepower in turf wars so the local police forces wouldn't get too serious about shutting them down had been difficult to work around. Sometimes the only way to convince someone not to fight was to let him know that he didn't have any chance of winning. And that was hard to do when armed with pistols and a few subguns.

"The men will be very glad to hear you say that, General. They don't like losing gun battles to drug dealers and common criminals."

"The men I'm expecting might not be criminals, Dinkic," the general said. "I wouldn't be surprised to find that the Yankees weren't on our trail. They have taken most of the casualties so far and they are afraid of what might be coming their way. It is what I would do if our situations were reversed."

"Who do you think it would be, their CIA or Special Forces?"

Bladislav thought for a moment. "You know, I used to hear stories from our Russian advisers about some kind of deep cover strike force the Yankees used to fight terrorists. No one had anything firm on them and they told the tales among themselves like children telling ghost stories scaring one another. Most of the reports were discounted, but I don't know. It would be stupid for a country as great as America not to have a way to effectively deal with the things that threatened it."

"But," Dinkic said, "the Yankees are such a strange people. They are always talking about stupid things like their so-called 'human rights' and at the same time they let their own people wallow in crime and drugs like animals. If they had such a force, why don't they use it at home and clean up their own country first? I have heard some of those stories, too, but I don't believe a word of them.''

He shook his head. ''They are like their television programs, fantasy.''

''Nonetheless,'' Bladislav said, ''tell the men that even though we don't know where it's coming from, the threat is real. I want them to take all precautions and stay on their guard. If they get ambushed again and somehow survive, I will kill them myself.''

Dinkic chuckled. ''They already know that, General.''

''How much longer will it be before Germaine is ready?'' Bradislav asked.

''He has almost enough of the virus now,'' Dinkic reported. ''The vaccine, however, has proved more difficult to perfect. His last report said that it would be at least another month, if not longer.''

''Keep on him,'' Bladislav said. ''Now that Marina's with him, he should be able to work harder. If he doesn't, I will make her go away.''

''Do you think he knows that you sent her to him?''

"I doubt it." Bladislav laughed. "He is a brilliant scientist, no doubt about that. But, for being a Frenchman, he is very stupid about women."

"Most men are very stupid about women," Dinkic said.

"You wound me, Zoran." The General laughed.

"The General excepted, of course," the operations officer replied. "Using her to get him to join us was an act of pure genius."

"Wasn't it just?"

# CHAPTER TWELVE

*Stony Man Farm, Virginia*

Having an immediate field operation to support took Aaron Kurtzman's mind away from his troubles, namely not being able to grab the guy who was behind the smallpox attacks. He wasn't satisfied with just having identified the researcher who was more then likely responsible for loosing the terror of mutated smallpox on United States forces. Knowing that André Germaine as the arch-criminal behind this lethal outrage wasn't near enough to satisfy him. He wouldn't rest until Germaine was located and killed or captured.

For now, though, he would push that to the back of the stove. The menu Bolan was cooking would require the best efforts of the entire Stony Man crew to support. The weapons and equipment list alone would be a major undertaking. Switching gears, he went into operational support mode and rang up Cowboy Kissinger to get things rolling.

GETTING THE WEAPONS and operational equipment into Budapest required the assistance of the United States Air Force and the State Department. But with the President in his current frame of mind, it went smoothly and arrived on time.

For this outing, McCarter and Bolan had decided to go full kit. Their information indicated that they would be going up against well-armed opponents and would be severely outnumbered, so they fell back on the tried and true solution. Nothing succeeds like superior battlefield information and firepower.

Along with their standard weapons shipment, they added one of the advanced IOCW 20 mm weapons systems, a couple of 5.56 mm SAWs and an increased ammunition load.

"What in the hell are those things?" Rafael Encizo asked as Bolan opened a metal box to reveal what looked for all the world like a kid's small radio-controlled model airplane crossed with a science-fiction flying saucer. The matte charcoal-gray finish, though, took it out of the kid's toy category and IDed it as some kind of weapon of war.

Bolan grinned. "That's one of those new Mosquito mini-UAVs. They're going to be our top cover over Budapest. I couldn't get them to loan us a Stealth fighter."

Gadgets Schwarz saw the small plane and broke out in a broad grin.

"Damn, Striker!" he said. "I saw a photo of one of things in a magazine once and I was real disappointed when I found out I couldn't buy one. There's this apartment building next to mine see, and I wanted to keep an eye on their midnight pool parties."

"You and every other man in the country." Bolan chuckled. "Those things are better than a set of ten-power night-vision goggles and you get much better angles."

He opened a smaller box to reveal what looked like the world's greatest computer game control center. "I'll let you launch them," he added.

"Great." Schwarz grinned. "Maybe there's an apartment pool around here somewhere I can check in on."

McCarter laughed. "Good luck in this weather, boyo. If you find any Hungarian bathing beauties this time of year, they'll be wearing fur coats over their wet suits, not birthday suits."

"Maybe we can hang around till summer?"

McCarter shook his head.

HAL BROGNOLA CAME DOWN from Washington to watch from the Annex as this involved scenario half way around the world played out. He'd told the President that this was a good chance to get the lead they were desperately looking for, and he wanted to be able to call him the second they had it.

Even with the high-tech battlefield aides that had been sent to Budapest, the Farm's Computer Room crew still had a critical role to play in this scenario. In fact, nothing would happen unless they were able to identify the target train carrying the heroin, tape the transfer of the shipment and then follow the trucks to their destination.

Rather than tie up the NRO spy birds by having them watch every train making its way west out of Eastern Europe, Kurtzman had asked them to key in on the trains traveling the rail line that passed close to the Serbian border McCarter had pointed out. Everything rode on his tactical assessment and if his guess was wrong, they'd look like idiots.

Using Kurtzman's search program, the NRO satellites picked up the train as soon as it pulled off onto the siding right outside the Hungarian border. It wasn't until the three trucks pulled up and the men stepped out, though, that Kurtzman knew he had what he wanted. Once more, McCarter's years of good guesses had proved to be golden again.

"We have it," he announced. "We're good to go."

Brognola reached for his roll of antacid tabs.

"I'll notify Striker," Hunt Wethers replied, "and send him the tapes on the down link."

BOLAN RAN THE TAPES from the NRO bird for McCarter and Lyons.

"There's more than a dozen men there alone," McCarter said as he watched the transfer of the packages to the trucks go down.

"And there'll be at least that many more at the warehouse, if not more," Bolan added. "The Russians aren't going to let anything keep them from getting those goods."

"Let the games begin," Lyons wisecracked.

IT WAS SEVERAL HUNDRED miles from the Hungarian border to Budapest so the three trucks drove in a convoy and kept to the speed limit. The long drive gave the Stony Man warriors more than enough time to get ready to meet them when they arrived in the city.

With the real-time streaming video feed from the NRO spy bird there was no way that they would lose the trucks when they reached Budapest and ducked into the city streets and back alleys. But, even the NRO birds could go off-line at any moment. So, when the trucks approached the eastern outskirts of the city, it was time for Bolan to put his own eyes in the night sky. Eyes that wouldn't go off-line for four hours.

"Get the UAV's ready," Bolan told Gadgets Schwarz.

"One aerial minispy coming up."

Schwarz took the first Mosquito from its carrying case, placed it in the launcher and started its small motor. As soon as its prop was spinning, he called out to Bolan, "Ready to fire off the first one," he called out from the UAV launch control console.

"Go for one," Bolan replied.

Schwarz hit the button, the compressed air launch piston fired and the little UAV leaped into the air. "Running hot," he reported.

"I've got video feed and control on number one," Bolan reported. "Get the rest of them ready."

"Number Two ready to launch."

"Hold till I get the link."

BACK AT THE FARM, Kurtzman got the report of the first UAV launch and keyed in the preprogrammed, deep space, target designator program he had laid on. Using the same satellite hardware that had allowed the B-2s to launch two-thousand-pound laser-guided bombs from miles away during the Kosovo air campaign, the spy bird's laser designator sought out and invisibly marked each of the trucks.

He watched as the first Mosquito was guided to its truck. The cyber brain in the mini-UAV was small, but powerful. When its sensors picked up the laser mark on the lead truck, it inputted the truck's shape into its memory. Now, even if the satellite lost the designator link, the minibird would still remember which truck it was following.

"The first one is locked on target," he told Brognola.

"WE HAVE A LOCK ON number one," Bolan called out. "Launch number two."

"On the way," Schwarz called out.

The second Mosquito quickly acquired its truck as did the third when it was launched.

"I've got all three locked up," Bolan announced. "Launch the two free flyers."

The last two mini-UAVs were launched on an orbital search program. As soon as the truck's destination was identified, they would circle above it like a miniflock of crows and send back anything they saw on the ground with their night-vision video pickups.

BROGNOLA SAT WATCHING the night scene over the city on the Annex's big-screen monitors. One screen gave him the NRO feed and the other a split screen view from the Mosquito UAVs with a map of the city and the paths of the trucks marked in red. There was no way they were going to disappear.

"That's got to be it," Kurtzman said as the first truck pulled into a walled factory compound in the eastern suburbs of Budapest. A large building in the center of the compound was the destination as the truck was quickly driven inside out of sight. The other two trucks quickly followed it.

The factory was typically European in that a masonry wall surrounded the open grounds blocking the view from outsiders. That could be good or bad, but if the gangsters didn't have it covered by surveillance cameras, it would let the Stony Man warriors get that far unseen.

"Tell Striker that they're a go," Brognola said.

THE STONY MAN COMMANDOS had broken down into two teams for the assault. Bolan went with Lyons and Able Team while McCarter led his Phoenix Force warriors. Even though there was danger in their traveling through the city in full gear, they were suited up. The risk of being spotted had to be balanced with their need to hit the warehouse before the goods disappeared again.

Now that the target had been identified, it took mere seconds for a plan map of the compound to be downloaded to the men's HUDs. McCarter studied the plan for a moment and marked two sites on the far side of the compound as their entry points.

"Striker," he said, "you and Carl take the one in the back. We'll hit the one closest to the gate."

"You guys get to have all the fun," Lyons said. "That gate's likely to be guarded."

"That's the point," McCarter replied. "We draw the fire away from you guys because we have most of the heavy firepower."

A last check of their weapons and com links and they were ready to go.

THE TWO MERCEDES sedans the team had rented were loaded and waiting to be their battle taxies. With McCarter behind the wheel of the lead car, it was a fast trip through the night streets of Budapest to the factory compound on the southern outskirts of town. Parking the cars two blocks away from the factory, the commandos quickly made their way up to the compound wall unseen.

When they arrived, the Mosquitos were already on station five hundred feet above the factory. James reported that there were only a few men on the grounds that he could see, but Manning wanted to make a close-up survey of their section of the perimeter wall. Unsnapping the remote eye from his harness, he held it up to look over the wall. The fiber optics worked through his night-vision gear and gave him a view of what was behind the concrete without exposing himself over the top of the wall. "It's clear here," he sent to McCarter.

"Do it."

Hawkins and Manning went over the wall first

followed by James with the heavy firepower of the OICW. Their night vision showed that their immediate surroundings were clear.

BOLAN AND ABLE TEAM were supposed to have had the easy entry, but as soon as they came over the wall they were spotted. Hearing the shouts in Russian removed all doubt about who they were up against. The characteristic sound of the incoming fire backed up the language identification.

"That sounds like AKSUs," Bolan radioed.

"That means this isn't your street corner Mob operation," McCarter cut in. "The Russians are keeping a close eye on those things and aren't letting them go out the back door of their armories."

"Okay, guys," Bolan informed his teammates. "We're up against the first team here. Keep sharp."

"COVER ME," HAWKINS transmitted as he took off to aid Able Team. He was halfway across the open ground when he took a round full in the chest. Giving a grunt as the breath was knocked out of him, he crumpled to the cobblestones.

"T.J.!" he heard James yell over his comlink.

"I'm okay," he gasped. "The armor soaked it up."

"You got hit by a sniper. Keep your ass down till I can get that bastard!"

"No problem."

# CHAPTER THIRTEEN

*Budapest*

Flipping his OICW combo-weapon to 20 mm, Calvin James used its passive IR seeker to look for the guy who'd shot his partner. The smoke stack, or whatever it was, towering above one of the smaller buildings seemed the most likely place to hide a sniper. It was square sectioned and had some kind of enclosure on top that could easily hide a shooter and give him the high ground over the whole compound. And, if that's where he was, he had to be very careful.

Considering the part of the world they were in, the gunner was more than likely using a Russian 7.62 mm Dragunov sniper rifle. That round was powerful enough to give his body armor a workout, and he wasn't in the market for a sucking chest wound tonight.

He was scoping for an IR track when Gary Manning cut in on his com link. "Need someone to keep his head down?"

"No," he replied. "Actually I need someone to draw his fire so I can spot the bastard. But chances are, he's got an SVD up there so be real careful."

"You need to work a little on your comedy routine, Cal." Manning chuckled. "It sucks. 'Draw his fire, Gary, but be careful.' Right."

"Dammit you two!" Hawkins radioed. "Knock off the stand-up routine and blast that asshole. I don't know if I'm bleeding to death yet, and I can't move to check or he'll know I'm still alive and whack me again."

"T.J.," James transmitted. "Get ready to move out of the line of fire as soon as I start to fire. Gary, light him up a little, I've got the IR on him."

"Here it goes," Manning said as he broke cover and laced the smoke stack with a sustained burst of full auto 5.56 mm from his SAW.

The Russian shooter couldn't resist the temptation of a new target and sent two shots after the Canadian as he dived back for cover. The first shot passed close enough for him to hear it sing past his head. The second round, though, was a clean miss.

"Did you spot him, Cal?" he called on the com link.

"I got the bastard," James sent back.

Even with the SVD's muzzle break hiding the

muzzle-flash, the hot gases from the two shots had lingered long enough to give him a good IR target. Standing to get a good firing stance, he took his shot. When he'd loaded his magazines, he'd alternated point detonating HE and AP rounds, and the first shot was armor piercing.

The solid shot round blasted a big chunk out of the brickwork the shooter was hiding behind.

The sniper tried a shot at him in return, but Manning sprang back into action and dumped the rest of his assault pack mag of 5.56 mm on full-auto, spraying the smoke stack and driving him back into cover.

That gave James his chance and he took it. His first 20 mm round was a point detonating HE that didn't do much damage to the bricks, but it made a lot of noise. His second round was another AP, which sent a second cascade of bricks flying and exposed the gunner. The next shot in the magazine was a PD HE round. It impacted the sniper's center body mass, and the detonation rained bloody chunks.

"T.J., Gary," James called out. "You're clear."

"Calvin," David McCarter's voice cut in on the com link, "if you and Gary are through screwing around out there, we could use a little help over here. Ironman and Striker have got a half a dozen of them on the run. T.J., are you okay?"

"I'm fine."

"We can use you, too."

Hawkins winced as he hauled himself erect. "On the way." He'd be bruised and battered in the morning, but right now he had work to do.

THE MINI-UAVs were giving Schwarz a better than bird's-eye view of the battlefield inside the factory walls. James's 20 mm barrage had done a lot to convince the gunmen that open ground was unhealthy, and they quickly broke contact and retreated into the main building. With the grounds cleared, the Stony Man commandos were closing in on the warehouse in two teams. The problem now was that with the grounds clear, the UAVs had become useless.

"Cal," Schwarz sent, "see if you can blow an opening in the roof of that building up toward the top. If you can make a hole, I'll see if I can get one of the birds inside."

"No sweat." James took aim at the middle of the roof and touched off a 20 mm round. The HE blew a hole in the roof three feet wide. "How's that?"

Schwarz used the spy bird's eye to check James's handiwork. "That should do it."

He selected Mosquito number three and, watching his screen, brought it down to roof level. Guiding it through his video link, he slipped it through the hole with no problem. He was pleased to find that the building's interior didn't have a ceiling and the UAV's video eye sent back a good view of the floor below.

"David," he sent over the com link, "we're back in business."

"What do you have?"

"It looks like you've got about two dozen gunmen cornered in there. Some of them are stacking crates by the north wall for cover. You've got at least two covering each entrance and the rest are taking cover behind the trucks. If you can take your guys around to the south and make the main effort there, Carl can come in on their flank from the east."

"Got it."

Keeping to their two squads, the Stony Man commandos closed in on the building. To start the assault, James opened a hole in the cinderblock wall with an HE round from his OICW as a diversion. Even before the dust settled, a barrage of return fire flashed through the opening. While the gunmen waited to see if they had any more business there, he sent another Twenty HE to open the door on their side of the building.

A 40 mm frag grenade from Rafael Encizo's M-16/M-203 and a long spray of 5.56 mm from Manning's SAW cleared the two entrances they had created. Now it was time to make their entry. With his SAW slung on his right hip, Manning rushed the hole in the wall proceeded by a blaze of fire from the mini-machinegun.

With Phoenix Force drawing the enemy's undivided attention, Bolan and the Able Team made their entrance through the service door. Once inside the darkened building, Bolan drew his .44 Desert Eagle. In a free-for-all like this, its one-shot stopping power would be useful.

Firing his 20 mm weapon from the cover of the edge of the hole in the cinderblock wall, James was doing fearsome work inside the warehouse. Clipping a magazine of time-fused HE rounds into the magazine well of the OICW, he set the time for zero and fired a round right over the top of a makeshift barricade inside.

The round detonated almost as soon as it left the muzzle, but it flew far enough to rain its wire frag on the gunmen behind the barricade. A follow-up with a PD HE blew several of the crates aside, setting them up for a long burst of 5.56 mm rounds.

The gunmen hiding behind the vehicles turned their fire on James, giving Bolan a target-rich environment. His first shot punched through a truck's door and took out the gunman inside the cab. A second shot punched all the way through another truck's front fender and hood to take out the guy who thought that he was safe behind that much metal. Apparently, he'd never seen the power of a .44 before.

The bark of the Desert Eagle sounded loud over the clatter of the AKs and drew the attention of several gunmen to the sudden danger from their rear. A burst of AK fire slammed into the wall by Bolan's head, sending concrete chips slashing into his face.

Dropping down, he saw a pair of legs behind the wheel of another truck and put a shot into the gunman's knee. When the man screamed and tried to crawl away, a second shot put him facedown on the concrete.

With two groups of attackers, the gunmen were whipsawed back and forth trying to cover both fronts. Even though they were on the losing end of this dustup, the enemy gunners had no intention of surrendering. There was simply too much at stake, and that didn't include their lives. No one walked away from a multimillion-dollar shipment of heroin. And that put them right where the Stony Man commandos wanted them.

With Bolan and James the star attractions of the moment, Lyons made his move, racing out of the shadows for the cover of a huge machine tool halfway across the open floor.

When a burst of AK fire bounced off the concrete floor inches away from Lyons's churning boots, he dived the last few feet for cover. Not taking time to reload his shotgun, he whipped out his .357 Colt Python and added its roar to the din. His first target was the guy who had put him flat on the concrete. This particular gunman got too enthusiastic and stood to try to get a clear shot. Lyons's Python put him back down with a shot in the chest.

The Able Team Leader's play gave Phoenix Force an opening to get back into play themselves. James broke cover and sent another 20 mm burst into the biggest group of them. A full magazine of 5.56 mm from the same weapon made sure that those he had only nicked with the HE's wire frag got their full measure of grief.

The renewed assault finally sent the surviving gunmen scrambling, but there was no safe haven. The last man on his feet spun as he ran to try to spray Lyons, but Bolan spotted him and dropped him with a head shot.

WHEN THE LAST SHOT echoed away, the Phoenix Force commandos broke cover to sweep the kill zone. As they expected, none of the casualties were still alive. Several of them were wearing Russian-style camouflage uniforms, but without rank or unit insignia as would be expected of someone's army or police. Nonetheless, they had been well-armed and equipped, so there was money behind them. Maybe they were some kind of private army, a crime lord's bodyguard. Searching them, however, didn't reveal much.

"David," Hawkins called out, "over here."

"What'd you have?"

Hawkins handed over a black, Euro-style beret with a embroidered cloth patch sewn into the lining. It showed a red-and-white shield with a black castle in the middle and a motto in yellow.

"I got it off that guy." He pointed to a camouflage clad body draped over a pile of rubble.

McCarter looked closely at the badge. "It's nothing I've ever seen before," he said. "But, the lettering on it is Cyrillic."

"Russian?"

"I don't think so, it has the flavor of the Balkans. I'd guess some kind of special Serb unit, but why is it sewn on the inside of the beret?"

"That's an old American Special Ops trick," Hawkins said. "Even if you're trying to keep a low profile, you don't want to go to war without your colors so you sew it on the inside of your headgear. If things go wrong and you buy it—" he shrugged "—at least you'll be buried with it. Damned near every guy I knew who'd been sheep-dipped did that."

McCarter looked perplexed. "You know, T.J., I've heard you say many things that I've had to have sent out for translation before I could understand them, but you really have me stumped this time. What does dipping sheep have to do with special forces operations?''

''Easy.'' Hawkins grinned. ''It's the process where you put a wolf in sheep's clothing before sending him off to war. Like making the Green Berets and Rangers wear UN uniforms when they worked clandestine missions in Africa in the seventies. They'd been sheep dipped.''

McCarter shook his head. ''The things you bloody Yanks do to butcher perfectly good English.''

''Hey!'' Hawkins sounded indignant. ''I'm not bloody. I didn't even get a scratch, just a bruise.''

McCarter shook his head.

''What're we going to do with this stuff,'' Manning asked, pointing to the neatly stacked bundles of heroin in the backs of the trucks.

''Burn it,'' Lyons said. ''If we leave it here, it'll 'disappear' from the evidence room in a flash. This is just too much shit to leave behind.''

''This isn't L.A., Ironman,'' Schwarz said over the com link. ''Let's give the Hungarians something to brag about.''

''Not on your life,'' Lyons insisted. ''The Hungarians are great people, but let's remove the temptation, okay? We've got better than ten percent of the annual gross national product of Hungary here.''

''He has a point,'' McCarter said. ''My take is that the local police have been bought off.''

Unlike what had happened in both France and Germany, there were no wails of police sirens immediately responding to the firefight this time. And with the smuggler's weapons not being silenced, there could be no doubt that a firefight had been going on.

Hungary was on board with the EU fight against international drug smuggling, but it was still a poor country. A very small percentage of the total value of the shipment in the right pockets had given the smugglers complete immunity to conduct their business. It was an old story in most of the world and it wasn't about to change any time soon.

''Good point,'' Bolan agreed. ''Burn it.''

AFTER RAMPAGING THROUGH half of Europe, the beret badge from Budapest was the first possible concrete lead the Stony Man teams had uncovered. It could also, though, be another dead end if it was merely a keepsake of a mercenary who had signed on to guard a drug shipment. Nonetheless, it merited a full-court press and Aaron Kurtzman dug into it.

No one had ever sat down and compiled a proper Order of Battle for the various warring factions in the Balkan War theater. Considering that many of the units—Serb, Croat and Muslim—were little more than armed, uniformed gangs, or the personal guards of political leaders, it would have been a difficult task. Simply stated, Order of Battle information was intelligence about a specific unit—its history, current strength, weapons and who commanded it. Minor details such as their distinctive insignia and the background of its principal officers was also included if known.

It took some time to download all of the Order of Battle reports that had been gathered during more than ten years of conflict in what had once been Yugoslavia. Once compiled, it was a short trip to what he was looking for.

"I found it," Kurtzman said. "It's the badge of the Serbian Iron Guard, Milosevic's butchers. They called themselves special forces, but the only thing they specialized in was ethnic cleansing."

"Like the SS?" Price asked.

"More like that, yes."

"Who's on record as their commander?"

Kurtzman scrolled down. "It appears to be a General Viktor Bladislav."

"What's the story on him?"

"I'll find out as soon as I can."

It didn't take long for Kurtzman to find the file on ex-Serbian General Viktor Bladislav. It was toward the top of the pile in the UN's wanted war criminal's stack.

"If this is the guy man behind this," Kurtzman

told Price, "it all starts to make a kind of twisted sense. According to this, Bladislav bailed out on Milosevic early when things started to go south, but he's a well-known Serb ultranationalist. And look at the targets he's chosen to attack so far— Muslim villages and American forces. He could be doing this to get both us and NATO out of his homeland. His tie-in with the Serbian Mob in Europe also makes sense. A man with a plan like that is going to need a lot of money to pull it off and quick money would be real attractive to him."

"That seems to fit the bill for me," she said. "And Hal's going to love it. Now we have someone to focus on."

"Apparently, though," Kurtzman added, "he's one of those guys who never allowed his picture to be taken. There's a report from one of those Brit combat junkie, photojournalists covering the Bosnian War that says he had his film confiscated because Bladislav thought he'd taken his picture. That's a well-known dodge for guys who don't want to see their picture on a wanted poster someday."

"What do you have on his current haunts?"

"Absolute zip," Kurtzman said. "Interpol's looking for him as is the UN War Crimes Tribunal. According to this, the minute things started turning sticky for Slobodan, he completely evaporated and nothing's been reported since then."

"That also figures," she said.

"It also adds a dimension we haven't counted on, though," Kurtzman pointed out.

"What's that?"

"The guy's a Milosevic general, so we could have high-level Serbian military involvement in this."

"We need to get Hal in on this immediately to work the political end."

"I'll get it to him right away."

## CHAPTER FOURTEEN

*Stony Man Farm, Virginia*

Hal Brognola held a conference call after seeing Kurtzman's evidence and taking it to the Oval Office. "The president has the assurances of the new Serbian government that they're not involved in this incident in any way. They say that they're looking for Bladislav as well so they can hang him for war crimes."

"And you believe them?" Price asked.

"They have a big incentive to tell the truth," Brognola said. "U.S. aid money. We're shipping it to them by the ton and if they piss us off, that'll dry up real fast. They're still trying to get their economy back together again, and foreign aid is all that's feeding most of their people. They can't risk losing that."

"We keep running into Serbs, though," she replied. "That's the one thing that's stayed consistent right from the first with everything we've looked into.''

''How about all those ex-Milosevic war criminals in Serbia we keep hearing about?'' Kurtzman asked. ''Isn't there supposed to be a couple brigades of them still unaccounted for? For God's sake, from what I understand, there's a large chunk of that country that's still not under the control of the new government, and that's a perfect place for this guy to hide his little operation.''

Brognola had to admit that Kurtzman had a good point there. Serbia wasn't even close to being what anyone could call a stabilized situation yet. And, if history was any judge, their chances of achieving anything approaching stability was somewhere between slim and none. Having a connection to a Serb war criminal made it an ironclad case for him.

''Good point,'' he said. ''I assume that you have a recommendation?''

''I want to let Hunt start having the NRO birds take a real close look at that place. Hiding a lab there wouldn't be too much of a trick, but finding it will be.''

That wasn't exactly what Brognola wanted to hear, but it was what they had to work with. ''Go ahead.''

''We'll be in touch,'' Kurtzman promised.

THE LOSS OF THE BUDAPEST shipment had created an instant crisis for Viktor Bladislav. It hadn't been his property, but its transportation had been entrusted to him by his Russian allies. It was true that it had been delivered to them in Budapest as ordered, but they accused the Iron Guard escort of having led the attackers to the meeting place and demanded that Bladislav cover their losses.

As extensive as the general's holdings were, there was simply no way he could give them the cash that the sale of the heroin would have netted them in Europe. The amount was in the hundreds of millions of U.S. dollars, and he didn't have that kind of ready cash on hand. He would have to liquidate all his holdings to meet the demand.

"I don't know what to say, General." Zoran Dinkic shook his head and laid the report from the Hungarian police on the desk. "We had paid off the Budapest police, and there should have been no problem. I had a full Iron Guard detachment escorting it and they were well-armed."

The operations officer shook his head. "For this to have happened as it did, the enemy would have to have had a fifty-man assault unit and supporting weapons. A force like that could have only been sent in by the Americans. Their Rangers could have done something like that."

"I will not let this stop me," the ex-general vowed. "I will see victory for Greater Serbia and our people."

Bladislav was more than merely a criminal mind. His love for his country wasn't opportunistic. While pragmatic in many ways, at the core, he was a man from a culture where *vendetta* was more than a obsolete word. He truly believed that his ancestors had fought to wrest their lands from the iron-shod boot of murderous Turks. He wanted nothing more than to free them from the iron boot of the Western nations. Those who had brutally wounded his nation were owed for the blood they had spilled, and he was the man who now had the means to repay that blood debt.

Working with his new criminal allies had put him in touch with like-minded Slavs who sympathized with the plight of the traumatized Serbian people. They saw what the United States and NATO nations had done in Bosnia and Kosovo as naked aggression in what should have been a purely national affair. If he was successful in his venture, he had no doubt that he would be given the official recognition of the Orthodox states of Eastern Europe.

When he was done, the Balkan Slavs would finally be free of meddling foragers and he would be able to create a Greater Serbia where so many others had tried and failed. Under his leadership, the historically fragmented land could finally come together and take its place in the world. Linking up with the other Slavic nations, the Ukraine, Croatia, Romania, would ensure that the West could never again be able to interfere in the region again.

"It will happen, Zoran," Bladislav said firmly. "A thousand years from now, schoolchildren will read of us and sing our names in prayers."

Dinkic frowned. He believed in his boss's plans, but he was an operations officer and his focus was on the hardware and men required to carry them out. "If we can get the damned Russian tanks and missiles delivered in time and that does not look good right now, General. Not now that the heroin shipment has been destroyed."

"We will get what we need to take our rightful place in the world," Bladislav promised. "Dr. Germaine will see to that. When the Russians see what he can do on a large scale, they will be happy to support us fully. In fact, I expect that they will want to share my secret weapon."

"What do we do until it's ready?" the ever pragmatic Dinkic asked. "If the Yankees are onto us, they might find the lab as well."

The ex-general walked over to his map. "We will put every Iron Guard we have around the castle and built up our defenses. Until we can get the tanks from the Russians, see if we can 'borrow' a couple from our Romanian army contacts."

"I will try again," Dinkic replied. "But they did not want to consider that the last time I asked.

They see their armored forces as their guarantee of staying in power.''

''They are smarter than they look,'' Bladislav admitted. ''Try doubling our offer.''

''Yes, sir.''

''And Zoran...'' Bladislav said.

Dinkic turned back.

''We will win.''

''Yes, sir.''

WITH HUNT WETHERS working with the NRO on the search of Serbia for the elusive lab, Aaron Kurtzman went back to trying to track down Dr. André Germaine. It was as if the earth had opened up and swallowed the man and his mistress as well. He knew, though, that Germaine hadn't stopped cooking up mutated death. The *Bunker Hill* attack had proved that.

The first step toward finding him—running through all the known facilities capable of doing the job—had already been done by someone else. The WHO had invited the CDC to participate in a series of no-notice inspections of labs from Singapore to Finland. Flying squads had hit all of them within twenty-four hours so word of the raids would not get out. It had been a job well done. But, as had been found with the investigation of the known viral researchers, their labs all came up clean.

It was true that the inspection teams hadn't been able to get into the "outlaw nations," Iraq, Iran, Afghanistan, North Korea, but Kurtzman's gut kept telling him that these incidents were centered around the Balkans. So far, Serbs had been involved in this every step of the way, and he felt that they were the key. Plus, he had a feeling that making smallpox in the Middle East or Asia would be counterproductive from the viewpoint of the perpetrators. There was too great a risk of it getting loose. And, if it did, the primitive sanitary conditions and medical expertise in both regions would insure that it would eradicate the populations.

While it was difficult to set up a rouge bio-war agent lab, it wasn't impossible. Saddam Hussain had done it right under the eyes, and surveillance cameras, of the UN observers. He'd been making Anthrax, a simpler material to manufacture, and he hadn't been mutating it. Nonetheless, the principle was the same and would only be a little more difficult to manufacture the mutated smallpox. He just had to figure out how to spot such a facility from space and positively identify it.

Kurtzman's mind raced through the procedures for growing and gene splicing viruses, and started counting off the machinery and procedures necessary to do the job. When he started considering the media necessary for growing the deadly bugs, things fell into place.

"I'll be damned. Hunt!" he almost shouted across the room. "Start tracking viral media shipments within Europe. Go back two months...no three...four!"

Wethers didn't need a long explanation as to why he'd been asked to do this job. Kurtzman had come up with something, and that always took priority over whatever else was cooking. Also, the request was so obvious he was surprised that none of them had thought of it before. Like all living organisms, the smallpox virus needed to eat to stay alive. And a virus ate culture medium. Find the food, find the bugs. Simple.

"I'm on it."

EVEN WITH THE ANNEX'S mainframes being equal to the legendary machines of the NRO, it took some time before the results started coming in. Operating at the speed of light in cyberspace was all fine and good. But if the information you were sorting through hadn't been inputted into someone's database, you might as well be fumbling around with hard copy instead of bytes. Fortunately, most of the scientific supply houses in Europe and the United States were on-line. And little that was in cyberspace could remain hidden from Stony Man for very long.

"I have a list of possibles," Wethers said by the end of the day.

"How are they ranked?"

"The top three are here." Wethers handed over a pile of paper. "But my pick is Consolidated Scientific Supply. As you can see, they've been sending tons of top-grade viral media to a distributor in Prague. Who, by the way, is a new customer for them."

"Who owns Consolidated?"

"We're having a little trouble tracking that down," Wethers admitted. "It looks like it might be a front company."

"Serb Mob?"

"That or Russian."

Since the Russians also kept popping up in this investigation, a tie-in with them was again not unexpected. In fact, he'd have been surprised if they weren't in it up to their belt buckles. The Cold War was over, but peace hadn't now, nor would it ever, be declared until the last Russian mobster was cold in his grave.

"Where're they sending the stuff?"

"To Romania of all places," Wethers said. "At least that's what it looks like now. I had expected that it would be going to Belgrade or somewhere else in Serbia, but I have copies of the manifests to Bucharest."

"Interesting," Kurtzman said. "I'll look this over and send it to Striker. And have the NRO break off the Serbia search and start checking Romania for anything that looks like it might be a clandestine lab.''

Since the lab, if it existed, could be anywhere from an old factory to an abandoned house, that was as tall an order as the search of Serbia had been. Satellite recon could produce almost magical results, but it was not magic, only applied science. But he had the best America had to offer working for him now and they might just be able to pull it off. Fortunately, with the President fully behind them this time, he could simply order the NRO to shift their focus and not have to steal a satellite to do it.

MACK BOLAN KNEW full well that Kurtzman's hunches were better than most men's cold hard facts. When he heard of the Romania lead, he decided to relocate their operation to Bucharest even before the computer wizard came up with a specific target for them. And, since they had kind of worn out their welcome in Hungary anyway, it might be a wise move to make.

It had taken the Hungarian cops until the next morning before they had moved in to investigate the shoot-out and fire at the warehouse. But once they did, it became the biggest thing in the country since the Communist government had fallen. It would be only a matter of time before someone stopped their van on the streets, and then they'd have to have Brognola spring them.

A quick call to the Farm got them on board for the move and they started packing up.

ROMANIA HAD AN INTERESTING history. The nation's name referred to the Romans who had colonized the region in the first century AD. Even today, the Romanian language was a debased form of Latin. To most in the West, though, it was a country few thought of even if they knew of it. It was just one more of the dirt-poor ex-Communist states that was slowly emerging from a decades-long nightmare. That it was having a very difficult time doing that also wasn't news to the Western world. And, it wouldn't become news until people started dying of something more spectacular than mere starvation.

To non-Romanians, the most well-known part of the remote country was Transylvania, the place across the forest. In fact, people who had never even heard of Romania knew the legends of the vampires of Transylvania. But Vlad Dracul's castle aside, Transylvania was a real place and being both remote as well as sparsely populated made it a good place to put something that you didn't want anyone to find.

The Russian Mafia had noted that early on and, in conjunction with their Romanian Mob allies, had built a modern drug production facility in Transylvania. Since the Russians had the main franchise for the Afghan poppy production, it made sense that they would want a place to convert the raw opium into the finished product. Kilo for kilo, selling heroin was much more profitable than the raw product. And, what better place to site a drug lab than in a ruined castle in the wild vastness of the Transylvanian Alps?

Early in the planning stages of his nation-building operation, Viktor Bladislav had learned about the clandestine lab in Romania from his dealings with the Russian Mafia and decided that it was the perfect place for what he had in mind. With the scientific equipment already on hand, it wouldn't be that great a leap from making heroin to producing viral cultures. To be sure, the protective measures needed to produce deadly disease were far greater than those needed to refine heroin, but the principals were the same, and much of the equipment already there could do double duty.

After extensive negotiations with the Russians, he ended up running the heroin lab for them in return for a cut of the final product. He didn't tell them what else he was going to manufacture there. The viral production section of the lab had been finished three months before Dr. Germaine had been "killed" in France, and now it was in full production.

He could almost taste victory, but it wasn't his yet, nor was the struggle over. He had covered his tracks as well as he had known how, but it was clear that someone was after him.

# CHAPTER FIFTEEN

*Transylvania*

Dr. André Germaine was pleased with the results of the test of the first batch of his new M-2 virus as he was calling it. From what he had learned on CNN, the death toll on the USS *Bunker Hill* was everything he could have wanted and more. And, the American decision to incinerate the warship would do much to spread panic about it in the West. The M-2 was a killer, there was no doubt about that, but the panic it would cause was just as much a weapon as the virus itself.

The original mutated smallpox he had developed in France had worked well enough on the primitive peasants of Kosovo and Bosnia, but he hadn't liked the results he had gotten in the attack on the American unit in Germany. It had had a higher lethality rate than natural smallpox would have had, but the vaccines that had been given the troops had been somewhat effective against it. His new product was able to overcome any known smallpox vaccine.

Germaine took great pride in his work, but he was enough of a scientist to give most of the credit for the design of the M-2 virus to one the ex-Soviet scientists working with him. Viktor Bladislav had been able to get two researchers from the now defunct Russian Bio-War program to assist him. It was one of them who had spotted the report from Australia on a gene-splicing experiment gone bad that had given him the critical clue he had needed to create it.

Not even he could have imagined that grafting the Interleukin 4 gene to the virus would have the effect it did. IL-4 was supposed to boost the human immune system and had been used as an experimental cancer treatment. In his gene-spliced use of it, however, it completely destroyed the body's immunity to all viruses. If the M-2 didn't kill someone exposed to it, they would surely succumb to the next flu or cold virus they were exposed to. The rare individual might escape death, as nothing worked at a hundred percent efficiency in human biology. But his calculations indicated that he would have a ninety-six percent kill rate and that was better than Ebola.

Along with the killer bugs, Germaine was also manufacturing a new M-2-specific vaccine to protect the Serbian population when the major attacks were made. The virus had been created to achieve a specific limited political goal, not to depopulate the planet. There was no point in driving the Americans and Western Europeans out of Greater Serbia if the native population all died as well.

As soon as a large enough supply of the vaccine was ready, it would be distributed to the Serbian people well before the M-2 was sent to selected military targets all over Western Europe. The casualties would be heavy and would include a large percent of the civilian population as well. That wasn't necessary to Bladislav's plans, but it would be unavoidable and would be revenge for all the Serb civilians who had been killed in the Western bombing raids.

And once the political situation had stabilized and the new Greater Serbia formed, the M-2 virus would be for the Serbs what nuclear missiles had been for the old Soviet Union and the United States during the Cold War. Having a stockpile of it on hand would ensure that no one would ever again agress against the new nation. He had no idea what the Serb people would make of themselves in the future, but at least they would have a future. He and Bladislav would see to that.

MARINA STOMBOLIC entered the basement lab's hot room in a full biohazard suit. Among the equipment André Germaine had managed to secret out of the Doumer lab before his ''death'' was enough state-of-the-art, French biohazard gear to protect him and his workers.

''André?'' she asked as she walked up behind the doctor. ''How much longer will you be working tonight?''

Germaine turned to see the main reason he was doing what he was doing. He couldn't see Marina's glossy back hair inside the helmet of the suit, but her startling deep-blue eyes were clear through the helmet visor and he smiled.

Before meeting Marina, he hadn't been political since his university days. But meeting her had changed all that. She had told him the true plight of the Serbian people and had made him aware of the crimes against them that had been committed in the name of the ''New World Order.'' The tears in her blue eyes as she'd spoken of her homeland would have moved a statue, and he finally told her the nature of his secret work for the French government.

From there, it had been a short leap to his realizing that he could use the mutated virus he was developing for the French to help Marina's embattled countrymen and -women. A meeting with General Bladislav had moved his idea forward even more, and the Serb leader had offered all the support he would need to make it happen.

Along with being nonpolitical, Germaine had

had no idea of the extent of the role the criminal underworld played in modern Europe. His reading material had been all medical journals, not the popular newspapers. When the general told him how much money he would be paid to fake his death and come to work for the Serbs, it had been an easy choice to make on that level as well. Having Marina with him made his temporary circumstances here in Romania much more bearable that they would have been if he had come alone.

For a man of science, this wasn't the way he intended to live the rest of his life. It was primitive, and he severely missed the culture of his native land. But, for now, with her to go back to every night made it bearable. When this project was finished, he would be able to live in comfort with her anywhere in the world.

"I will be done very soon, dear," he said. "I need to make sure that my current batch is cooking properly, then I will be done."

"Don't be too late." She smiled. "You work too hard, and I have fixed a special dinner for you."

He smiled back. "I will be on time."

As soon as Marina cleared the decontamination chamber, she headed for the suite in the castle—if you could call three drafty rooms with stone walls a suite—she shared with Germaine. She, too, wasn't impressed with the accommodations, but she also knew that it wouldn't be much longer before she could live anywhere she wanted in the style she craved. Bladislav had promised to ensure that she would never again have to want for anything she desired and as far as she was concerned, she had more than earned anything she might ever want.

Germaine wasn't a bad man, but he had to be one of the most absolutely boring men she had ever known. And, even for her, playing the role of an old man's mistress hadn't been easy. Were it not for a couple of the Iron Guard troops in the castle's garrison, she'd be going out of her mind right now. But, for the payoff Bladislav had promised her, she was willing to play the game for a while longer. Just as long as it didn't take too much longer. She wanted the smell of old man out of her face.

FOR HIS FIRST OFFICIAL appearance in Bucharest, Romania's capital, Mack Bolan had decided to pose as a European Mob boss.

Compared to Budapest, Bucharest was lackluster. Kurtzman's Interpol guy had provided a couple of tips about the worst districts in town, and that's where Bolan took his show. It was easy to find the district police station; it was in the block that was completely empty of foot traffic.

Parking at the curb, Able Team got out of its

Mercedes to escort the ''boss'' into the police station.

The police commandant was straight out of central casting for the part of a corrupt official in a fifth rate, Third World pesthole. He was corpulent, but moved his bulk well enough to signal that it wasn't all fat. His head needed a shave as did the rest of his face and ears. His uniform was rumpled and not all that clean. In short, the guy was a human slug, but Bolan had not come to make deals with the local aristocracy. To establish his bona fides, he had to make his play to the other players.

''I understand,'' Bolan said in Russian, ''that if I wish to do business in this part of Bucharest I need to introduce myself to you.''

''That may be,'' the commandant said, ''but who are you and what do you want to do?''

''I am Sergi Butovik,'' Bolan replied. ''And this is my business card.''

He nodded to Lyons, who stepped forward to place his briefcase on the commandant's desk. When one of the cop's side boys moved in to intercept him, Lyons switched hands on the case and had his Python in the man's face before the switch registered.

The tough skidded to a halt. The commandant's pig eyes narrowed as he motioned the man back to his place. With his way clear again, Lyons holstered his weapon and delivered the briefcase.

Now that the first gun had been shown, Blancanales whipped back his long coat to reveal his MP-5 hanging from its shoulder sling. Slowly moving his right hand to the pistol grip established the rules of the game. They were here to pay off the local chief grafter, but they weren't going to deal with anyone's morons. It wouldn't be good for business. The next moron cop who burped wrong was going to get his head blown off.

The commandant popped the latches on the case and opened it. For a moment, he sat motionless, stunned at the stacks of twenty-dollar bills.

"It is a truly a pleasure meeting a man who knows how to do business, Mr. Butovik." The commandant beamed and it wasn't a pretty sight. Usually people had more teeth and those they had weren't so discolored.

"I like to observe local customs," Bolan replied. "And I understand the value of making new friends everywhere I go. It keeps minor misunderstandings from getting in the way of conducting business."

"That it does." The commandant nodded as if that was the wisest thing he'd ever heard anyone say as well as being the first time he had ever heard of such a concept. "If you do not mind my asking, how much business do you think you will be doing here in Bucharest?"

"As much as I can," Bolan answered. "I understand that your city is a crossroads for all sorts of trade.''

''It is.'' The commandant leaned back in his chair. ''And I am in a unique position to help you meet the people involved in whatever trade you are interested in.''

Bolan studied him for a moment. ''At what fee?''

The man shrugged. ''I usually get a six percent fee for facilitating these transactions.''

''Two and a half.''

''Three,'' the commandant replied.

''Three it is. Please consider my introduction gift a payment in advance for your services.''

A pained look crossed the commandant's face. He'd thought it would be the cream on the top of his usual take.

''But—'' Bolan caught the look ''—your percentage should grow quickly if I meet the right people.''

''You will meet them soon. I assure you.''

''I'm counting on it.''

''What else can I do for you?''

''I'll need a place to conduct my business,'' Bolan replied. ''Nothing too flashy and somewhere I can safeguard my goods.''

''I know of just such a place,'' the commandant replied. ''In fact, my brother-in-law handles the property. I will send him to see you today.''

Bolan glanced at his watch. "Make it quickly. I want to get set up as soon as I can."

"Of course." The cop scribbled something on a scrap of paper. "This is the address, and he will meet you within the hour."

"I'll be there." Bolan took the paper. "And I'm sure we'll meet often."

"I look forward to it," the commandant said.

THE PROPERTY BOLAN was shown was a semi-crumbling two-story building. It's lower portion dated back centuries while half of the top story was badly laid cinderblocks. But it had good fields of fire all the way around and would do nicely for what Bolan had in mind.

Another, but smaller, briefcase full of U.S. dollars secured the "lease" on the property. He was aware that for half that price, he could have purchased the building outright, but that wasn't the way the game was being played. He had to look like he had more money than brains to bring out the worst in the commandant. Letting the brother-in-law see several bundles of what looked like one hundred dollar bills laying around casually should fuel that belief.

As soon as the brother-in-law was clear of the premises, David McCarter appeared with Phoenix Force in the van.

T. J. Hawkins stepped out of the vehicle carrying a bag of Russian-made RDG-5 hand grenades. "I got two dozen of these puppies for ten bucks," he said, grinning. "And they're the latest issue. The guy offered me a mortar and a dozen rounds for fifty bucks, but I didn't think we needed it."

"There was a weapons mall at the checkpoint," McCarter explained. "You might let Hal know that he can probably buy this whole country for a few million. We should be able to do business here very well."

"We've already started," Lyons said. "We bought a dirty cop for five grand."

McCarter laughed.

Now that the Phoenix Force had arrived, the first order of business was to off-load the van and set up a command post in their new digs. While that was being done, Gadgets Schwarz went to work securing the area. The first thing he put in was the early-warning surveillance equipment. Much of what he was laying in was fiber-optic pickups. They didn't give as good a picture as the minicams he used back in the States, but worked good enough for what they might be facing here.

While Schwarz was emplacing the eyes, Gary Manning was laying demo charges. Explosive booby traps were one of his specialties and this was a great location to work with. To start off, he laid in a half a dozen command detonated mini-Claymore mines as the first line of defense. Fiber optics tied to the antipersonnel devices would give him a picture of what he had in his sights before he pulled the trigger on them.

Closer in, he emplaced a few more of them to cover possible hiding places for the attackers. These, too, were put in with fiber optics covering their kill zones.

SCHWARZ WAS AT THE SECURITY console that night when he spotted the first sign of interest. "Striker," he called out, "it looks like we've got company, and they didn't even call ahead for a reservation."

Bolan walked over and studied the images. "Didn't take long to fall for it, did he? Too bad, I was just starting to warm up to him a little. I thought he was going to stay bought, but no, he had to get greedy."

"What can you expect from a slug like him?"

Bolan shrugged. "I guess I expected him wait a couple of days before trying to rip us off."

"Fat chance."

"Speaking of fat, have you spotted our boy yet?"

"No," Schwarz replied. "These are all hard-men."

"Good. We can use them to send the fat man a message."

# CHAPTER SIXTEEN

*Bucharest*

The Stony Man commandos silently went to their battle stations. Unlike the knockdown brawl they'd gotten into in Budapest, they would try for silent kills this time. Now even Brognola's connections wouldn't likely to get them sprung quickly if they ended up in a Bucharest jail. Particularly the fat man's lockup.

Bolan and Rafael Encizo had taken positions in the two buildings closest to their own. Lyons and Able Team had the forward flanks covered while Phoenix Force took care of the rear approach.

Manning's fiber-optic network gave Bolan good enough coverage on his minireceiver to see who had come calling. The pickup placed at the head of the alley leading to the rear of their building showed half a dozen gunmen moving into position to block their escape.

"David," Bolan sent over the com link, "I have

six or seven of them coming up behind us. You want them?''

"Yes, I'll take them.''

"Rafe and I have the bulk of them. I see a dozen coming our way.''

"I'm going to let them get in close enough so the Ironman can help us make a clean sweep. I'll open, Carl.''

"Gotcha covered,'' Lyons sent back.

The Executioner waited patiently until the first of the gunmen walked up to the front door of their building. The gunman tried to peer through the window and seeing nothing, waved the rest of his men forward.

Bolan got him in his sights, and when he turned back to kick down the door, took him out with a head shot.

Seeing their leader go down apparently to a silenced shot, the others froze for a moment before trying to take cover. It was a short moment, but it was long enough.

Rosario Blancanales and Gadget Schwarz both had a good field of fire and swept the kill zone with long bursts from their silenced MP-5 SDs. Encizo and Bolan stayed out of that waiting to see which way their targets jumped.

One or two of the gunmen returned fire with AKs, but only got off short bursts before being taken down. The rest of them turned and fled.

One of the gunmen wasn't smart enough to know that he'd been given his life back and spun around to try to cover his comrade's retreat. Bolan snapped a short burst of silenced 9 mm rounds after him and was rewarded by the thug going down face-first, his AK clattering on the cobblestones.

In the alley at the rear of the building, Phoenix Force's targets hesitated when they heard the AKs from the front. It was only when they heard a yell in Romanian that they realized something was amiss. Unfortunately for them, Phoenix Force didn't miss.

Caught in a cross fire, the four leading gunmen went down without firing a shot. The remaining three proved that they, too, were fast on their feet.

The battle was over almost before it got started.

CLEARING THE KILL ZONE didn't take very long this time. Whoever their visitors were, they hadn't come expecting to get into a full-blown firefight from the four men they'd been told were in the building. When they started dying, they'd pulled back leaving eight casualties behind.

Most of the bodies were in civilian clothing, but two of them were dressed in well-worn Russian pattern camouflage fatigues with full military harnesses. Hawkins walked over to the first cammie-clad body and leaned down.

"Here's another one of those Serb beret

badges." He held the hat out to McCarter. "It's on the front of the beret this time. This guy's up-front with who he is, no more playacting."

"Serbian special forces in Romania," McCarter said.

The Serbs and the Romanians were of different ethnic groups, but they were both Orthodox and therefore natural allies in the twisted politics of the Balkans. "I think this is what Hal has been looking for."

"I sure as hell hope so," Hawkins said. "Not that this gig hasn't been fun. But, man, I'd sure like to get this thing wrapped up."

"What's the matter, T.J., got a hot date?"

Hawkins shook his head. "I'm just tired of Euro cuisine, man. I haven't had a decent steak and baked potato since we got over here."

"I'll see if Barbara can have one flown in for you."

"Will you?" Hawkins grinned. "Gee, David, that'd be great. Can you talk her into throwing in a six-pack while she's at it?"

"Bloody Yank."

"I've got our real-estate agent over here," Lyons called out. "Looks like he was moonlighting as a punk."

"What can you expect from the commandant's brother-in-law?" Hawkins answered.

"It's hard to pick good in-laws."

HAL BROGNOLA WAS ELATED that the Bucharest probe had shown results so soon. He'd felt that going there had been a long shot, but the gamble had paid off. Finding that ex-General Bladislav's Iron Guard had been put in play again confirmed the earlier information and made locating the man their central focus now. Unfortunately, though, that was proving to be as difficult as the rest of this exercise had been.

Aaron Kurtzman and his computer room team was ripping through databases like Attila the Hun in a snit. He, himself, had used the magic words, *Oval Office,* to kick start a search through the hard copy files and reports of every U.S. agency that might have a clue. So far, though, all they knew was that he had vanished years ago.

"The thing that bothers me," Kurtzman mused as he and Brognola went over the negative information they had recovered a second time, "is why Germaine and Bladislav have held off on more bio attacks. They have to know that the virus works well enough for what they have in mind. The coverage of the *Bunker Hill* debacle has been extensive enough that they can't have missed it."

His eyes focused on Brognola. "They know the damned thing works, but they're holding back. Why?"

Before Brognola could think of a reply, Kurtzman continued with his monologue. "I think we've missed one very important factor here. And, one, I might add, that works in our favor for a change.''

"And that is?'' Brognola asked.

"Vaccines,'' he said. "When they loose that virus on a wide scale, they're going to need to have a way to keep from killing their own people. Assuming, of course, that their purpose really is what we've assumed it is, to get the Western nations out of the Serbian Balkans. Fortunately for us, it's more difficult to create an effective vaccine than it is to mutate the bug. The CDC is finding that to be the case and they've got to be better at it than some damned renegade Frenchman working in primitive conditions in Eastern Europe.''

Brognola brightened up at the possibility of a reprieve from the ax hanging over the collective heads of the Western world. "How long do you think it might take them?''

Kurtzman hated to rain on the big Fed's parade when the sun had just come out, but that was part of his job as truth teller. "There's no telling.''

STONY MAN'S DEBUT in Bucharest could only be called a smashing success. Having visitors come calling after less than twenty-four hours was some kind of record, even for them. And, now that the ball was in play, the next move was up to Bolan, and he decided to pay another visit to their new friend, the district police commandant.

"Carl," he said. "I'd like you, Gadgets and Pol to come with me to make a house call on the commandant. He has some explaining to do."

"David," he said, turning to McCarter, "since our visitors were Iron Guard, keep an eye out in case they decide to come back and try again."

"I think we can handle them."

"We'll take the Mercedes. The van might attract too much attention."

Everyone went silenced this time as they absolutely didn't want any interruptions. Even in a place like Bucharest, someone might get alarmed at a major firefight erupting inside a police station.

After parking halfway up the block, Bolan and his team entered the building. Screams from the rear told them that the commandant was entertaining a female visitor, and the laughing male voices told him that he had help doing it. Fanning out, they headed toward the sounds. They found the iron-barred cell blocks empty except for a couple of drunks sleeping it off. They continued on unchallenged.

From the rifle racks against the wall, the back room was apparently the armory, but no one was cleaning his weapon tonight. The cigarette smoke filled armory had been turned into a party room and the guest of honor was tied in a chair under a bare lightbulb. The woman in a chair appeared to be in her mid-twenties, but it was hard to tell.

She'd been knocked around pretty well and was scared out of her mind. That treatment was enough to age anyone.

The commandant had one of his meaty hands in her hair twisting her head to face him while his other hand pawed at her breasts. When he remembered that his fly wasn't opened yet, he took his hand from her breasts and went for his belt buckle, letting his pants fall to his feet.

The cop closest to the commandant was also opening his pants and four more like him waited off to the side patiently. It seemed that their boss wasn't adverse to sharing the perks of being a Romanian cop.

To get this stopped before it went any further, Bolan got a sight lock on the man standing in line for seconds and popped him in the head.

The sound, and the sight of the man's ruined head put an immediate damper on the party. Even so, the commandant and his thugs were slow to react; the half-filled liquor bottles on the nearby table probably had a lot to do with their reaction time.

Since the Stony Man warriors were stone cold sober, they did just fine. Four more short bursts eliminated the remaining lower ranking cops, leaving the commandant with his eyes bulging and his unzipped pants still on his feet.

Bolan quickly crossed to the young woman and

a swipe of his Tanto knife freed her. He helped her to her feet. Rather than dissolving in tears, she reared back and delivered a kick between the commandant's legs. He screamed, grabbed his crotch and doubled over. Then the young woman started to cry.

"Do you speak Russian?" Bolan asked her.

*"Da,"* she answered through her tears.

"Is there somewhere you can go and be safe?"

She nodded. "My sister lives in Prognia. I can go back there. I only came to Bucharest to look for work."

She pointed at the commandant still bent at his waist. "That filthy pig said that he would give me a work permit."

Reaching into his pocket, Bolan pulled out a handful of twenty-dollar bills. "Use this to go to your sister's place. And," he added. "Forget that you saw us."

Grabbing his hand, the young woman wet it with her tears. "God bless you, sir. God bless all of you."

"Go now."

Blancanales walked her to the door and saw her away safely into the night.

WHEN BLANCANALES walked back in the police station "party room," the commandant was now occupying the guest chair. It was a tight squeeze, but he had been stuffed in it and tied down.

"This can be as difficult for you as you want it to be," Bolan said as he walked in front of the man. "Or it can be easy. It's up to you. I want answers to some questions." The Executioner unsheathed the Tanto knife. "If you tell me what I want to hear, you will still have your eyes and tongue in your head when we are done. If not…"

The commandant was a brutal coward, but he wasn't stupid. "I will tell you anything you want to know," he said, his eyes going to the blade.

"First off," Bolan asked as he pulled the black beret out of his pocket, "what is this insignia?"

"It's from General Viktor Bladislav's Serbian Iron Guard," he said. "They are Serbs."

"What are Serbs doing here in Romania?"

"There are thousands of Serbs living here now." The commandant shrugged. "Like everyone else, the war has driven them from their homelands."

"And the Iron Guard?"

"The general brought them here as bodyguards."

"What is he guarding?"

"That I do not know," the commandant said.

"Is it worth one of your eyes not to know?" Bolan asked.

"I swear I do not know what they are doing here."

"Then why did they attack me?" Bolan snapped.

"For your money." The commandant shrugged. "For a businessman, you do not hide your business very well. When someone has large amounts of money like you do, word of it gets around quickly."

"Where does this general have his headquarters?"

"He has a building on the northern side of my district. It is a small compound for his troops, but I do not know what else he does there."

"Is it big enough to hold a drug processing lab?" Bolan asked.

"I don't think so," the commandant replied. "The rumor is that he is working with the Russians somewhere in Transylvania in that business."

"The Russian Mafia?"

"Of course. To process the Afghan opium."

"Where exactly in Transylvania is this lab?" Bolan asked.

Now the commandant balked. This was obviously what these people were after, and information like that was valuable to a man like him.

Bolan eased his Beretta 93-R from its holster and placed the barrel an inch from the man's temple. "You can tell me what I want to know right now or you can die. And, to be honest with you, I don't care which you decide to do.''

The policeman gulped. Bladislav wasn't a man to cross, but the renegade Serb didn't have a gun to the commandant's head. The choice was easy for him to make.

"It is in a castle in the Rusca Valley. You can't miss it because it's the only one in that valley.''

"Does this place have a name?''

"The locals call it the castle.''

As the Executioner lowered his silenced Beretta 93-R, the commandant made his play. He was almost fast enough for a man his size. His intention was to catch Bolan in a head lock, but he hadn't counted on Carl Lyons getting off two shots first. The policeman collapsed to the floor. The commandos left the police station as quickly as they had come.

IT DIDN'T TAKE LONG for word of the Bucharest shoot-out to reach Bladislav in Milan. The ex-General's eyes narrowed as he read the report. "That is the second time now that these people have cost me valuable men.''

"It may be more than that,'' Zoran Dinkic said. "My feeling is that they are the ones who attacked our operations in Western Europe as well. It is obvious now that they have been working their way to us, picking up information along the way and it had now brought them to Bucharest.''

"You had the district police commandant on the payroll, right?''

"Yes.'' Dinkic nodded. "He was well paid to protect our rear area there.''

"Do you think he might have told these men about our operation to the north?''

"That is difficult to tell,'' Dinkic said. "But it is a possibility. Regardless of what it looked like, there was no firefight at the police station, it was an assassination. Our men who escaped the attack on the building those men leased confirm that. My take is that the police station was attacked in retaliation, the police killed and the commandant might have been taken alive. If so, with his worthless life on the line, there's no telling what that pig might have told them before he was killed.''

Bladislav walked over to his wall map. "Whoever those people are, Zoran, I cannot allow them to stop me. I will have a victory for our people.''

He turned back to his operations officer. "Have the major at the castle put his men in the woods immediately. I want the patrols in the security zone doubled and on a twenty-four hour schedule.''

"Yes, sir.''

"And I want every man we have left in Bucharest sent up there as well. Lastly, have the commissioner raise the issue of UN protection for the castle in the General Assembly again.''

''Won't that draw attention to us?''

''It might, but it will also make whoever is doing this think twice before attacking.''

He laughed. ''Particularly if it is the Americans like you think they are. They are very 'sensitive' to matters of cultural heritage. Particularly when those fools in the United Nation gets involved. What fools! They have the power to rule the world and they piss it away on trivia like that.''

The ex-general took on his national leader voice. ''I can assure you, Zoran, that I will not let my Serbia wallow in the past like that. When I am standing at the head of the people, I will lead them into a glorious future, not keep them in the dead past.''

Dinkic worried more about the here and now, not the future that might be if everything went as Bladislav had planned, so he left to pass on the general's orders for the defense of the castle.

# CHAPTER SEVENTEEN

*Stony Man Farm*

The confirmation of finding General Viktor Bladislav's troops in action again and getting the possible location of his secret lab had put the mission
on a fast track.

"Good work, guys," Brognola said as he slid
into his chair at the Annex break table. "The pres
ident is very pleased. However—" he opened his
briefcase "—we have a couple of problems about
your going against that particular castle."

"Let me see," Aaron Kurtzman said. "I wonder
what it might be this time. Hmmm? Could it be
that the United Nations General Assembly has declared that Transylvania is off-limits to operations
against terrorists making mutated smallpox. Something about Romanian vampires being on the endangered species list, right?"

Brognola looked blank. "Almost," he said.

"Give me a break! We've been rampaging

through half of Europe looking for this damned place. We've left a string of cleaned-out whorehouses and drug joints behind and that's not saying anything about the body count. What's wrong now?''

''Well, it turns out that the castle Striker thinks Bladislav's using happens to be a highly valued cultural monument.''

''The home of Dracula's little brother, right?''

''His uncle, actually,'' Brognola replied. ''And it turns out that he was a major hero in the Serb war against the Turks. Before that, the place was a monastery used as a headquarters by Saint Cyril, the founder of the Russian Orthodox church, when he undertook the conversion of the pagan Russians. Kind of their Vatican, they say.''

''That's cute, real cute,'' Kurtzman was completely disgusted, and few things could get him in that state faster than the international bureaucracy of the United Nations. ''Vampires get their own saint. And, to quote our favorite Brit, 'that's not too bloody likely.' Next you're going to tell me that the Russians made the identification of this particular pile of rocks out of a dozen in the area just like it and worked to promote the 'cultural heritage' designation in the General Assembly, right?''

''How the hell did you know?'' Brognola knew better than to be surprised by anything that came out of Kurtzman's mouth. But he hadn't known that he had any interest in cultural minutia like heritage sites.

"I didn't. What I do know, however, is how those bastards work."

"The UN?"

"The Russians."

Kurtzman leaned across the table. "I'll tell you what, Hal, let me run through a couple of things for you here, James Burke–style."

Brognola didn't know who in the hell James Burke was, but he was willing to find out. "Okay."

"Serbs and Russians are Slavs, they share the same general cultural background. The Russians are royally pissed at the U.S. and NATO for their recent 'interventions' in what they've considered as purely Serbian affairs. In fact, had it not been for their army having been in complete disarray at the time, we might have gone to war with them in Bosnia. Fast forward. We have good evidence linking the Serb Mob to these attacks on U.S. forces, and my gut tells me that they aren't doing it completely on their own. They don't have the resources. Ergo, they turn to their cultural Big Brother."

"You mean Moscow's helping them?"

"Moscow's not the only government in what

used to be the Soviet Union, and it sure as hell isn't the most effective of the two they have.''

''The Russian Mafia.''

''Bingo.''

Brognola looked puzzled. ''But we haven't run into any Russians in this so far.''

''Oh, yes, we did,'' Kurtzman reminded him. ''The Budapest hit. That was a huge shipment of heroin by anyone's standards. And, as we all know, the Russian Mafia has the Afghan franchise locked up. But, we knocked over the processed product, not raw opium. That means that it was refined somewhere to the east of Hungary, i.e., Romania. Then, to lock it up, Serb Iron Guard troops brought the shipment into Hungry to hand it off to their Russian buddies and we run into those same scumbags again in Bucharest. Russians, Serbs, Romania and to me that's a wrap. The Russian Mob is doing something at that 'cultural heritage' site, for damned sure. But I can tell you for sure that it's not archaeology.''

Kurtzman bore in for the kill. ''If that 'heritage site' is the Russian heroin production facility that every drug task force in Western Europe has been looking for since the early nineties, it's also a perfect place to make a mutated smallpox virus. That shipment of culturing media I pinpointed being shipped into Bucharest tells me that's exactly what they're doing there.'' He snorted. ''And that gives an entirely new definition to the concept of 'cultural heritage.'

Brognola could be a hard sell, but once he was sold, there was no buyer's remorse. "How soon can Striker get a recon up there?"

"It's a long way from Bucharest to Transylvania, but they're ready to move out now."

Brognola took a deep breath. "Do it," he said. "I'll square it with the Man."

"You'd better. Because if that place's what I think it is, it's not going to be a walk in the park to get close to it."

He leaned closer. "That's why the Iron Guard is mixed up in this."

OPERATING IN WHAT had once been Eastern Europe's most repressive Communist police states was a mixed blessing. On the one hand, very few Romanians were bold enough to question anything the Stony Man warriors did unless they were government officials. On the other hand, this was a country where spying on even your own family and turning them in for rewards was a time-honored national pastime. Even though the rewards weren't what they had once been, the custom was still followed.

That said, it was high time for the Stony Man warriors to get out of town before someone ratted them out.

"Okay," Bolan said. "We're leaving town, and we've got the go-ahead to make a recon of the castle."

"Why screw around with that?" Lyons asked. "If you haven't noticed, we're a little thin on the ground around here. This is a hostile country, and along with standing out like a Mariachi band at a bar mitzvah, we're far from any kind of meaningful support."

"The problem is that while we have Hal on board with this place as most likely being our target, the President is being cautious because it's a listed UN cultural heritage site."

"So?"

"The 'so' is that it's a Russian cultural site and they're a little protective of it. The Man's still trying hard not to restart the Cold War."

"Man," Lyons said, looking totally disgusted, "I get so tired of this shit. If we find that they're making that smallpox there, I'm going to grab a bottle of it and visit the United Nations building when we get back."

Bolan suppressed a grin. "That's called bioterrorism, Carl, and we're supposed to be fighting against people doing things like that."

"I'm against assholes hiding behind crap like that while they're trying to kill me."

"David—" Bolan turned to McCarter "—what's your thoughts on a recon?"

The ex-SAS man studied the map for a moment. "If we do it, we're going to need to relocate our base closer to the target. I want to be close enough to reinforce if needed. I'd say—" he tapped the map "—maybe this mountain meadow on the other side of the ridge line."

"And, since we're in Romania, not Switzerland," McCarter stated, thinking aloud, "it's got to be an armed recon. If we went out as backpackers, we'd disappear within the day. If the Iron Guard didn't get us, the locals probably would whack us for our shoes if nothing else."

"For this…" He looked over at James. "Cal, you feel up to doing a walkabout?"

"Sure."

"Gary?"

"Why not?" the Canadian asked. "Looks like it might be interesting country."

"Except for the vampires," Hawkins said.

James laughed. "Man, those blood suckers know better than to mess with me. Back on the block, we ate vampires for a light snack."

"And had werewolves for dessert, right?"

James high fived. "You got that right, homey."

"I don't think you'll need to pack wooden stakes for this outing," McCarter said. "Seven point six two should take care of it quite nicely."

"You'd still better pack a couple of tent stakes," Hawkins cautioned.

HATEG WAS THE LAST LITTLE town on the map before Calvin James and Gary Manning got into the hills around the castle, so they decided to check it out on their way in. The town itself wasn't much, two dozen medium-size houses around a white-washed Orthodox church. Right outside that, though, was a small military compound consisting of a small headquarters building, a couple of barracks, a sizable tank park and vehicle maintenance sheds.

"That's a nice little collection of hardware," James said as he peered through his field glasses at the company-size tank park.

"Anything we can use?" Manning asked.

"Actually," James said as he watched black diesel smoke fill the air as a mechanic cranked up a Russian-built T-72 tank, "if it turns out that we're going to have to get serious with that rock pile, this's the place to borrow the tools to do it with. Tank guns in 125 mm firing AP rounds should just about handle anything we come up against in the line of Medieval rock fortifications."

"Or modern field fortifications," Manning added. "Don't forget the Iron Guard."

Kurtzman had faxed Bolan a series of satellite recon photos of their target castle, but persistent cloud cover had prevented the K-12 from getting really clear shots. A number of terrain mapping readouts had come with the less than perfect photos, but they too were difficult to read. It did, however, look like someone had been digging in around the approaches to the castle. If that turned out to be the case, they might need a tank.

IT WAS LATE AFTERNOON when James and Manning broke through the tree line on a ridge two and a half miles from the castle. Keeping low, they moved to the edge of the woodline for a good look.

The castle sat on a low hill at the northern end of the valley several miles away. The keep itself was impressive enough, surrounded by a number of outbuildings and a second wall enclosing the entire complex. A paved road led through the valley from the south right up to the main gate in the outer wall. For a site dating back to Byzantine times, it was in a pretty good state of repair. The shades of the patina on different sections of the complex, though, made it obvious that some of the work was recent.

"I didn't realize that Dracula had so many neighbors," James said as he scanned the target.

Manning grinned. "That's supposed to be just the home of Drac's uncle, remember? He must not have been so hard on the neighbors."

"And such nice neighbors," James said. "I'm picking up guys all over the place in cammie battle dress and what looks like black berets."

"Iron Guard troops?"

"Sure looks like it."

A green-and-black camouflaged truck with troops in the back appeared at the main gate of the outer wall. A guard waved it through and it drove on trailing a cloud of diesel smoke.

"They sure as hell aren't transportation corps guys," James replied. "Or that truck would be running better."

The paved road curved in right below the ridge line they were occupying and the truck stopped half a mile away. As they watched from cover, a five-man unit got down and, after checking over their weapons and gear, started up a path leading to the ridge.

"We need to evaporate," Manning said.

"You got that right."

The two Stony Man commandos pulled well back into the trees. James flipped out his map and looked for a way around the security team.

"You have a truck stopped on the road below you," Bolan's voice came in over the com link.

"We know," James replied. "It dropped off some kind of roving security squad, and we're evacuating the premises at this moment."

"Try going east for a mile or so and then hooking around to the north. It looks like you'll have good cover all the way."

James looked at his map and spotted the route Bolan had suggested. "That looks as good as anything," he said. "We'll try it."

"Have Aaron see if he can pick those guy's weapons up on his MAD sensors," Manning asked. "So he can keep an eye on them. We don't need to be followed right now."

Magnetic Anomaly Detectors worked by detecting minute changes in Earth's magnetic fields. It worked best for things like tracking submarines, but had been known to pick up men packing small arms.

"There's a lot of scrap iron in those hills," Bolan came back a moment later. "So he's not getting the kind of readings he'd like. In fact, the only way he's tracking you is through your locator beacons."

"I thought all this high-tech stuff was supposed to cut trough the cloud cover and ground clutter."

"Not yet," Bolan said. "We're going to have to wait for Version 2.0."

"Shit."

James had inputted their new route into his GPS system and was ready to move out. "Let's go," he said.

The two commandos headed west though the woods. They moved as quickly as they could, but with a tracking team coming in behind them, they had to be careful not to leave a trail. Finding a well used game track winding up the ridge line, they took off on it.

A HALF HOUR LATER, James almost skidded to a stop as he flashed a hand sign. Manning was beside him instantly, his H&K assault rifle at the ready.

The five-man patrol heading up the trail toward them was wearing Russian-style cammies with black berets and full combat packs with at least one radio. They were also packing AK-74s and AKSU subguns. Like the men who had come in the truck, these guys were someone's regular troops, not some ragtag militia or a local war lord's followers.

They were still following the game trail leading up the side of a steep slope so their options of evading these guys wasn't good. Looking around, James spotted a dark area between two boulders on the cliff above them.

"Up the cliff," he whispered over the com link. "I think there's a cave up there."

Manning saw that if it wasn't a cave, it was at least deep shadows they would hide in. "Go."

Moving quickly, but carefully so as not to leave sign of their passing, they worked their way up through the rocks to the cliff face. The cave James had spotted turned out to be a four-foot opening between two huge boulders. They slipped inside right as the patrol approached the place on the trail where they had been at before heading up to the cave. Then the patrol stopped.

The two commandos figured they'd been spotted and snapped their weapons up to their shoulders. They were outnumbered, but not that badly and they had a good fighting position. Their only problem was that damned radio. James started tracking the man carrying it on his back, planning to take him out first when the shooting started.

"Ah, shit!" James said when he saw the patrol start taking off their packs and finding a place to sit. "Now they're taking a fucking coffee break."

Manning brought his assault rifle down. "At least they're not coming after us."

"Not right now," James pointed out the obvious. "But we're stuck here till they leave."

## CHAPTER EIGHTEEN

*Transylvania*

The Stony Man command-and-control van had been pulled in under the trees in a wooded area a few miles from where Calvin James and Gary Manning were doing their recon. The remaining Stony Man warriors were in security positions around it and, so far, they had avoided being spotted. That, however, could change at any moment.

They hadn't seen all that many civilians in the area, but all it would take would be for some local farmer to take off after his missing sheep to stumble on them and they'd be on the run again.

Inside the van, David McCarter and Mack Bolan watched the NRO satellite sensor readings stream in from the Farm. As Carl Lyons had so aptly pointed out, they were too thin on the ground to have two of the team miles away on an unsupported recon like that. Particularly with poor satellite surveillance of the operational area. The cloud cover was blanking out most of the visual imagery, and they were having to rely on MAD sensings which weren't all that helpful, either.

"Aaron picked up more vehicle movements a little while ago," Bolan said as yet another satellite MAD readout came in over the fax. The worst thing about the MAD sensors they were hooked up to was that it wasn't real time like the video images were. It took some time for the satellite's processors to go through the MAD data and plot it out before sending it back to earth.

"Where?"

"On the road going east from the castle."

"Bloody hell! That's heading right into the area Calvin and Gary are evading into."

Bolan keyed the com limk. "Cal, you have more traffic heading your way."

When he received no answer, he tried again. "Cal, this is Striker. Come in."

Still, there was no reply.

"It's these mountains," he said. "Aaron promised that com sat of his would relay everything we sent."

"Well, it bloody well isn't working, is it?" McCarter started up.

"No," Bolan agreed as he punched in a code on his keyboard, "It's not. And the locator beacons aren't transmitting, either."

"Are you getting the killed signal?"

"I'm not getting anything."

"We'll go after them in a couple of hours, after nightfall. They may be holed up somewhere that's blocking their transmissions. And I'll take the jeep."

On their way out of Bucharest, Gadgets Schwarz had managed to come across a Korean War-vintage American M-38 jeep in remarkably good condition. For a mere hundred bucks, they'd added it to their convoy.

McCarter hated to sit on his butt waiting for the two to surface or for darkness to fall. "I'll go out and relieve one of the guys."

Bolan nodded. "I'll give you a shout as soon as I get something from them."

"Do that."

CALVIN JAMES and Gary Manning hugged the walls of the cave, their weapons trained on the entrance. Getting caught by the enemy patrol like this was real cherry crap. They'd been so focused on trying to get away from the first patrol coming up behind them that they'd almost stumbled over the second one. The worst thing was that the rocks were blanking out their com link with the others, so there was no way to report what had happened to them.

The sound of rocks clicking together echoed from the back of the cave sending both commandos spinning, their fingers on their triggers. James activated his night-vision goggles and saw a civilian with his finger held up to his lips standing right behind them. Damn, that guy could move silently and, if he'd been armed, they'd both be dog meat.

"Jesus," he said softly as he lowered his weapon.

The man looked to be a hundred if he was a day and was dressed in rough peasant's clothing with what looked like a sheep's fleece vest. They could smell him as he got closer, but most of it was goat.

"Germani," he whispered and pointed to the entrance of the cave.

"Germani?" Manning said quietly.

The man nodded emphatically and tugged on his sleeve to draw him deeper into the cave. With the Serbs parked outside, not looking like they were going anywhere anytime soon, rather than wait for one of them to decide to do a little cave exploring, it was the best option they had.

"Let's do it," he whispered to James.

The old man led them to the rear of the cave where two pillars of rock reaching to the roof flanked what looked like a depression in the rock. Going around the right-hand pillar, however, revealed a narrow passageway that seemed to continue even deeper.

The old man had to have had eyes like a cat because he plunged into darkness that even the

NVGs didn't illuminate well. James and Manning followed him blindly.

After what seemed like ten minutes, the narrow tunnel suddenly turned a corner into a larger cave lit by candles. Flipping up his NVGs, James saw that it was furnished as a small shepherd's hut with crude handmade furniture and not much of it, either. A bed of thick blankets was against one wall and a wooden door on the far side probably led back out into the open. The door had a large carved Orthodox crucifix attached to it and icons flanked it on both sides.

A young man dressed in woolen clothing stood waiting for them. "Welcome," he said in English. "I am Danic."

"He said something about Germani?" Manning nodded at the old man.

"My grandfather," the young man said proudly. "He fight Germans in the Great War. The new soldiers, he call them Germans, but they are Serbs." The man spit. "Iron Guard. Bad men."

"Bingo," James muttered.

"You are Americans." Danic looked long at James. "Do you come to kill Serbs?"

"We want to see what they are doing at the castle."

The man crossed himself. "That is a bad place. They do bad things there."

"Looks like we found ourselves an ally," James said.

"What kind of bad things are they doing?" Manning prompted him.

"They take our sheep and do not give us money. They shoot at us if they see us. Russians are there too, and they are bad men, too."

"This is starting to sound real familiar," James said.

Danic gestured to the table where a loaf of bread, a half round of cheese and a couple bottles of wine sat. "Will you eat?"

"Thank you," Manning said, "but is there another way out of here? We have to go as soon as we can."

"You not go now!" The men looked panicked. "Night come soon and bad things live in the woods at night. The evil ones who drink blood."

"Man," James said, "it sounds to me like this neighborhood could use a thorough housecleaning. The Iron Guard, Russians and now vampires."

"Don't forget smallpox."

"Right."

"You eat now, sleep here with us tonight and go out in the morning," Danic urgently insisted. "The evil ones see in the dark."

"We'll be safe in the woods," Manning said. "We can see in the dark, too."

The man recoiled and his hand moved to cross himself again.

Manning tapped his NVGs. "This makes us see in the dark," he explained and tapped the H&K slung at his side. "And we can kill the evil ones."

Danic nodded his understanding. "Even so," he said, "we will pray for you."

"Thanks," Manning said. "How do we get out of here?"

The shepherd moved to open the wooden door. "This is on the other side of the mountain," he said. "You will be safe from the Serbs who follow you."

Manning didn't ask how this guy knew they had been followed, but apparently, the locals knew enough to stay out of the way of the Bladislav's patrols.

"Thank you."

"Go with God, Americans."

THE STONY MAN COMMANDOS went into the twilight and waited until they were a quarter of a mile away from the shepherd's hut before they used tried to use their com links. "David," Manning said, "we're back online, but we're in some kind of vampire preserve."

"Where the hell have you been?" McCarter stated. "And what in the hell are you talking about?"

"We got trapped in a cave by an Iron Guard patrol and a friendly local showed us a back way out. We have confirmation that there are both Serbs and Russians in the castle, and the locals say they're up to no good."

"We also were warned about vampires in the woods," James broke in. "The locals were frantic when we said that we were going back out tonight. According to them, there are blood suckers out here that can see in the dark."

"Night-vision gear?" David suggested.

"That's what it sounds like to me, so we're going to be extra careful."

"Did you get the photos?"

"We got them covering the southern approach and it doesn't look good. I figured that we'd try to work our way around to the north side by morning and take a look at that as well."

"Cancel that," McCarter cut in. "Just get clear of the area and Rafe and I will pick you up just south of that village you called in."

"Roger," Manning called back.

Night had come quickly to the thick forests covering the mountain, but the glowing green scene through their night-vision goggles was distinct enough for the two commandos to move at almost daylight speed down the tree-covered mountain. The shepherd's warning of night stalkers on the loose made them cautious, though.

Two miles from the hut, James spotted something that brought him to an abrupt halt. A human skull had been nailed to a tree like a warning marker. The rest of the skeleton's bones were in a jumble below it as if they had fallen loose. The warning was plain enough and would scare the locals who had heard the ancient legends, but this wasn't the work of vampires.

The skull had a bullet hole in it, and the traditional blood suckers in the region hadn't been big on guns.

"Here be vampires," James whispered.

"With AKs."

"Thanks for the warning."

Not for the first time on this outing, the two wished that they were wearing the new ALOCS combat suits. Not only was the night vision better, they could have used the rest of the system they had been designed to work with. For one thing, the suits cut down on the wearer's IR signature. With night stalkers in the woods, that would have been very helpful, as would the GPS and terrain readouts that could be displayed on the helmet visor HUD.

As it was, they had their NVGs and hard earned experience at moving through unfriendly territory. Checking in with McCarter every half hour, they continued down off the ridge and linked with the jeep right before daybreak without spotting any vampires.

WHEN THEY ARRIVED back at the van, Bolan popped the disk out of Manning's video camera and plugged it into the port on his laptop. A few taps on the keyboard transferred the images to his hard drive.

"Good shots," he said as the first image came up on his monitor.

Using a video rather than a film camera on recons cut the time of processing the film to zip. Plus, it was easier to send them as jpeg images rather than faxes from developed film. The Farm would get these shots in the same detail and clarity that he was seeing them now. That was the good news. The bad news was what they were showing.

The castle itself would have been bad news enough. It had been built for combat back in the days when men moved on foot to fight, and it showed it. Those sword-and-shield guys had known how to make it difficult for men on foot to get over their walls. Adding modern weaponry to stone walls made it only more of a problem for a commando raid.

The second image was a telephoto shot of the trenches and weapons emplacements that had been dug in front of the walls. The old Yugoslavian State Industries had been known for making world-class artillery. Yugoslavia was defunct, but some of their excellent guns had been put to good use here. McCarter picked out a pair of 85 mm antitank guns in the direct support role as well as several 128 mm multiple barrel rocket launchers in general support.

"Since we are slightly less than an armored brigade," McCarter commented dryly, "I believe Hal would be well advised to rethink this entire affair. He's going to be out a couple of commando strike teams if we try to go up against that place."

"I'll pass that on," Bolan said, "but I'm afraid that we're going to have to at least give it a try."

The Brit studied the screen. "I was afraid you were going to say something like that."

WHEN WORD REACHED Viktor Bladislav that the mysterious westerners in Bucharest had disappeared, he became concerned. The Iron Guard officer who had gone along with the police commandant's idiotic idea to try to rob these people had been disciplined. His explanation that he thought he was just dealing with a drug gang hadn't saved him. His body had been buried in front of the entrance of his Bucharest headquarters so every man entering the building would have to step over him. It would serve as a reminder that his orders were to be obeyed without question and orders came only from him or Dinkic. Bladislav couldn't afford to have his junior officers getting personally ambitious and thinking for themselves.

While he was sure that there would be no more such lapses in the near future, Bladislav now faced having to locate those men before they caused him any more problems. Zoran Dinkic still held to his belief that they were American Rangers, and Bladislav was beginning to believe that his operations officer was right. The United States was the only major Western nation where he didn't have someone in a position of importance to feed him information on their counter terrorist activities.

Dinkic had reported that the patrols were ranging far out into the mountains to give him early warning and the castle had been reinforced as he had ordered. That done, it should be able to withstand anything short of a major attack, either from the ground or the air.

But he was also fully aware that given enough time the circumstances would inevitably change. They wouldn't, however, change in his favor until after the virus attacks had been made. Until such time as he was fully ready to launch them, he was completely at the mercy of Dr. André Germaine.

Working with Germaine had been a frustrating exercise for Bladislav. Being a man of science, the doctor's motivations were different from most other men's. Bladislav had learned early on of Germaine's work for the French from his man in Bureau Two, and the idea to try to turn him had come to him then. The problem turned out to be that the doctor wasn't a man who was susceptible to the usual bribes. Money for money's sake wasn't of interest to him.

Investigating his background turned up the fact that he had had a torrid affaire with a young Serbian woman, a fellow medical student. After several fevered months, the woman's family had called her back to Yugoslavia for an arranged marriage. Germaine had never loved again, and Marina Strombolic had been exactly the right kind of bait to use to snare him. She was a good look alike for his lost love, and Bladislav sincerely doubted that Germaine had known a woman like little Marina. Her approach to sensual pleasures had completely rearranged his thinking and woken him to something he thought he'd lost for all time. After she had been with the researcher for only a couple of weeks, it had been child's play for her to bring him into the plan.

The money he had been offered for successful completion of his project wasn't high on Germaine's list of concerns. He saw it only as the means he would have to keep Marina happy when this was over. The old fool had no idea that she couldn't wait to get away from him and back to her playgrounds in Western Europe. She hadn't said anything to Bladislav about her post-Germaine plans, but he knew her mind well. After all, she had been his mistress for years before he'd loaned her to the Frenchman to promote his plans.

The problem he was having with Germaine was that the man didn't really comprehend the urgency they all were facing right now. He saw his work as something that entailed measured steps that couldn't be hurried. As he had said, "Science cannot be hurried for the needs of men." That was all fine and good for a man of science, but it was not the way Bladislav thought. He was a man of action, and he needed to get into action now.

Reaching out, he hit the intercom button on his phone. "Yes, sir," Dinkic answered.

"Get my helicopter ready, Zoran," Bladislav said. "I want to go to the castle and light a fire under the doctor."

"When do you wish to leave?"

"As soon as you can get flight clearance."

"That will take a day."

"Just take care of it as soon as you can."

"Yes, sir."

# CHAPTER NINETEEN

*Stony Man Farm*

The digital photos Manning had taken of the Transylvanian castle were displayed on the big screen monitors in the Annex for the briefing. The defensive positions that had been hidden from the spy satellites by the cloud cover were nicely laid out for all to see in glowing color. But while clear, the photos didn't look good. In fact, the forbidding rock pile looked more like the set for a World War II movie than a rebuilt medieval castle.

"That's about as good a target as I've ever seen for a half a dozen, two-thousand-pound, laser-guided bombs," Aaron Kurtzman grumbled as he studied the bad news. "No, make that an even dozen. With our guys lighting up the targets for the Stealth fighters, they could take that place out right down to bedrock and no one would ever be the wiser."

"The President's not going to let us do that,

Aaron.'' Hal Brognola shook his head. ''And you know that because laser-guided bombs are our trademark response. That's the sort of attack that only the United States can make and it's like leaving a calling card behind with the Presidential Seal on it. We're going to have to do it on the ground this time and blame someone else for the damage.''

''You're saying that a rational alternative to having someone denounce us in the UN General Assembly is to ask our guys to go toe-to-toe with fifty or sixty Iron Guard troops and dug in support weapons? Tell the Man to get real, Brognola!'' Price stated.

Brognola had been expecting her response and stayed calm. ''Part of the problem is that both the Ukrainian and Russian UN ambassadors brought up the issue of war damage to the cultural sites in the Balkans again yesterday. If I didn't know better, I'd almost say that Bladislav prompted that to keep us from doing exactly what you've suggested.''

''Well, how about that?'' Price said. ''The bad guys are using the UN to keep us from doing our jobs. What a novel concept!''

''I may be able to get our guys a little help, though. The Man's authorized weapons and equipment drops if they need them.''

''How about authorizing a battalion of the 101st while you're at it? Or a Marine landing force?

Maybe air drop a company of Abrams and Bradleys in as an escort. Hal, that stone castle's guarded by shock troops and modern weapons this time, not a couple dozen drug lord scumbags.''

"Let's bring Striker in on this,'' Brognola continued, trying to pour oil on the troubled waters. "He may have something useful cooking.''

"Just as long as it's not suicide stew.''

Brognola didn't bother responding to that as he placed his call to Romania. As the signal went up to the comsat and back down, he thumbed off a couple of antacid tabs from his roll and swallowed them dry.

"WE CAN TRY A BIT OF razzle-dazzle here,'' Bolan suggested when he connected on the satcom call. "Gary and Cal found a tank park on their way into the target area. We can borrow a tank and do a standoff attack as a diversion while a demo team works its way inside to blow the place up. On the way out, we'll go with two exfiltration routes to expedite the recovery of the teams.''

"Go with any plan you think might work,'' Brognola said. "As the man on the ground, I'll leave that completely up to you. But work up a list for the resupply you'll need as soon as you can. I've got a C-17 waiting on the tarmac at Fort Stewart to bring it to you.''

"Is there a limit on the number of drops we can get?"

"Not that I've been told."

"First off then," Bolan thought out loud, "I want ALOCS suits for the team with full armor inserts."

The Advanced Low Observable Combat Suit, shortened to the acronym ALOCS and pronounced "A-Locks," was the army's latest application of digital technology to military requirements. Among the high-tech suit's abilities was that it reduced the wearer's infrared signature to that of a small animal. If that wasn't enough, the suit could also camouflage itself against whatever terrain the soldier was moving through. Peizoelectronic circuitry woven into the suit's fabric allowed it to change shades of color depending on the man's immediate surroundings. At night, of course, the colors darkened.

The accessories that came with the suit were what really made the system the wonder of modern technology that it was. The communications system worked off of a keypad worn on the right wrist as well as the throat mike. That allowed both voice and data transmission and gave the commandos a silent way to communicate with one another and, through satellites, with the Farm.

The ALOCS helmet was also a marvel of microchip technology. Its Kevlar face shield worked like a fighter pilot's HUD—Heads Up Display—screen. It could display a map of the terrain they were moving through and GPS could be slaved to the HUD to read out range and azimuth to anything the soldier could see. It also kept track of the other men wearing the suits as well through the personal locator, pinpointing their locations on the HUD display.

When the helmet was used in conjunction with the OICW, the heavy weapon's targeting and sighting electronics could be slaved to the visor allowing the gunner to aim and fire without having to even look through his weapons sight.

"Okay," Brognola told him, "I'll do everything I can to see that you get them."

"Then," Bolan continued, "for the ordnance request, along with all the 20-mm rounds you can get for the OICW, I want all the Dragon's Breath 40 stuff you have in stock, both the M-19 and M-203 loads. We're going to need to burn that place, and the Dragon's Breath will be a good way to light it up. Oh yeah, make sure to toss in Gary's sniper rifle."

"I don't see a problem there," Brognola replied.

"For the bigger pieces," Bolan said, "I want one of those Spec Ops Dune Buggies with a M-19 40 mm mounted on it. Along with it, I want a Hummer so we can stay mobile on the exfiltration phase."

"I'll make sure it's one of the sterile Spec Ops vehicles, too."

"Give it an M-2 .50-caliber so we'll have some reach."

"Will do."

"On the rest, The demo and the bits and pieces, I'll get with the guys and work up a list."

"Get that to me as soon as you can," Brognola said. "Needless to say, the President wants to see this concluded as quickly as possible."

"And," Bolan added, "Hal, you might want to let the President know right now that if we fail, he'd better get the Stealth bombers cranked up. A Plan B, if you will, to fall back on. If we can't take that place out, we're going to have mutated small-pox racing through the States and Western Europe."

PUTTING ALL THE Stony Man team's resupply into one C-17A Globemaster II jet assault transport was a trick, but the Spec Ops cargo handlers at Fort Stewart, Georgia, were really good at what they did. Grimaldi's CIA credentials made sure that few questions were asked and even fewer answered. As was always the case with a Stony Man mission, the fewer who knew what was going on right in front of their eyes, the better.

With all of the Stony Man commandos occupied in Romania, Brognola had authorized Jack Grimaldi to select a four man cargo kicking team from the Farm's blacksuit security force. For the first leg of the trip, the long flight across the Atlantic, a properly cleared air force major was coming along as the copilot.

The C-17A was a relatively new, state-of-the-art bird and Flying Jack hadn't yet been checked out in it. By the time they reached Italy, however, he'd be as at home in it as he was in everything else he strapped himself into.

After a final check, Grimaldi, the copilot and the blacksuits boarded the jet, got immediate clearance for takeoff and flew east.

After a fairly fast transatlantic flight with his air force copilot, Grimaldi landed the C-17A Globemaster II at the UN airbase at Aviano, Italy, for a quick refueling. The copilot left the plane there, and Grimaldi would take it in alone from that point. Since the one-way distance was just over seven hundred miles, he could do that one-handed.

His flight path was going to take him over Croatia, Bosnia and what was left of the former Yugoslavia before flying the border between Hungary and the former Yugoslavia. UN Profor intelligence indicated that most of the jet fighters of those splinter nations were grounded for lack of fuel or maintenance. Nonetheless, they all were well equipped with Russian designed antiaircraft missiles and were a bit touchy about strange aircraft flying overhead. And there was always enough JP-4 fuel drums lying around the fuel dump for a curious MiG pilot to scope out an aerial intruder crossing over his homeland.

The pilot planned to make much of his trip to Romania under the radar, but while flying low would protect him from MiG patrols, it put him in the danger zone from antiaircraft fire. One of the blacksuits along for the ride was ex-air force, and he was riding Grimaldi's right-hand seat to keep track of the threat warning systems.

The last countermeasure he'd taken before leaving the States was to have the C-17's markings painted out. He'd thought of having big red Russian stars painted over the U.S. insignia, but decided that might cause him too much grief on the way back into Italy. This was supposed to be a classified flight, and he didn't need every UN MiG Cap jockey in Southern Europe making a gun run on him before he could get him waved off over the radio. As it was, he'd end up coming back with a F-15 escort anyway, but at least they wouldn't be tracking him with their weapons hot.

After a last aircrew pit stop, Grimaldi and the blacksuits boarded again, and it was wheels up for Romania and the Transylvanian Alps.

WITH THE RUGGED, densely forested, terrain of the region, David McCarter had been hard-pressed to find a good drop zone for the incoming resupply flight. The spots that were large enough were forested, and the clearings were too small to get something as big as a C-17 in.

He'd been forced to settle for a remote high mountain valley with only one access road leading into it. Blocking that road should keep the Romanians and the Iron Guard out, but the DZ was so big there was no way to keep out wandering locals. If a sheepherder or two did stumble into the DZ, they'd be scooped up and held until they were ready to move out.

The only problem was that with a single road, if the Iron Guard did come in force, they'd be trapped. They'd have to abandon their vehicles to evade through the woods, screaming for help as they ran. The only good thing was that the deep woods ran all the way to the Hungarian border.

McCarter was prowling the perimeter when Mack Bolan's voice broke in on his com link. "David," he said, "I have confirmation on Jack's liftoff from Italy. His ETA is an hour forty-five."

"We're ready for it," McCarter replied.

"T.J., Cal?" The Briton transmitted, "you've got an ETA in less than two hours."

"We're set, boss," Hawkins sent back. "Tell him to bring it on."

# CHAPTER TWENTY

*Transylvania*

Jack Grimaldi entered the rugged northern Transylvanian Alps. So far, the trip hadn't been as exciting as he had expected, but there had been a couple of tense moments as he kept the huge transport down in the dirt on a terrain-following flight path.

Getting lit up by a SAM-6 missile battery had required a few minutes of fancy flying to break the radar lock. And the battery of 85 mm Triple A guns on the mountaintop he had flown past had been a giggle. He'd been flying so low through the valley beneath them that the gunners hadn't been able to depress their tubes far enough to take him under fire before he'd flown out of sight.

He'd flipped the gun crew the bird as he'd motored past at better then four hundred knots. But they'd been so busy cranking the elevation gears on their pieces, they hadn't noticed the defiant one-fingered salute.

Of all that, though, getting in and making the supply drop was going to be the critical part of this excursion. Checking his GPS readout confirming his current position, he keyed his throat mike.

"Vampire, this is Flyboy," he radioed. "I'm inbound ten miles out from your GPS Delta Zulu. Pop smoke to confirm, over."

"This is Vampire." T.J. Hawkins chuckled at Grimaldi's choice of their call sign as he pulled a smoke grenade from his assault harness. "Smoke out on a cold Delta Zulu."

He pulled the pin on the grenade and tossed it out in front of his feet. Three seconds later, a cloud of green smoke billowed up into the air. The colored smoke wasn't only to confirm the drop zone location, it also gave the pilot an accurate assessment of the ground winds over it.

"Roger Lime," Grimaldi replied when he saw the smoke. "I've got you covered and I'm coming in."

"Bring it on."

Looking to the north, Hawkins spotted the big cargo jet on final approach, its gear and flaps down. Unlike the smaller C-130 Hercules turbo prop assault transports they used whenever they could, this monster seemed too big to be flying that low. The angle to the wings and the four underslung jet engines gave it the look of a predator, not a deliverer.

Looks aside, he knew that Grimaldi would deliver the goods, assault transport-style.

EVEN THOUGH THIS was a cold DZ, Grimaldi brought the C-17 straight in on a deep dive. He had his landing gear, flaps and rear ramp down as he lined up with the trees at the far end of the DZ. The valley was long enough that he wouldn't have to do any fancy maneuvers here today, just accurate flying. As always with a LAPES delivery, the essence of the art was to get the pallets on the ground, in the right place, intact. Miss any of those three, and he might as well have stayed home.

LAPES was military jargon for Low Altitude Parachute Extraction System, and it was the fastest way to transfer something from inside an airplane to the ground that had ever been invented. This time, though, he wouldn't be able to touch his wheels down to steady the delivery while the pallets were being whisked out the back by the drag chutes. The ground was too rough, and even a plane that had been designed for rough terrain landing risked breaking something at that speed. He would, however, be close enough to the ground to use his landing gear if something went wrong.

In the cargo hold of the C-17, the four blacksuits along for the ride as cargo kickers were at their stations. Unlike with a Hercules, the LAPES on this plane was semi-automated so human error wouldn't screw up the critical timing. As the heaviest of the two large pallets, the M-198 Hummer would exit first followed by the dune buggy.

"Stand by to initiate the drop," Grimaldi sent over the intercom.

"Roger," the blacksuit acting as cargo master responded. "Standing by."

The blacksuit stood by his control panel while the others manually released the pallet lock down pins. Out the open rear ramp, they could see Grimaldi bringing the plane closer and closer to the ground. It almost looked as if he were trying to land in the grass and brush, but he was going much too fast for that.

"On my count," Grimaldi called back again. "Three...two...one, do it!"

On command, the cargo master hit his switch, which caused the pilot chute from the first pallet to deploy out the open rear ramp. Caught in the roiling slip stream behind the plane, it instantly jerked the drag chutes out of their packs. The risers on the larger chutes snapped tight and the palletized Hummer shot out the back like it had a retrorocket strapped to it.

No sooner had the vehicle hit the ground than the auto delivery system sent the dune buggy pallet flying out the rear after it. With the second pallet clear of the plane, Grimaldi jammed his four throttles up to a hundred and ten percent power and the four fan jets howled in response. Sucking his gear up, he hauled back on the control column to clear the trees at the end of the valley.

Once he had a couple of hundred feet of air under his belly, he keyed his com link. "Vampire, I'll hang around up here while you get that stuff outta the way."

"Roger," Hawkins sent. "We're moving now."

FROM THE EDGE of the DZ, Hawkins, Manning, James and Schwarz raced across the grass to get the palletized vehicles off the drop zone.

Reaching the Hummer first, Hawkins slid into the driver's seat, hit the starter and the vehicle fired right up. Dropping vehicles full of gas had been a necessary risk this time. Manning raced around the Hummer hitting the tie-down releases holding it to the pallet. When the last one kicked free, he leaped into the passenger seat.

"Hit it!"

Grabbing first gear, Hawkins popped the clutch and got the hell out of the line of the second drop.

Behind him, Schwarz cranked up the dune buggy as James freed it from the nylon tie-down straps.

"Go!" James yelled as he grabbed the roll cage and swung himself on board.

Schwarz hit the throttle, spinning the tires as the nimble little vehicle sped away.

As soon as the two Stony Man vehicles were safely under the trees, David McCarter hit his com link. "Flyboy," he said, "the Delta Zulu is green."

"Roger, Vampire," Grimaldi sent back. "Coming around to do it again."

Again, coming in from the north, the pilot dropped his gear and flaps to deliver the remainder of his load. Once again he held the huge plane a bare three feet off the ground at two hundred and fifty miles an hour as the parachutes snatched the pallets out one at a time and sent them crashing to the ground.

When the drag chute snapped tight jerking the last load off of the hold, the cargo master hit the switch to close the rear ramp as Grimaldi applied power to his four screaming jets for his climb out.

Now that the drop was completed, all he had to do was thread his way back past all the missile batteries and patrolling fighters to get back to Italy. With his right-hand guy strapped back into his seat and working the threat warning chores, he banked the C-17 around and set up to start running the gauntlet through the Balkans again. The beer was in the cooler back at the Aviano "O" Club, and he didn't want to be late for happy hour. They did great nachos.

Just another day at the office for the ace pilot. Checking his GPS against his terrain following nav system, he settled back for the return commute.

AT THE DROP ZONE, the Stony Man commandos quickly broke down the LAPES drop and reloaded all the weapons, ammo and equipment into their vehicles. They hadn't seen any signs of the opposition having any kind of air support, but erasing all traces of their activities was second nature to a commando unit. Rather than burn the parachutes and pallets and have someone notice the smoke plume and come to investigate a forest fire, McCarter had the teams dig a hole in the ground and bury the debris.

Now that they had the resupply, the Stony Man warriors had to go to work in earnest. The first part of that was to get their two new tactical vehicles armed, loaded and ready to move out.

Manning, Hawkins and James won the toss to man the dune buggy and started outfitting it for combat. When James mounted his .50-caliber and loaded the ammo for it, he found that Cowboy Kissinger had packed two different ammo mixes for the big fifty. One was the standard ground combat ammunition, one tracer to every four ball rounds. The other cans were loaded with the mix of AP, incendiary and tracer usually seen in aircraft guns. When it came to working on night targets, the incendiary might come in handy.

The other ammo pallet had the Dragon's Breath rounds for both the OICW and the 40 mm M-19 grenade launcher in the Hummer. The Dragon Breath ammunition had originally been developed for artillery during the Vietnam War as a weapon to defend base camps against human wave attacks. Loaded with up to a thousand pounds of the combustible magnesium mixture, the 155 mm version reportedly was able to burn a path two hundred meters wide and almost two miles long through any kind of terrain.

Worried about the public perception of such a weapon as being ''inhumane,'' the Army had decided not to develop the Dragon's Breath round beyond the test phase. In the mid-nineties, however, the concept reappeared in the form of a 12-gauge shotgun round sold as a novelty item. And what a novelty they were. Dragon's Breath turned any shotgun into a flame thrower with a hundred-meter range.

Recently, the concept had reappeared as a Spec Ops round for the 40 mm grenade launcher and the OICW, but with a slight difference. In those loads, the incendiary mixture didn't ignite until well clear of the muzzle. Mixed in with the standard HE frag projos, these flame rounds would turn their Hummer mounted M-19 launcher into a weapon few troops had ever faced.

Once their weapons and vehicles were ready, the commandos suited up in their high-tech battle gear. The ALOCS suits came in individualized containers with all the com and nav add-ons as a unit.

"You're not dressing for the party?" McCarter asked when he saw that Bolan wasn't unpacking his ALOCS.

The soldier smiled. "No Zoot Suit for me this time, thanks. I'll stick to basic black."

"But you're missing out on all the goodies you get with it."

"I'll just use the headset and NVGs."

The ALOCS com link data pad and night-vision system could be used separately with or without the HUD helmet display. Even wearing only the headset, he would be in full communication with his comrades and the Farm.

After donning the battle suits, they tested their com and data links to ensure that they were working. From the moment they cleared the safety of their isolated valley, they would be in enemy territory.

WHEN THE SMALL Stony Man convoy left the valley, Hawkins and Manning took the lead in the dune buggy. He and Manning would trade off behind the wheel while James rode shotgun on the

.50-caliber M-2. Lyons and his partners followed in the Hummer with the grenade launcher while Encizo took the M-38 jeep and Bolan and McCarter rode in the van.

The agile dune buggy ranged out up to a mile in front of the others finding a clear path through the forests as they advanced by leap frogging. Even though they hadn't been bothered during the time it had taken them to get the resupply, that didn't mean that these hills were uninhabited. All it meant was that the locals had learned not to intrude in things that didn't concern them. Armed men and jet planes dropping things on parachutes were surely nothing of their concern. In fact, they had learned in a brutal school that men with guns were best left to their own affairs.

Bolan kept the Farm updated on their movements from the back of the van. Right now, their first objective was to find an out-of-the-way place to hole up while they did some up close recon and worked up an attack plan. As they drove, he, McCarter and Kurtzman kept war-gaming the situation over the satcom link, but they'd not been able to come up with a workable plan yet. The negatives of the situation loomed so large that nothing jumped out to them as a clever way of reducing the odds. Even factoring in the "loan" of a tank or two from that Romanian army depot and the use of the ALOCS equipment didn't shift the balance near enough.

"You know," Bolan finally said, "you could do this as a diversionary attack to keep them occupied while I go in alone to take out the lab."

"No, Striker." McCarter automatically shook his head. "You'd never survive in there."

"If we go for a frontal assault," Bolan stated, "none of us will."

"I was thinking more of a multiaxis infiltration," the Briton replied. "Maybe with a two-man diversion team."

The former SAS commando was good at planning raids, but this was more than a lightning raid against a site that wasn't expecting trouble. Achieving surprise was one of the most critical elements of any raid and there was no hope that they'd be able to achieve that this time. As far as they knew, the enemy had no way of knowing that they were gunning for them. But James and Manning's preliminary recon had shown that they looked to be expecting something and were alert for whatever might show up.

"We have to do a more through ground recon," Bolan said as he flipped through a stack of printouts showing broken cloud cover instead of clear images of the approaches to their target. "We can't work with this. We have to know exactly what we're going up against."

"I've already told them that this is going to take time," McCarter said.

"Hal isn't bouncing up and down wanting us to go charging into the Valley of Death like the Light Brigade, is he?"

"No, he's restraining himself this time."

"About bloody time."

DUSK FOUND THE Stony Man warriors on a ridge line five miles from the castle. When the dark made further driving too dangerous, they laggered the vehicles for the night. After posting security around their RON site, they made a cold camp. Until this was over, there would be no hot food and no lights showing.

# CHAPTER TWENTY-ONE

*Transylvania*

Viktor Bladislav's Russian Mi-8 helicopter was painted in olive-and-dark-green camouflage, but bore no national markings. Flying low over the dense forests of the Translyvanian Alps, it blended in with the terrain nicely. He was in the copilot's seat when the forest ended, and he caught the first glimpse of his destination.

"We have clearance, sir," the pilot reported.

"Put us down."

Bladislav smiled when he stepped out of his chopper on the helipad in the courtyard of the castle and looked around. As they always did, the massive stone walls looming around him gave him a sense of personal strength.

Walls such as these had strengthened and protected his people in their long years of struggle against those who would have enslaved them. That was why a stone fortress was the centerpiece of the insignia of his Iron Guard. It was a different kind of war he was trying to fight now, but as if he were an ancient warrior, his strength was being gathered inside these medieval walls.

Zoran Dinkic stepped out of the machine to stand beside his boss. He, too, liked stone fortresses, but only as historical monuments. He knew how vulnerable they were to modern weapons and tactics. Bladislav loved this place, but the only thing that was really protecting them here was the United Nations' declaration that was a historic site. If that changed or if the Americans decided that they would risk UN censure and world opinion by attacking, the walls would be no protection, only a death trap.

He knew better, though, thàn to remind his general of that inconvenient fact. Bladislav's almost mystical belief in the symbols of the Serbian people's struggle was far too strong to be shaken by mere modern realities. All Dinkic could do was to make sure that the Iron Guard troops and the modern weapons he had brought to these ancient killing grounds were ready to take on all comers. And, so far, the only threat he had identified was that mysterious commando unit.

There was only the slimmest of chances that they would follow them from Bucharest to this remote location. But they had somehow managed to track the operation to Romania, and every Serb knew that a Romanian would sell his mother out for pocket change. The fact that the Bucharest police commandant had been found dead with his officers wasn't good news.

There were no signs that the man had been tortured, but there was still a chance that the fat man had been interrogated before he died. If that was the case, the commandos might have learned of the castle from him.

As he had pointed out to Bladislav several times, far too many people knew that Afghan opium was being refined into heroin at the castle. His fear was that someone might make a leap from that to the production of mutated smallpox. It wasn't likely, but it was not entirely impossible. And in his line of work, anything that was in any way possible had to be taken seriously and planned for.

"Sir," he said, turning to Bladislav, "if you don't have anything else for me to do right now, I'd like to inspect the defenses and check in at the operations center. Now that you're here, I don't want anything to go wrong."

"Nothing will go wrong here, Zoran," the ex-general said confidently, his eyes still taking in the battlements. "Not on this hallowed ground. This is the place of destiny both for me and the people of Greater Serbia. Our fight to regain our rightful place in the world will begin and end with what we are doing here."

He flung his arms wide to encompass the walls. "I can feel our strength gathering around me."

He back turned to his deputy. "And, Zoran, now that we are strong, I want you to expand our reach a little."

"Sir?"

"After we have driven these new Western invaders from our land, I want to pay a tribute to all of our ancestors who held the line for so long against the godless Turks of the past years."

Now Dinkic was really confused. For one, the medieval Turkish Ottoman Empire had swallowed up the Serbs along with damned near everyone else in the Balkans regardless of their ethnicity. The Serbs had fallen to them as quickly as had their neighbors. Secondly, the Turks were far from being godless. If anything they were more God mad than even the Serbs; it was just a different God.

"How do you mean, General?"

Bladislav's face hardened. "I mean that I am going to have Dr. Germaine make enough of his virus to eradicate the Turks as well as our Muslim enemies here in Europe. We will never be safe as long as there is a single Turk left alive. We Serbs have had that point driven home to us for hundreds of years. With NATO and the American forces neutralized and in retreat, there will be nothing to stop them from attempting to take our lands from us again."

Over the years, Dinkic had learned to keep a straight face when Bladislav went off on one of his rants about the danger of the Turks or whoever his enemy of the week was. But he had never heard this particular rant before. Not only was it insane idea, it was completely unnecessary.

"But sir," he said, "the Turks have problems of their own right now and they aren't likely to be planning an invasion of Europe."

Bladislav's eyes glittered. "The Turks have long memories, Zoran, and they have not forgotten the taste of Serbian blood. When they see that the Western Forces are no longer protecting us from them, they will return. I tell you, I have seen it. Hordes of screaming Janissaries will flood across the Bosporus and drive straight to Belgrade, raping and killing as they did of old."

Now Dinkic really started to get worried. The legendary Turkish Jannisary Corps that had been the vanguard of the medieval Turkish armies hadn't been in existence for a century or two. In fact, the doomed Jannisary revolt had been one of the last gasps of the old Ottoman Empire before reform was forced upon it. The current Turkish army had no such slave corps of shock troops and was as modern as any in the region.

Trying to defuse this line of thought, Dinkic hurriedly replied, "I'll pass that on to Dr. Germaine, sir."

"I will do that myself," Bladislav said.

Dinkic had been afraid of that.

AS EXPECTED, BLADISLAV found his virus researcher in his basement laboratory. Here the raw stone walls had been plastered and painted white and fluorescent lights hung from the ceiling to provide a well-lit place for him to work. An expensive German-made climate-control system kept the heat and humidity within the specified guidelines for such a place. Were it not for the fact that it was situated below a medieval castle, Germaine's workplace could have been in any Western European drug company lab.

"General," Germaine greeted him warmly, "how fortunate that you are here. You are just in time to celebrate the success of the vaccine tests."

Bladislav glanced over at the glass enclosure full of the small pigs that were used to test the effectiveness of the doctor's deadly concoctions.

"I have broken the ninety-percent effectiveness barrier with the current vaccine. Ninety-two percent, to be exact. If that meets with your approval, I can put it into production in a couple of days."

Ninety-two percent meant that eight percent of the Serbian population would die when the virus was released. Bladislav had hoped for something more effective than that. But great revolutions required great sacrifices if they were to be successful.

When this was all over, he would erect a monument to the Serbs who were martyred so their brothers and sisters could live free.

"But to do that," the doctor went on, "I need another shipment of the medium. I do not have enough on hand to start full production."

"You will have it," Bladislav promised. As with any military endeavor, logistics always played a key role in its success. In the kind of warfare he was waging, viral media was as important as ammunition.

"And while we wait for that to be delivered," Bladislav continued, "I have another task for you."

Germaine didn't like the sound of that at all. He had been promised that as soon as his work on the vaccine was completed, the actual production chores would be turned over to his Russian assistants. He would be paid his promised reward and allowed to go free with Marina to live out the rest of his life.

"What is that?"

"I need to have even more of the M-2 virus."

Germaine frowned. "But, sir, we have enough on hand to drive the Americans away and still be an effective deterrent to a return of European union and NATO forces."

"I forgot to include Turkey on the target list," the General stated. "They, too, are in NATO, and they are just waiting for the Americans to pull out so they can reconquer the Balkans. The only way we will be safe will be to completely destroy them.''

Now the doctor was really confused. He wasn't up-to-date on the details of Turkish politics, but he had heard nothing of this. All he knew was that the Turks had trouble enough within their own homeland to keep them busy for decades. The stockpile of M-2 he had produced was sufficient only for the original plan and Turkey was a large country.

''That presents a problem, General,'' he said cautiously. The last thing he needed was to anger this volatile man and remain trapped in Transylvania for any longer than absolutely necessary. ''The medium needed to grow the virus is the same one I use to produce the vaccine. And because of the limited facilities here, even if I have enough medium, I cannot make both of them at the same time.''

This wasn't what Bladislav wanted to hear. He was a general, and his men never told him that they couldn't do something that he wanted done. Even loyal Dinkic would think twice before telling him that one of his ideas was impossible.

''You will find a way to do it,'' Bladislav commanded. ''Work up a plan and present it to me by tomorrow.''

''Yes, sir.''

ZORAN DINKIC WAS FINDING that the defenses he had ordered to be prepared hadn't been done as he had requested. The main problem was that too many of the current officers and NCOs of the Iron Guard weren't the veterans of the Bosnian War who had fled Serbia with Bladislav. Attrition had cut into those ranks, and many of the younger officers didn't have the field experience needed to read the terrain and prepare adequate defenses.

He had laid out the plans he wanted implemented and had forwarded them, but shortcuts had been taken and he wasn't happy. Grouping the artillery by the main gate was the biggest mistake that would have to be corrected.

Calling for the major in charge of the guns, he started reading the man the riot act.

AS SOON AS BLADISLAV left the lab, Germaine took the elevator up to the living area to the apartment suite he shared with Marina.

"The man's mad, I tell you, mad," Germaine said as he stormed into their living room. "I never should have allowed myself to get involved in this scheme. He's gone too far and he's going to take all of us down with him."

Marina was alarmed. She had never seen Germaine this agitated. In fact, she had never seen him get excited about much of anything that didn't involve his work. Even their lovemaking, for lack of a better word for it, was workmanlike rather than exciting.

"What does he want, André?"

"What does he want?" Germaine spun. "I'll tell you what he wants. He wants me to produce enough of the M-2 to kill all the Turks."

She frowned. "Turks? I do not understand."

"I don't, either," he said. "He's completely mad. He says they are just waiting for the Americans to leave so they can invade the Balkans and kill all the Christians. He's mad, I tell you, and he is going to get all of us killed before this is over."

She knew that she had to get him calmed down and back to work. If Bladislav was as fired up about this as Germaine said, they were all in trouble. Back in their days together in Yugoslavia, she had used Bladislav to protect her and promote her career. But it had been a pact with the Devil, and she had been lucky to escape to France intact.

Her letting herself be talked into helping her one-time lover snare the Frenchman had also been another pact with evil. But the pay she'd been promised to seduce him had helped her overlook what she was doing.

Germaine looked anguished as he walked over and took her hand. "I only agreed to do this, my love," he said, "so we could live in comfort together. It was to be a simple job, but it has become too complicated.''

He glanced around the suite as if looking for Iron Guards. ''We need to try to escape here while we still can. We won't have the money we had counted on, but we will be together. I can find work as a doctor in some little town where he can't find us. Say you will come with me.''

Marina had no intention of living as anything but a wealthy woman. She was no child to live on dreams and love; she wanted cold hard cash, loads of it. And she would live with a younger lover, not some crazy old man.

''What do you mean?''

''I want to leave here tonight,'' he said. ''Will you come with me?''

Marina was shocked. Seeing her plans go up in smoke, she quickly decided her course of action. ''Of course I will go with you. I promised you that I will always go with you. Go back down now and pretend that you are going to cooperate.''

Germaine's face softened. ''I knew I could count on you, my love.''

As soon as Marina heard him take the elevator back down to his lab, she took the stairs down herself.

''I CAN'T CONTROL HIM any longer,'' Marina told Bladislav. ''He is as frightened as a child and is not listening to reason. To calm him down, I told him that I would try to escape with him tonight.''

She snorted. ''He has some idea of becoming a country doctor and me living with him in some peasant's cottage.''

Bladislav smiled. Under the exceedingly attractive package, Marina Stombolic had the temperament of a viper. As long as he had known her, and that was since she had been seventeen, her only real interest had ever been in herself. That was what had originally attracted him to her, but it had grown wearying after a while. He hadn't been upset when she had fled him to live in Paris.

''Go with him tonight,'' he said. ''I will let you get to the outer walls before the Iron Guard find you.''

''Will there be shooting?'' she asked.

Bladislav smiled at her concern for her own safety. ''You will be safe, Marina,'' he said. ''Never fear. And, if you do this for me, I will give you the payment that was to be his.''

Her dark eyes glittered. Germaine's payoff was to have been a million dollars, and she could live quite nicely on that. ''I will do it.''

''Good girl.''

WITH HIS ALOCS SUIT changing colors and patterns to blend in with his surroundings, Gary Manning didn't need one of the traditional sniper's ghillie suits to hide himself. He had put his standard barrel wraps on the silenced 7.62 mm sniper rifle, however, and had his optics hooded.

Leaving most of the vehicles behind the Stony Man warriors had fanned out to work their way close enough to the castle to continue the recon and to find attack positions. This was the third firing position he had scoped out today and the one that would be the most important. From here, he was in position to fire on the gun crews of the Iron Guard's artillery.

The distance from his target was just long of half a mile and, even with his long-range weapon and superb optics, if he wanted a first-round hit, he needed to range a shot for that distance. Firing a ranging round at the actual targets would, of course, spoil the surprise so that was out.

Instead, after getting the bearing, distance and drop to his target area, he searched well off to the left for another area at the same distance that had the same vertical drop. Finding a patch of boulders that matched the intended target ballistically he zoomed in on it.

"See that rock?" he asked Rafael Encizo. "Vector 727, range just beyond one thousand five hundred." He read the numbers off his scope to Encizo. "The one that looks like it has ears on it?"

"The third from the right?" The Cuban ranged his powerful spotting glasses in on it.

"That's it." Manning went back to his scope. "I'm going to try to put a round in the middle of the right-hand ear. It's about man-size."

Encizo zoomed his field glasses in. "Got it."

Manning fired a silenced shot.

"Drop one zero, right two," Encizo called the impact.

Manning made the adjustments to his scope settings and tried again.

"Add one point five," Encizo caught the strike of the bullet again.

Manning adjusted his scope to bring the strike of the round up a meter and a half.

"That's within six inches."

"Which way?"

"Low."

Manning tweaked his scope again and fired.

"That's center body mass."

Manning pulled his rifle back and wrote the scope settings in his notebook. With the ranging shots he had taken, when it came time to do it for real, all he'd have to worry about was the wind. At those ranges, the wind could throw his round off as much as a foot.

"Okay," he said. "Let's get the hell outta here."

The two commandos pulled back into the woods.

## CHAPTER TWENTY-TWO

*At the Castle*

Zoran Dinkic had been tasked with intercepting André Germaine and Marina Stombolic before they made good their escape that night. It would be no great feat to intercept them, the old man wasn't an athlete, and the woman wouldn't let him get away on any account. The part he wasn't sure of was what Viktor Bladislav intended to do with the pair.

The general wasn't a man who allowed himself to be crossed. The Iron Guard had only remained as strong as it was because of the general's unwavering discipline. A military unit in exile usually fell apart, but not this one. He rewarded his men generously, but he was unforgiving with those who failed him. And no one had ever failed him twice.

Dinkic had a pair of Russian surplus night-vision goggles over his eyes as he scanned the cleared ground between the inner and outer walls at the rear of the castle. That was where Marina had said they would try to make their escape. A dozen men waited in the darkness for his command with another dozen ready to take up hot pursuit should the pair somehow manage to slip past him.

Bladislav wouldn't forgive any of them who failed him tonight.

Right on cue, the sally port in the inner wall opened, and he saw the green figures of the two emerge. Germaine had some kind of pack over his shoulder and Marina kept looking back at the walls behind her. Keying his handheld radio, Dinkic spoke, "Give me the lights."

Two spotlights on the outer wall snapped on, illuminating Germaine and Marina like they were on stage. The doctor looked like a deer on a mountain road caught in the headlights of an oncoming car. Marina screamed loudly and pretended to be frightened.

"Doctor," Dinkic called down, "stop where you are or you will be shot."

Dropping his pack, Germaine enfolded Marina in his arms.

Bladislav stepped out of the darkness and walked to where the two stood in the cone of light. A squad of Iron Guard approached from the other side, took the two into custody and hustled Marina away.

"You tried to betray me," the general told the scientist, "but you will not pay for this betrayal with your death as you should. No, you will be allowed to live so you can continue to work for me."

"I will not," the Frenchman said. "You are insane and I simply cannot do this anymore."

Bladislav's eyes blazed. "No man calls me insane," he hissed. "I will go down in history and be called the savior of my people."

"And I will be known as a mass murderer."

"You will be called the man who let his lover be put to death because he could not keep his agreement," Bladislav said. "That is how you will be known."

"She has nothing to do with this," Germaine said, panicked. "She only came because she loves me."

"She is in love with a fool," Bladislav replied. "And she will pay for that if you do not do as you are told."

He spoke into his handheld radio and a piercing female scream echoed from the rock walls.

"No!" Germaine screamed. "Don't hurt her! Please! I will do what you want, just don't hurt her."

"Her safety depends on your doing exactly what

you are told," Bladislav said. "If you oppose me ever again in any manner, you will watch as I have her killed."

Germaine had tears in his eyes. "I hear you," he said. "I will obey."

"Good." Bladislav signaled for the guards to take him away. "Back to the lab with him. He has work to do."

AFTER TAKING GERMAINE back down to his lab and posting a trio of guards to make sure that he stayed there, Bladislav went up to his office. Marina was waiting for him with a smile on her face.

"Was I convincing?" she asked.

"Very," Bladislav replied. "The good doctor is in his lab at this moment working diligently for Serbian independence. I do not expect that I will have any more trouble from him on this matter."

"When do I get my money?" she said. "I want to leave this rock pile tomorrow. I can't wait to breathe the air of civilization and eat decent food."

"I'm sorry that you haven't enjoyed your stay here." Bladislav didn't smile.

"I am sick of peasant food." She grimaced. "And, frankly, Viktor, I don't see how you can stand being here. You have lived in the West, you know better. How can you do this to yourself?"

"This is my place of destiny," he replied.

"Well," she said, tossing her head. "You can have it. I just want to get out of here."

"You want Germaine's payment, do you?"

"Please, Viktor," she said. "Don't play with me. You promised."

"I did promise payment, didn't I?" he said as his hand went to the holstered Makarov pistol on his belt. "Here it is, whore."

"Oh God, Viktor." Her eyes flashed as she spun to escape, but he was standing in front of the door. "Please!"

He triggered the Makarov and the round struck her in the back. She gave a little gasp and slumped facedown on the floor.

Bladislav stared at her body for a long moment. It was a shame that one so beautiful had to die, but heroic endeavors always took their toll among the fighters. Her name, too, would go on the monument he would erect to the Martyrs of the Struggle.

Dinkic crashed through the door of Bladislav's office, his Makarov in his hand. "General! Are you…"

He lowered his weapon when he saw Marina.

"She betrayed me, Zoran." Bladislav's voice was strained. "Me, the man who made her everything she was. Women are born treacherous, they can't help it."

"I'll have the body removed, sir."

"No." Bladislav turned back to her. "Leave her

for a while. I will call you when she's ready to leave.''

"Yes, sir.'' Dinkic went out and quietly closed the door behind him.

*Stony Man Farm*

WHEN HAL BROGNOLA stepped down from his chopper early that morning, he had a look of grim determination that Barbara Price hadn't seen from him in a long time. Although he'd said that he was going to remain at the Farm until this operation was concluded, he had taken off yesterday afternoon without telling her why.

"I had a long meeting with the President last night,'' he said before she could ask. "I showed him the photos Striker sent and the satellite radar and MAD readouts. I must say that seeing it in black-and-white shocked him.''

"Did it shock him enough to call this damned thing off?''

"No,'' he said with an odd tone to his voice. "He didn't. He did, however, send a War Shot alert to the USS *Guardfish* on patrol in the Med.''

"Isn't that a Boomer?''

"It is.'' He nodded. "A missile attack sub armed with Tomahawk III cruise missiles. Two of them with 1.5 KT warheads are being readied for a strike in case Striker decides to call off this mission. His feeling is that we don't have too much time left to deal with this.''

It wasn't exactly what she'd wanted to hear, but a taste was better than no bite at all. It gave hope. Striker knew when to fold a losing hand. She'd feel better, though, if she didn't also know that he could be obstinate when it came to the so-called "weapons of mass destruction.'' Slaughtering noncombatants wasn't high on his list of acceptable things to do for any reason. Knowing that nukes were waiting to be used if he failed would only spur him on. When the innocent were imperiled, Mack Bolan wasn't known to back off. In fact, she wasn't sure that he was even capable of bowing to superior force in those circumstances.

At least, though, with the Boomer alerted, when they failed, the situation wouldn't be lost. There would be retribution, Bladislav and his virus would be incinerated. But it would come in time to save the men she loved.

She followed Brognola into the farmhouse and down to the tram in silence. There wasn't a damned thing she could say that would make this any better. She hated feeling that way.

AARON KURTZMAN caught the mood instantly when Brognola and Price walked into the Computer Room. He had worked with the two of them long enough to know when it was crunch time.

"Hunt,'' he called out as he scooped up his latest printouts to show Brognola, "skull session.''

Hunt Wethers was a grinder. Regardless of the inequity of the balance of force that was about to come into play in Romania, he felt that battlefield intelligence was the key. He also knew that the cloud cover wasn't letting the satellites give the Stony Man commandos what they needed and that situation had to be rectified immediately. The long range weather forecasts didn't hold hope for a better outlook any time soon, so it was time to go to intel Plan B.

The problem was that they had no Plan B for intel gathering. They had the first team on line now, but they weren't giving them what they needed. That meant that they had to look for another solution and he'd thought of something that should have been long forgotten. But trying to introduce it would cause a firestorm.

Wethers had the reputation for being a mild-mannered intellectual. It went with his academic credentials. Nonetheless, he hadn't survived his years at UC Berkeley by being a candy ass. He could go to the wall and take his shots when he had to, he just didn't see the need to do it very often. He would, however, make an exception for this circumstance.

"You know, Hal," he said casually as he took his seat at the table, "there's a way to give our guys a little better chance of handling this situation."

"What's that?"

"Geopulse."

Brognola caught his breath. There were a few things that even Stony Man Farm wasn't supposed to know about, and Geopulse was right at the top of that list. "I don't know what you're talking about." The big Fed tried to brazen it out.

"That's bull! You know damned good and well what I'm talking about."

"Damn!" Kurtzman said quietly. "I forgot all about that little bugger."

Seeing that he was about to get shot down in flames, Brognola changed tack fast. "That's been nonoperational for years now."

"Want to target it on the Annex here and see if it still works?" Wethers didn't smile.

"I don't even know if the President is even aware of it," Brognola tried again.

Price glanced from one of the men to the next in complete bewilderment. "Will someone please tell me what you're talking about?"

Wethers was happy to. "Geopulse," he said, "was the brainstorm of a rather demented weapons research team back in the late seventies, early eighties. It's a satellite weapon that was designed to cause devastating earthquakes in enemy territory."

When Price continued to look blank, he continued. "It's a kinetic energy weapon. It fires diamond-tipped depleted uranium arrows at hypersonic speeds deep into the earth where their velocity is converted into explosive heat energy. If fired into a fault zone, they cause an earthquake. At least that's what the designer claimed it would do. Fortunately, after the first test shot into the Pacific cooler heads prevailed and the damned thing was supposedly scrapped.''

''You said supposedly?''

Wethers nodded to Brognola. ''Ask him.''

''It was kept in standby mode,'' Brognola explained. ''In case of a national emergency that couldn't be handled by any other means. Kind of a doomsday weapon.''

''Cute, if the megaton nukes don't kill 'em all, triggering an earthquake will.''

''More or less.''

''Why was it canceled?''

''The thought was that it was too dangerous,'' he explained. ''The shock wave from the first test scared the hell out of seisemologists all over the world for weeks. There's a new volcanic island in the ocean floor that owes its origin to that one test shot. The designer said that only happened because Earth's crust is so thin there, but the geologists were afraid of further tests creating the Big One all over the world.''

She turned to Wethers. ''And you think that firing this thing like artillery is going to help our guys out?''

He shrugged. ''It's a way of dealing with that lab that doesn't call for taking Stony Man casualties. And since the Man's panicked about anyone finding out that we've bombed a historic site this is a perfect alternative, it's untraceable. One shot and the problem's taken care of. At best, there's a little earthquake in the Transylvanian Alps and the castle turns into a pile of rubble. Worst case—'' he shrugged ''—there's a new volcano in Romania.''

''THERE'S BEEN A SLIGHT change in plans,'' Bolan said as McCarter entered the van. ''The Bear's come up with a Plan C so we're going to stand down and see if he can pull it off.''

''What happened to bloody Plan B?'' McCarter asked.

''It's still in the fire, but Aaron—Hunt Wethers, actually—pulled one out of the long-dead doomsday files and they're going to try it instead.''

''Doomsday files?''

''It's called Geopulse, a kinetic energy space weapon.''

''I don't know if I like the sound of that.''

''Not if you're in the line of fire of the damned thing,'' Bolan said as he launched into an explanation of exactly what was involved.

"Bloody hell!" McCarter shook his head when the Executioner had finished. "Why don't they just nuke the bloody place and bloody well be done with it?"

"That was my question. But, the answer was that the kinetic energy arrow doesn't leave radioactive traces behind that could be traced to the United States. This will look like it was an act of God."

"Or Satan."

Bolan wasn't adverse to using high-tech solutions to solve age-old problems. Eradicating evil was the always the goal, not the method used to do it. There was, though, something apocalyptic about sending a missile, for that's what it was, crashing deep into the core of the earth. Using an earthquake as a weapon seemed excessive. Even a nuke could, more or less, be controlled by man. Blasting a hole in Earth's crust could have consequences far beyond the objective of protecting people from a virulent virus.

"Has this been passed by the Oval Office?" McCarter asked.

"Apparently."

"And we're to pull back?"

"Yes."

"How far?"

"That's what they're looking into right now. Aaron says that the Transylvanian Alps are stable.

A massif, he calls them, and he doesn't think that they'll start spouting volcanoes when that damned thing hits.''

"That's comforting," McCarter said. "I've been told that having a volcano suddenly erupt under your bum can be rather unpleasant. I'll give the guys a warning order to pull back to the rallying point on order. God help us all."

"I'll give the safety zone to pull back behind," Bolan said, "as soon as they figure it out."

"Whatever it is, add a mile to it."

# CHAPTER TWENTY-THREE

*Transylvania*

It wasn't as easy as it sounded for the Stony Man warriors to stand down in Transylvania. After infiltrating as close to the castle as they had, to pull back out of the hills ran the risk of their being spotted by one of Bladislav's roving patrols. Even if they did get away clean, they would then have to turn and try to work their way back when they were ready to go for it again. But while remaining where they were seemed the best course of action, it also wasn't without serious risks.

An army could stand down, dig in and remain in place if they needed to pause an operation. It had the armor, artillery and air support for defense if they were attacked. The Stony Man crew wasn't an army, and they didn't have battalions of tanks, batteries of guns and squadrons of gunships to call upon if they were attacked. Their best defense would be to remain well hidden, but carefully mobile.

Since they had to be concerned about hiding four vehicles, Bolan decided to get Gadgets Schwarz's M-38 jeep out of the equation. It had been a damned good buy and would have been a useful addition in another scenario, but was it just one more thing to hide now.

"Okay," Schwarz grumbled when Bolan gave him the bad news. "I'll get rid of it. But I'm not going to just leave it by the side of the road with the keys in the ignition for the first goat herder who walks by. I paid good money for that damned thing."

"Sabotage it then," the Executioner stated, "but just get rid of it. We're going to have a hard enough time hiding what we're keeping."

"I'll follow you in the dune buggy," Calvin James said, grinning, "so you don't have to walk back."

"Gee, thanks."

WITH THE COMMANDOS stood down, it was time for the Stony Man Annex crew to get to work before they were discovered by one of Bladislav's patrols. But bringing the Geopulse online to shoot wasn't as simple as it had sounded when the idea had been tossed around.

For one, the system hadn't been designed to be

a pinpoint precision weapon. Unlike the more modern space-based lasers, it didn't need to hit its target within a few millimeters of its aiming point to be effective. In fact, striking anywhere within a mile or so of the target would do for its design purpose. That was because it was a doomsday weapon and the projectile wasn't guided.

Once the kinetic arrow was aimed and launched, it couldn't be deviated from the flight path it had been sent on. Like any cannon, it was simply aim and shoot. And, like a cannon, it was the aiming that counted. Its streamlined shape and extreme velocity ensured that atmospheric pressures wouldn't force it off its trajectory as it streaked to Earth like a meteor caught in the gravity well.

To further complicate things, Geopulse had been put in orbit before the birth of the GPS system of pinpointing locations anywhere on Earth to within three feet. Instead, it used an eighties optical-mapping system to determine its aim point and that was turning out to be more of a problem than they had thought it would be. GPS had made missile guidance so simple that they had forgotten how difficult it could be to pinpoint a target on the Earth from deep space.

Kurtzman had gotten a GPS reading from Phoenix Force to the center of the target, the courtyard inside the castle's inner walls. Converting that to a map grid coordinate from a map of Romania dating from when the satellite weapon had been launched gave him his aiming point. When fired on that coordinate, the kinetic arrow would have a thousand-meter CPE, Circular Probable Error, meaning that it should impact within a thousand-meter circle, better than half a mile, of the aim point.

That wasn't bad for a pre-GPS targeting system, but it wasn't too accurate when compared to a modern laser or GPS guided bomb. But this thing was designed to trigger an earthquake that would be felt hundreds, if not thousands, of miles away.

The main concern, though, was the radius of destruction after it hit. No one knew what that would be because the system had never been tested on dry land. Even if it had, the individual geology of the target area would still be the greatest determinant of the result the impact would have. The result of it hitting the Sahara Desert wouldn't be the same as targeting the San Andreas Fault.

On deciding the safety zone needed to keep their guys out of danger from the weapon, Brognola was opting for a best-case scenario while Kurtzman was arguing for the worst. They ended up agreeing on something somewhere in the middle of those two extremes and hoped that it would be far enough away.

While the Stony Man commandos were moving to safety, the Annex crew started bringing their weapon up to firing condition. "I'm starting the countdown to activate the system," Kurtzman announced.

THE COLD, AIRLESS environment of space was supposed to be the perfect place to park something, nonorganic of course, that you wanted to remain perfectly preserved. At least that was the theory. It was expected that would be the case with the twenty-year storage the Geopulse satellite had been through. Upon receipt of the coded signal from Stony Man Farm, the launch platform awoke from its long sleep and sent a signal to its nuclear power plant to power up.

The series of self-checks the satellite performed took longer than they would have with a more modern machine, though. The microprocessor brain on board the satellite was an ancestor type that didn't blaze with the speed of the twenty-first century. In fact, in PC terms, it was barely a 286 running at twelve megahertz. In time, though, it completed its diagnostics and sent a signal to the Farm that it was back in business and ready to do its master's bidding.

"OKAY!" AARON KURTZMAN called out. "Geopulse says that it's up and running. Time for the maneuvering burns."

He was playing mission control for this shoot

and had a NASA Houston Cap Com–style orbital graphic up on the big-screen monitor. It displayed the satellite's orbital path as it crossed Earth's surface. Bringing the launch station in line to hit the target required nudging it out of its current orbit and into one that would bring it over a remote corner of Romania at the proper time and place.

Watching the orbital numbers stream past on his monitor, he sat with his finger poised on the button that would send the signal to the Geopulse's maneuvering rockets. He had already programmed in the time lag to compensate for the microsecond it would take for the signal to reach deep space.

"Zero three to initial burn," he called out. When the number rolled up, he fired. "Contact."

"It's moving," Hunt Wethers called out.

Kurtzman watched the numbers stream by, his finger poised to fire the second burn that would hold the bird in its new orbit.

"Coming up on the second burn," Wethers reminded him.

"Burn on zero three," Kurtzman said as he counted down the seconds. "Contact."

"You have target lock," Wethers said.

"Initiating the weapon," Kurtzman replied.

In the satellite's weapons bay, a twenty-four-inch-long projectile looking for all the world like a high-school kid's model rocket was pulled from its storage container by a mechanical arm and inserted into the firing chamber of a linear accelerator.

This was an expensive model rocket, though. Its nose cone and tail fins were both fabricated from artificially grown diamond crystals cut to shape with a laser. The body of the projectile was machined from depleted uranium covered with tungsten carbide giving it a weight of almost a hundred pounds. When it impacted Earth at better than fifty thousand miles an hour, that hundred-pound mass moving at that velocity would convert into kinetic energy with the explosive force of a rather large megaton-size nuclear bomb.

The launch tube it was loaded into was also more than a rocket launcher. Often called a Rail Gun, a linear accelerator was a simple device with no moving parts beyond a few microswitches. It was, in effect, a series of powerful electromagnets set in a line around a tube or rail, hence the nickname. On command, the electromagnets driven by power supplied by the on-board nuclear reactor would switch on or off at microsecond frequency to push or pull the object being propelled with magnetic energy.

While space by definition was airless and empty, in reality it was anything but. Particularly the part of space within several thousand miles of Earth. Near the planet, space was full of man-made junk. Bits and pieces of discarded rockets, dropped spacewalk tools, dead satellites and anything else that man had launched into orbit, and lost track of, could be found circling endlessly.

There was less man-made debris the farther you got away from Earth, but that was the zone where you started running into "natural" space debris. Since the planet was a gravity well, it attracted the detritus of comets, meteors and anything else that passed close enough to Earth to be pulled into orbit. Comets in particular tended to shed bits and pieces in their passage like a dog shedding fleas. Many of these chunks of debris were no more than chunks of ice since comets are largely composed of space ice.

Several years earlier, one of these pieces of ice, about the size of a hardball, had come in contact with Geopulse. This ice ball hadn't hit the satellite hard enough to cause damage, the collision had been more like a sideswipe. But because the launch platform was large enough to have a microgravity of its own, rather than the ice chunk bouncing off and flying off on its way, it had been moving at such a low relative velocity, it had stuck there.

Had Geopulse been in a fixed orbit away from the sun, the ice ball might have remained a ball. But, the heating and cooling caused by the satellite's constant moving in and out of the sun's light caused the ice ball to do something it wouldn't have done on Earth's surface. It didn't melt and refreeze, but it slowly flowed. This gradual flowing as the ice moved toward the warmer sections of the satellite caused it to move enough to obstruct the end of the Rail Gun tube.

None of this, of course, showed up on the system checks Kurtzman had performed. The designers of Geopulse had never envisioned a need for such a check.

"CONFIRM TARGETING," Kurtzman called over to Wethers as he continued the launch procedure.

"On target confirmed."

"Launching on zero five," Kurtzman said. "...four...three...two...launch!"

He stabbed the firing button.

The signal reached Geopulse a microsecond later and flashed through its microprocessor sending a signal to the relay that controlled the Rail Gun. In the vacuum of space, there was no sound as the projectile launched.

The kinetic arrow was moving at better than forty Gs when it hit the ice blockage at the end of the launch tube and that was unfortunate. What was even worse was that the instant it hit, the electromagnet ring closest to the end of the tube energized.

The physical damage of the arrow going "off track" in the launcher right as the last electromagnet was firing combined to send the energy that would have added even more acceleration to the projectile into the airframe of the launcher instead.

The result was like a bomb had gone off in the satellite.

The NORAD radar tracking the Geopulse indicated that Geopulse had been completely destroyed. What had been a solid return was now showing as multiple returns streaking through space. One of them might have been the errant kinetic arrow, but it was hard to tell.

BARBARA PRICE FELT her breath catch in her throat as Plan C died in the deep blackness of space. That meant that the Stony Man warriors would have to put Plan A, as flawed as it was, back into action. She turned away from the big-screen monitor and headed for the elevator.

Aaron Kurtzman saw her go and unlocked the wheels of his chair. "Wait up," he said.

She turned and he saw that she was fighting to keep her mission controller game face on.

"Wanna go for a walk?" he asked. "I need to see the sun for a while."

"Sure." She attempted a smile and halfway succeeded.

They made their way to the tram and remained silent during the trip to the farmhouse.

When they went out on the front porch, the sun was shining and all seemed well with the world.

"Where do you want to go?" She looked out onto the orchards.

"This is fine, actually," he said. "I just wanted to breathe clean air, smell the blossoms."

She leaned her hands down against the porch railing, arched her back, slowly turned her head from side to side and rolled her shoulders to relieve the tension in her neck.

"We've come to expect that technology's always supposed to make it easier," he said. "And it's a bitch when it doesn't work as advertised."

"The gods of war are pissed," she said. "The bastards don't like it when we try to substitute some hotshot gadget for the blood offerings."

"The technology of modern war gives them lots of blood," he said.

"But sometimes they like to get it the old-fashioned way, from brave men 'facing fearful odds for the ashes of their fathers and the altars of their gods.'"

"It's been a long time since I heard Horace," Kurtzman said.

"It never changes. And I should know better by now."

"It's not a suicide mission," he said lamely.

"I'm not putting our guys down," she told him, "but it might as well be. I can't believe that we got sucked into this with our eyes wide-open."

There was nothing he could answer to that.

"But we did." She took a deep breath and turned to face him. "You had about enough fresh air?"

"Sure," he replied.

"Good." She grabbed the handles of his chair and swung him around. "We've got work to do."

When he looked blank, she grinned. "We gotta make a silk purse out of this sow's ear."

CARL LYONS, DAVID MCCARTER and Bolan were jammed in the van, clustered around the monitor when the Farm tried to fire the Geopulse.

"So much for high-tech doomsday weapons and Plan C." McCarter stood after watching the NORAD radar show-and-tell. "Now we'll go back to doing this the old-fashioned way."

"I'll get back to Aaron to see if there are any intel updates for us," Bolan said. "And I'm requesting that they make sure that we have everything they have on the radar probing of that place. Particularly anything they might have in ground-penetrating radar."

"What do you have in mind?" McCarter asked.

"I haven't liked our thinking on this operation from the very beginning. This isn't what we do well, and I don't like the idea of trying to infiltrate combat teams into a place like that."

McCarter had been playing the game long enough to know that any operations plan, no matter how well thought out, could be improved upon. And, most importantly, no attack plan should ever be set in concrete. When you planned to go in harm's way, you did the best you could right up to your launch time and went with it. As always, though, the plan rarely survived your first contact with the enemy.

In this instance, though, this plan had so many negatives going against it, it might not survive even that long.

"How do you want to do it, then?" he asked Bolan.

"I'm going in there alone while the rest of you race around out front and keep the Iron Guard busy."

"You're not going in there without me," Rafael Encizo spoke up.

"I can get in there easier by myself, Rafe," Bolan replied.

"Yeah." Encizo nodded. "I know you can. But the last time I checked, Striker, you still didn't have eyes in the back of your head."

Bolan grinned. "Okay, but just the two of us. To keep them thinking that they're under a real attack, David and Carl are going to need all the help they can get."

# CHAPTER TWENTY-FOUR

*Transylvania*

Rather than lose a day wasting time waiting for more information to come in from the Farm, Bolan and Encizo decided to make a personal recon. The plan was to spend most of the day working their way around the castle from one side to the other. On the way they would examine the Iron Guard defenses and the rock pile itself as they scouted out a route to take up to the walls.

Their walk through the woods went quickly. Finding high ground overlooking their objective, they settled down for a look-see.

The castle complex occupied a slight rise in the ground where two roughly east-west ridgelines came together at the north end of a broad valley. Its placement clearly showed that its orientation was to the south, the obvious avenue of approach the castle had been built to guard. The Iron Guard positions were also oriented to defend against attackers using the ancient invasion route up the road from the south. Had they been facing a conventional force, it would have made sense.

"You know," Encizo said as he took his field glasses from his eyes and made another entry in his field notebook, "I think that if we keep to the eastern ridge, we can get within two hundred meters without being seen."

He pointed to a small chapel halfway between the eastern wall and the tree line. "A hundred meters across the open to that building and we halt there. David starts his demonstration and we sprint to the base of the wall. From there, we work our way around to the back and look for a way in."

Bolan focused his field glasses in the small building. "That should do it," he agreed. "Let's check the route over to there."

"Have you noticed that we haven't seen any signs of recent patrolling?" Encizo asked as they moved out. "Gary and Cal ran into them in spades, but it looks like we have this particular piece of woods all to ourselves now. It's spooky. I like my opponents out in the open so I know what they're doing."

BOLAN'S REQUEST FOR everything they had on the target from the radar sensor readings put Aaron Kurtzman's crew to work retrieving, downloading and transmitting several days' worth of printouts.

As Kurtzman looked over the take before sending it to the Executioner, though, something started tickling a corner of his memory and he mentally clicked on it to download it into his forebrain. Bolan had specifically asked for ground-penetrating radar information for a reason.

Deep-space ground-penetrating radar systems had been originally developed for oil and mineral exploration. A couple of times they had even been used to survey archaeological sites to locate the good stuff for the diggers so they wouldn't waste their time digging blindly in the dirt.

The military application of this technology was limited, but it filled a vital need. Ground-penetrating radar had been used to map out the internal structure of Saddam Hussein's command bunker in Baghdad so the air force would know where to leave their high-explosive calling cards. Once they had the information, rocket-boosted four-thousand-pound bombs had blasted their way deep under layers of concrete to completely destroy the place. A number of buried Iraqi communication centers had received the same treatment.

That same technology could be used to scope out Bladislav's castle right now to the bedrock, and Kurtzman mentally kicked himself for not having thought of that before.

None of the satellites they were using at the moment had that particular radar system on board, only terrain-reading radars. And it was too late to move a specialized spy bird into position to take the readings Bolan wanted. But another mental bubble surfaced and burst in his consciousness like an aerial bomb. The boys and girls of NIMA, the national collecting point for obsessive-compulsive computer geeks, dweebs, nerds and other forms of chronic overachievers might have exactly what he needed.

NIMA—the National Imagery and Mapping Agency—was a branch of the Defense Intelligence Agency, and was tasked with providing imagery and geospatial information to the military. At least that's what it said in their PR handout. In reality, they were just another spook group working with the NRO's deep-space surveillance systems. Their job was go over the satellite intel take, in whatever form it came to them, and tease out the goodies.

In this case, "teasing" meant breaking the data down to the lowest possible component and examining each single pixel or frequency bleep to the point of obsession. No wacko had ever stalked a Hollywood starlet the way these people went after their projects. It was rumored that most of the NIMA operatives actually lived in cells onsite and rarely saw the light of day. Who needed a real life when they could totally immerse themselves in the wonders of cyberspace?

As a lark, they had spent thousands of man-hours on their off time to find that the missing Mars Polar Lander had actually reached the planet's surface intact. NASA had declared that it had burned up on entry and had been lost. To test their technology to its limits, the NIMA people had gone over thousands of photo and radar images of the Mars polar cap with a microscope until they found the missing space traveler.

When they weren't using their ground-penetrating radars to defend America and her allies from buried menaces, NIMA routinely did underground survey work for a number of peaceful ventures and organizations to keep their hands in. Much of this time was spent in mapping historic sites and archaeological surveying. They had found a legendary lost city in the Arabian desert from twenty-two thousand miles in space. Archaeologists had driven right over the exact site several times previously and had noticed nothing.

Another of their "peaceful" clients just happened to be the UN Cultural Heritage Commission.

"Hunt," Kurtzman called out, "who do you know in NIMA?"

Wethers thought for a moment. "There's a mathematician I worked once with on a problem of partial pixel resolution and reconstruction. Why?"

"I need to know," Kurtzman replied, "if

they've been doing any surveys of historical sites in the Balkans. Specifically a particular castle in Transylvania reputed to be a Romanian national treasure."

"Damn," Wethers said as he keyed in his phone list, "I should have thought of that. I'll get right on it."

ZORAN DINKIC WAS doing his best to keep out of the way of Viktor Bladislav as much as possible. Since killing Marina the previous night, the general seemed to have permanently moved into a zone he didn't want to have any more contact with than he absolutely had to. The general had gone off on occasion before, but it had only lasted for an hour or so and had never been this bad.

The first clear sign of his boss's dementia was when Bladislav had ordered the flag of medieval Transylvania raised over the castle. The flag raising ceremony had included most of the Iron Guard troops and had been presided over by Bladislav wearing a historic costume complete with a medieval broadsword strapped to his waist.

The Iron Guardsmen weren't accustomed to seeing their leader playing a role from the long-dead past and hadn't known what to think. When one of the officers came to talk to him about it later, Dinkic had been hard-pressed to explain the general's behavior.

Worse yet was that Bladislav had ordered the roaming security patrols in the mountains ended. He had decided that all of his troops should be in their positions around the castle ready to fight at a moment's notice. That, of course, robbed him of his "eyes," and an operations officer lived and died by what he knew and how soon he knew it. With this new order, he wouldn't know of enemy forces until they attacked.

Then, to go three for three, Bladislav had forbidden Dinkic to even talk to Dr. Germaine. He was overseeing the lab operations completely by himself and Dinkic was beginning to wonder what the two of them were cooking up down there. He seriously doubted that Bladislav had told the Frenchman that his lover had been killed. That would have been counterproductive. Instead, he was sure that the woman's fate was being held over the scientist's head to encourage him to do Bladislav's bidding. He also had no doubt that the general planned to eliminate Germaine as well when this was all over.

This entire affair had gone from being a thing of honor and national salvation to a tyrant's insane dream, and he was afraid.

Bladislav's plan had seemed doable at one time. Dinkic was as good a Serb as any man and knew well how badly his people had been treated for decades. Using the mutated smallpox to drive the

Westerners out of the Balkans was harsh, but it was the only weapon they had access to that had any possibility of working. He had once seen its use as justified for the greater good. Now he had serious doubts.

DR. ANDRÉ GERMAINE might have been an old fool besotted by a younger woman, but he wasn't a stupid man. He knew full well what had brought him to where he was. He had made a deal with the Devil, and now he would have to pay the price. He had no hope that Viktor Bladislav would honor his promise and release him when this was over. He was also certain that Marina wouldn't be released, either.

Now that the shock of being discovered and captured had passed, he was examining what had happened to him the previous night in detail. After all, he was a scientist trained to examine things. It couldn't be chance that Bladislav and his second in command, along with spotlights and a platoon of troops, had accidentally been in position to catch them. They had to have known that he was trying to escape and where.

They might have learned his plans from bugging his apartment in the castle, but he doubted that. The more likely way Bladislav had learned of it was that Marina had told him. He had often suspected that her connection with the general went far beyond what she had said it was. Her story was that she had met him at a meeting of Serbian expatriots in Paris, had been drawn to his plan for a Greater Serbia and had agreed to work for him.

He had doubted that story on occasion before, but he had simply not wanted to risk examining it. A man in love will suspend his belief whenever it suits his purposes. It was too late for him to rethink what he had done for the love of a young woman. He wasn't the first old man to fall that way. Like Sampson, his Delilah had brought him to his death. But he wouldn't die alone.

He knew there was no way that he could get to Bladislav and kill him. He wasn't a man of physical prowess. He had never been an athlete, and his poor eyesight had kept him from being drafted into the old French army. Fighting his way to Bladislav wasn't an option; he knew his limitations. His strengths were of the mind, and he had to figure out a way to avenge himself even if he couldn't be saved.

The best he could do was to ensure that the megalomaniac general would never see his dream of ruling over his Greater Serbia come true. Bladislav might escape the smallpox himself, but Germaine vowed that Serbia would become a wasteland, and that would be his vengeance. The weakest part of Bladislav's plan had always been the vaccine needed to protect the Serb population.

As with any bioweapon, his M-2 virus was completely indiscriminant of friend and foe. To preserve the Serbs Bladislav said he was trying to protect, he had to have the vaccine. Without it, much of Eastern Europe would become a barren wasteland littered with the rotting dead. And it was easy enough for him to ensure that would happen.

Walking out of his office, he went up to one of the Iron Guard watch dogs Bladislav had put on him and he said, "I have to go down and inspect the vats."

The man motioned with the muzzle of his assault rifle. "Go."

On the way to the basement, he picked up yet another guard, but he didn't mind. They could guard his body, but they didn't know what was in his thoughts.

The Iron Guards followed him as he went to the climate-controlled room where the smallpox vaccine was fermenting in sealed stainless-steel vats. Ignoring the guards, he went to the control panel and adjusted the PH factor in the media upward by introducing lactic acid into the mix. Once it was at the level he wanted, he recelebrated the sensor that read the PH levels so it would indicate what it had before he had introduced the additional acid.

A smallpox vaccine of sorts would still be produced from this spoiled batch, but it would lack the strength required to protect anyone from his

M-2 virus. In fact, it would be completely useless again this micromonster he had created. Better yet, even if Bladislav killed him right where he now stood, he was the victor. Since he had recelebrated the PH sensor, anyone else attempting to make new vaccine to his formulation would also grow garbage. No one would ever think to check the instrumentation values.

He still had the test batch of the full-strength vaccine and, walking over to the cabinet where it was stored, he took out the three vials. Going over to the sink, he turned his back on the guard and gave himself an IM injection. That left three more injections worth of the good vaccine in the vial, and he put it in his jacket pocket with a disposable syringe. The other two vials he broke in the sink and washed the vaccine down the drain.

"What are you doing?" one of the guards asked.

"Disposing of some bad vaccine," he said curtly. "A test lot. I am finished here now."

The guards followed him back to his office, and one of them remained outside his door as he listlessly pawed through his papers and waited.

HUNT WETHERS'S NIMA contact paid off by the end of the day. To record the destruction that had been inflicted on so many historical monuments in the Balkans over the past ten years, the UN had contracted with NIMA to conduct a survey of what remained as well as the ruins. Both terrain reading and ground penetrating radar as well as photo imaging techniques had been requested and the project had just been completed.

"I got it," Wethers said as he handed over a mainframe hard disk. "I had to promise to co-author a pixel restoration article with him in order to get this. But I talked him into it without having to spell out why I wanted it and got him to download a copy of the entire survey. It's in raw form, but I can extract what we need from the Romanian section and store the rest."

"Outstanding!" Kurtzman grinned. "Get that broken down and sent to Striker as soon as you can. I'll let him know it's on the way."

WETHERS HAD BEEN ABLE to isolate the radar readouts from the castle and surrounding area and send them as a series of images that Bolan could print out. When they were in hard copy, he called Lyons and McCarter in to go over them with him.

"I'll be damned," Bolan said as he ran his finger along a parallel pair of lines on the ground-penetrating radar printout of the eastern approach to the castle. "That looks a lot like a priest's hole."

"Okay," Carl Lyons said. "I'll bite. What's a priest's hole? A clerical crapper?"

"Actually," David McCarter said, "it's more of

an escape chute to hide in when the bad guys have broken into your castle with murder on their minds."

"Just for priests?"

"Usually for the lord of the manor and his family to use to get out," McCarter explained. "The priest's name comes from the religious wars of Europe when the various Christian groups were seriously targeting each other's religious leaders. Look at this. It leads from the castle and appears to come out inside that small building."

"Rafe and I saw that on our recon," Bolan said. "It looked like a chapel or a shrine. If it is a chapel, the tunnel is probably hidden under the altar."

"Where does it start?" Lyons asked.

"That's not quite clear," Bolan said as he pulled out a graphic of the entire castle compound and tried to make sense of it. "But at least it leads back under both the outer and inner walls."

The ground-penetrating radar plot showed depth and density as well as the form of the buried object it was looking at by shading the return. The problem in reading it came when there were too many solid objects, like rocks, piled on top of one another.

"That's good enough for me," Bolan said. "We had intended to try to make our entrance on that side anyway. If we can get through to the inner wall, we'll be halfway there."

"That does look like your way in," McCarter said. "But what if it doesn't come to the surface?"

"We'll take demo charges and make our own hole."

McCarter smiled. "So much for making a stealthy entrance."

"We'll blow our hole quietly and blame it on your demonstration out front."

"Right."

# CHAPTER TWENTY-FIVE

*Stony Man Farm*

Now that the operation was back on track, Hal Brognola had flown down to be in-house for the assault on the castle. Though their cause was just, and vitally necessary, the mood in the Annex was anything but upbeat. Along with the expected anticipatory tension that was part and parcel of every mission finale, there was a deep sense of foreboding as well. The target was chock-full of a deadly virus.

Eliminating the human perpetrators of this outrage was mandatory. Men who resorted to terrorism on this level had to die. And, when it was over, a carefully crafted version of the events that had taken place would be leaked to a selected handful of the world's governments as a warning in hopes of preventing a repeat. He was fully aware that it was a vain hope, but the effort had to be made, nonetheless.

That, however, was only part one of the exercise. The second, and even more important, thing that had to be done was the destruction or sterilization of the virus. As long as it existed, the threat remained.

No one was concerned with thoughts that the Stony Man warriors wouldn't be successful against their human enemies. The odds were great, but they had triumphed over greater many times before. This time, though, the unseeable foe might bring them low. A deadly virus wasn't brought down by a spray of full-metal-jacket rounds, nor by a well-placed grenade. After Stony Man had rendered retribution to Bladislav and his henchmen, there was still a possibility that the nuclear option would have to be employed to eradicate the virus.

Even if the containment room, or wherever the material was stored, had not been breached, as long as it existed it would remain a threat.

Brognola had pointed this out to the President earlier that day and had strongly suggested that he ready the nuclear option as a postoperation measure. It hadn't been a suggestion the Man had wanted to hear. To his credit, though, he realized the continuing threat of allowing such a bioweapon to exist. And, short of mounting a complicated, multinational, clean-up campaign, it was the quickest and most certain way to deal with it.

The president had finally agreed to seriously look into this aspect of the situation and Brognola left the White House. On the way to catch his chopper, he wished that he'd been able to convince the Man to take the nuclear option earlier. Sending the Stony Man warriors against a target that was going to be nuked anyway was a tragic lapse of logic.

AFTER WORKING THEIR WAY down the ridgeline in the dark, Bolan and Encizo held right inside the trees and surveyed the open ground between them and the chapel.

"We're ready to move out," Bolan called back to McCarter.

"Before you go," McCarter said, "scan what you can of the defensive positions on your side of the castle and GPS them so I can mark them on the HUD overlay."

Encizo clicked on his GPS and started taking readings of every enemy position he could see and transmitting them to McCarter. "That's everything we can see from here," he said.

"That helps fill it in," McCarter sent back as the positions popped up on Encizo's HUD display adding to the information that had been sent by the other commandos. "And you're good to go."

"We're on the way," Bolan sent.

The two men moved cautiously, but quickly.

There was little cover along the way, but they took advantage of what there was along with the dips in the ground to try to stay out of sight. Keeping the chapel between them and the fortress, they quickly reached the cover of its back wall. The entrance was on the side of the chapel facing the castle, and the two men kept low as they rounded the corner into the open. Finding the door not locked, they slipped on in and closed it after them.

The musty smell of old incense and burned wax was heavy inside. The interior walls of the shrine had once been adorned with icons and murals, but as expected, they had been defaced by vandals, ancient and modern. The Balkans was the historic birthplace of destroying the other guy's religious symbols. Whatever furniture might have once been present was also gone, as was everything else that could be carried off.

Only the carved stone altar remained. This massive six-by-four chunk of limestone had to have weighed several hundred pounds and was too big to have been easily destroyed or removed. Even so, it had been hacked at and pockmarked with bullet holes.

The men approached the alter, and Bolan put his right shoulder to the left front corner of the stone block. He attempted to move it aside, but it was as solid as the proverbial rock. He tried on the other front corner and got the same results.

"Try it from the back," Encizo suggested.

Again, pushing clockwise didn't budge it. But then that was the way most right-handed men would try. Shifting over to the right side, he put his left shoulder to the stone and felt it give. "Over here," he told Encizo.

It took both of them to pivot the massive stone block out of the way. Encizo's penlight showed a three-by-three hole under the base with steps cut into the stone leading down into darkness.

"We've found the tunnel," Bolan sent over the com link.

"You're clear to go," McCarter sent back. "There's no signs of movement in your sector at the moment."

With the penlight guiding them, the Stony Man warriors climbed into the tunnel. The steps ended twelve feet underground and, with no ambient light at all in the tunnel, Bolan switched to the active IR mode on his NVGs. The green glow showed the stone-lined passageway leading straight for the castle.

When he tried his com link again, the tunnel blocked both his com link with the other commandos and the GPS signal. "We're on our own," he told Encizo.

The Cuban grinned. "What's new?"

They moved out slowly in single file. They had no way of knowing if the tunnel was known to the castle's current occupants. If it was, they could expect to run into security sensors of some kind along the way.

HAWKINS HAD MANAGED to keep the dune buggy out of sight as he made a wide sweep to the south to come in on the enemy's left flank. Finding a good observation point, he and Calvin James dismounted and scanned what they could see of the enemy positions to add to the situation board. That done, they scouted out the easiest way down to the valley before going back to their vehicle.

James had his .50-caliber loaded with the HE, tracer and incendiary mix for their debut that night. The plan was that Gadgets Schwarz would open with a sound-and-light show courtesy of the ex-Romanian 128 mm rocket launcher. Eight rockets fired in pairs would cover their entry down to the valley and set them up to make their gun run across the enemy's front.

The big Fifty could deliver accurate fire well over a mile, which would keep him out of the range of small-arms return fire. He figured that Hawkins's Southern-boy moonshiner-style driving could keep them out of the sights of the 85 mm antitank guns when they made their charge.

The only thing that concerned him was that he had spotted at least two Russian-style ZU-23 twin barrel 23 mm antiaircraft guns. Though designed to kill low-flying aircraft, they also made good ground defense weapons, and they outranged his Fifty by a wide margin. If the opposition had good guncrews, this could get interesting.

On this first run, his protection from being decorated with 23 mm holes lay with Gary Manning's long-range shooting. The sniper was in position to lend a hand if the antiaircraft guns got into action. Manning had been given the GPS locations of the big guns and had put them at the top of his target list.

After their Banzai run, Schwarz would provide another eight rocket rounds to cover their withdrawal. As soon as they were out of the line of fire, Carl Lyons and Rosario Blancanales would race in and hit the other flank with their Hummer mounted 40 mm grenade launcher.

All of that was designed to keep the opposition busy while Bolan and Encizo tried to sneak into the castle. Since they couldn't talk to Bolan and know what kind of progress he was making, how effective they would be would be sheer guesswork. About the best he could say for the plan was that it looked good on paper. It reminded him, though, of gnats attacking an elephant. Futile and dangerous.

James keyed his com link. "You ready up there, Gary?"

"Gotcha covered," Manning sent back from his sniper's nest.

"You'd better be ready. I don't look good with holes in my body."

"You about ready, Gadgets?" Hawkins called.

"Locked and loaded," Schwarz replied. "Waiting on David to give me the word."

"Don't wait too long," Hawkins growled. "I just might change my mind."

ZORAN DINKIC BURST into Viktor Bladislav's command center. "General," he said. "One of the Russians in the lab reported that we have a problem down there."

"Why talk to me about it?" Bladislav replied curtly. "Get it taken care of."

Dinkic hesitated before answering. "You told me not to contact Dr. Germaine, General."

Bladislav looked puzzled for a moment. "Yes, I did.... What is the problem?"

"One of the fermenting vats is overflowing."

The ex-general rose and strapped on his pistol belt. "Let's go talk to Germaine."

As the two men hurried down to the lab, Bladislav ordered several of his Iron Guards to follow them.

They found Germaine at his desk in his small glass-walled office right outside the clean area.

Bladislav threw the door open and stormed in with Dinkic on his heels.

Germaine looked from his paperwork. "What can I do for you this evening, General?"

"Something is wrong in the lab," Bladislav snapped. "Why has something gone wrong?"

Germaine almost had a smile on his face. "And what might be wrong, General?"

"One of the Russians said the vat was overflowing."

"Did they? How strange." Germaine took off his glasses and placed them off to the side. "Give Marina my undying love, General."

Bladislav's hand flashed to the Makarov pistol in its holster, and he brought it up in one move. He fired, and the bullet drilled through the Frenchman's head, snapping it forward under the impact before he dropped face first on his desk.

Bladislav wondered why the doctor had been smiling as he'd been killed.

One of the Russian scientists working on the project rushed up to Bladislav. "We don't know what the problem is, sir," he stammered. "Something has contaminated the vaccine batch and it is ruined."

"Can it be fixed?"

The Russian hesitated. He and his comrades knew well the cost of passing on bad news to men with guns in their hands. It was a lesson every

Russian had learned well. "We are working on it at this moment, General."

"Liar," Bladislav said as he raised his pistol.

"General!" Dinkic said urgently. "With Germaine dead, you need these people."

Bladislav turned to him, his face unreadable. Dinkic backed toward the door.

"I do not need anyone," he said as he shot his operations officer in the face.

The Russian scientist turned to flee, but only collected a 9 mm bullet in the back for his efforts.

The other Russians in the lab had all ducked for cover behind the equipment.

The general looked at the weapon in his hand and slowly holstered it.

"Get these bodies out of here!" he snapped at the Iron Guard standing outside Germaine's office. "This is a lab and it must not be contaminated!"

"Yes, sir."

Just then, a pair of thunderous explosions sounded from the outer wall of the fortress. Dust showered from cracks in the stone and the lab's glassware tinkled.

Turning on his heel, Bladislav ran back up the stone steps. His Iron Guard ran after him.

# CHAPTER TWENTY-SIX

*Transylvania*

When the first pair of Gadgets Schwarz's 128 mm HE rockets roared up into the night sky, Hawkins took a deep breath and cranked up his dune buggy's engine.

"You ready, Cal?" He reached down to shift into first gear as he called up to Calvin James.

James tightened his grip on the spade grips of the .50-caliber M-2 in front of him. "Let's do it, homeboy."

Hawkins dropped the clutch and sent them skittering down the covered draw they'd scouted out into the valley. He kept to the left as he made his approach, hoping to get a little concealment from the brush-covered ridgeline.

For this little ride around, James had fitted all of the optional armor inserts into his ALOCS suit. Standing upright in the dune buggy with only the breech of the Fifty between him and a hundred

AKs, he would need all the help he could get. He tried not to think that the armor wouldn't be all that much help if he got popped by a 23 mm round.

By the time the second pair of rockets dropped out of the sky on the downside of their ballistic curve, Hawkins was within half a mile of the trenches in front of the walls.

"Do it to 'em, Cal!" he yelled.

Sighting through the night scope mounted on his gun, James laid down on the butterfly trigger and Ma Deuce begin to speak. Half-inch ball, HE, incendiary and tracer rounds fell like steel rain on the Iron Guard.

THE RUMBLE OF THE impacting 128 mm shells echoed through the stone walls of the tunnel.

"I've been keeping pace," Rafael Encizo whispered. "We should be passing under the outer wall right about now."

Bolan nodded.

A hundred yards farther on, the tunnel made a bend to the right before ending in a solid brick wall. Up close, their NVGs showed that the bricks were old, handmade, and the mortar in the joints was flaking in places.

"Damn," Encizo said as his fingers felt for gaps in the brickwork. "Look like someone did a little remodeling on the old place."

Looking up, Bolan saw a square of darkness above them. "Look up."

Encizo moved over under the hole. "Should I risk a light?" he asked.

"No," Bolan said. "Use active IR." The infrared light showed no end to the shaft, but the interior stones were uneven enough that they could be easily climbed.

"It looks like we have to go vertical," Bolan said as he reached up for a handhold.

Encizo slung his weapon over his back to follow suit.

HAWKINS WAS CONCENTRATING on his driving, trying to find the most level ground in front of him so Calvin James's hammering Fifty would do the most good. Hot brass cascaded down onto him in a steady stream, but he didn't flinch; he had driving to do.

When James sensed, more than saw, that his ammo belt was about to run out, he clicked in his com link. "Get us out of here, T.J.! I'm running dry!"

"Carl," Hawkins said into his com link as he spun the wheel and raced back out of the range of small arms fire, "we're pulling back."

"Roger. We're going in now."

Bracing his legs against the bounce of the vehicle, James opened one of the metal cans of Fifty ammo at his feet, another can of aircraft mix, and snapped it into place on the gun mount. Opening the feed tray, he pulled out the remnant of the old belt and dropped it. The new belt was laid in place and the feed tray snapped down over it.

Two pulls on the charging handle and he was back in business. "I'm up again," he yelled.

Hawkins found a dip in the ground and pulled into it.

VIKTOR BLADISLAV had rushed to the wall over the main gate and stood between the battlements like a medieval warlord to watch the battle raging on the plain below. The fact that he had his sword in his right hand and his Makarov in his left only added to the image. His radio operator, a young Iron Guardsman with no combat experience cowered behind one of the stone crenalations, hoping to stay out of the line of fire.

Even with his Russian night-vision goggles, the ex-general wasn't getting a clear picture of the size of the enemy force attacking him. The explosions and gunfire both incoming and outgoing rendered them almost useless. From the volume of the incoming muzzle-flashes, though, he felt that it was a relatively small force—maybe only thirty men—opposing him. That would square with Dinkic's contention that the American special operations unit that had been responsible for the firefight in

Budapest and the slaughter of the Romanian police in Bucharest had found him.

"Radio," he shouted over his shoulder and the radio operator stepped out to give him the handset.

"Dinkic," he screamed into it.

"He is dead, sir," the Iron Guard major who was acting as the new operations officer responded cautiously. Word of Dinkic's execution had flashed through the ranks of the Iron Guard putting everyone on edge. If Bladislav's closest comrade-in-arms could die at their leader's hands, what hope did that give the rest of them?

Bladislav seemed surprised. "How did he die?"

The major hesitated briefly. "Bravely, sir. What are your orders?"

"Get a mortar team out on the left flank," Bladislav. "Put some enfilading fire on them."

Like most of the Iron Guard officers, the major had little formal military training. He didn't know what in the hell enfilading fire was, but he knew well enough to follow orders. He didn't want to end up with a bullet in the head.

"Right away, sir."

THE ADVANCED OPTICS in the ALOCS NVGs allowed the Stony Man commandos to see clearly even with the battlefield illumination as explosive flashes and muzzle-blasts were referred to. From his sniper's nest on the east ridge Gary Manning had a good view of the proceedings in the valley below.

"We've got an assault force coming out on the right flank," he reported. "I'm counting an 82 mm mortar team, a couple of RPGs and a security squad."

"I'm on 'em," Lyons called back from the wheel of the Hummer.

"Get in there and give them a taste of the Dragon's Breath," David McCarter ordered.

Rosario Blancanales was behind the Hummer's M-19 grenade launcher and had a belt of incendiary rounds already loaded.

"We're on the way."

"I can give 'em a salvo of rockets for cover," Gadgets Schwarz suggested.

"Save those for the trenches," McCarter said. "Keep trying to take out their heavy guns."

"On the way," Schwarz replied Red Leg fashion as he hit the firing switch.

In response, the eight-barrel rocket launcher spouted rippling flame again, sending eight screaming 128 mm rockets flashing up into the air on ballistic curves. Free flight rockets weren't what one could call a pinpoint weapon, but Schwarz hoped they'd find something useful to destroy when they returned to earth.

LYONS HAD JUST cranked over the wheel of the Hummer and stood on the gas when he saw the muzzle-flash of one of the antitank guns. The 85 mm round impacted right where he would have been had he not turned.

"Gary!" he radioed. "Take that bastard out!"

"I'm on him."

Lyons abruptly swerved again, seeking a dip in the ground to hide him while Manning took out that gun crew.

Hanging on to the M-19 gun mount for dear life, Blancanales rode out Lyons's LAPD hot-pursuit-style turn.

"I'm still not in range," he said, reminding Lyons where they were supposed to be going.

"Shit!"

Lyons slammed the gearshift into first again and powered the Hummer out of his comfortable spot and aimed them at the enemy again.

"Gary," he called out, "are you on that AT gun?"

"Stay cool," Manning sent back. "And cut a hard left...now!"

Lyons did as he was told right as another high-velocity 85 mm round sang past his right front fender and exploded in a flash behind him.

"Get that fucker!" he roared.

Manning's com link was open and he heard the sniper rifle fire and cycle to load a fresh round. "...That's one," Manning said.

The antitank gun blazed again, but the round was far off target.

"That's two..." Manning said "...and three. You're clear to go ahead, Ironman."

"Gee, thanks," Lyons said. "Can I stop and clear my shorts first?"

"Better make it quick," Manning said. "That mortar crew is setting up and we don't need that."

"On the way."

THE HUMMER HAD BEEN fitted with a Spec Ops muffler, but it still wasn't completely silent, particularly when it was charging over open ground at better than fifty miles an hour. The Iron Guard sergeant in charge of the mortar and RPG detachment heard it over all the gunfire and was alarmed. With the cloud cover hiding the moon, there was no backlight to show them what kind of enemy vehicle was approaching. Or even how many of them.

"RPGs!" he yelled.

Two of his troops raised their loaded 58 mm antitank rocket launchers to their shoulders. Peering into the darkness through their optics they saw nothing, so they aimed at the oncoming sound. Suddenly, the sound changed as if the vehicle had slowed or turned.

LYONS LOCKED THE BREAKS and cranked the wheel, slewing the Hummer around to the right.

Blancanales had been expecting him to pull that one, though, and rode out the turn. When the dust cleared from in front of his NVGs, he had his target locked and pressed the trigger on the M-19. The characteristic heavy cough of the 40 mm round sounded loud as he traversed the weapon from left to right. Fifty meters out of the muzzle, the 40 mm Dragon's Breath rounds detonated.

It looked like an ancient god was throwing fiery thunderbolts into the night. But these thunderbolts flew in straight, ordered lines and washed flame over everything they touched.

The first tongue of flame washed over one of the Iron Guard RPG teams preparing to fire at the Hummer. The intense heat set off the rocket warheads in the launch tubes, but the sound of their detonation was lost in the screams of the crew.

The Dragon's Breath also touched the ready-to-fire pile of 82 mm mortar rounds next to the tube. Their detonation sent a sheet of red-hot frag slashing into the crew, flaying them.

The Iron Guard would stand and fight against anyone armed with normal weapons, but they broke and ran like schoolgirls when the Dragon roared.

Blancanales sent a few more rounds after them before shifting his aim to the trenches beyond.

THE ENEMY'S FOCUSING its attention on the Hummer created an opening for the dune buggy to come in again on the other flank. "Go for it again," James called out to Hawkins behind the wheel. "Run across their front."

Hawkins grabbed first gear and spun his tires as the nimble little battle car leaped forward. "How do you want to do it this time?" he asked.

"What ever looks easiest!" James replied. "But don't get too damned close."

"Hang on!"

When he spotted a clump of Iron Guard in his NVGs he headed straight for them.

With a five-hundred round belt of aircraft ammo mix in his breech, James laid down on the butterfly trigger. He was walking the Fifty's fire across the top of the trenches when he saw the twinkle of a muzzle-blast from the berm line. The combat center in his brain identified it as being from a machinegun, probably a 7.62 mm PKM. The thinking part of his brain also told him that it was far too late to duck.

Hawkins saw the tracers flash over his head and couldn't help ducking as James grunted over the com link. He spun the battle car and floored it.

Finding a dip in the ground, he hit the brakes, skidded to a halt in it and turned in his seat. "Cal?"

"I'm okay," James said. "The armor soaked up most of it."

"You sure?"

"Keep going, dammit!"

Hawkins hit the gas and they were rolling again.

McCARTER HAD ARMED himself for his solo evening's activities with Calvin James's OICW and all the 20 mm ammunition he could carry. With his ALOCS suit dialed up for night camo effect, he had been able to provide a little high-powered, close-in sniping to back up Gary Manning's long range surgical shooting.

He was a hundred yards from the Iron Guard's front line trace when he saw the machine-gun nest open up on Hawkins's dune buggy. Flipping the weapon's selector switch to 20 mm feed, he selected the airburst mode and targeted it for a 3-round burst.

The 20 mm rounds blossomed into deadly frag right over the gun crew. The wire frag struck like hundreds of hornets with razor-sharp stingers. One strike hurt and drew blood, but take too many and one would kill. These men were riddled and died in place.

With the MG crew out of action, McCarter selected HE PD and sent the rest of the magazine on the weapon itself.

Satisfied with his effort, he went hunting for other machine guns they might have emplaced.

# CHAPTER TWENTY-SEVEN

*Transylvania*

After speeding completely out of range of small-arms fire, Hawkins pulled his dune buggy behind a rise in the ground to check on Calvin James.

"You okay, buddy?" he asked as he started to get out of his seat.

"I'm okay, man, I'm okay." James took a deep breath. "Damn! I'm gonna be bruised like a mother in the morning, but the armor held up."

"Let me take a look."

"I said I'm okay, dammit. I need to reload the gun."

"Okay."

Not wanting to argue, Hawkins dropped back into his seat to give James room to feed a fresh belt into his smoking Fifty. The barrel wasn't glowing the characteristic dull red of being shot out yet, so they were still in business.

"Let's do it again," James said when he was

done. "But take it slowly on the approach this time, okay?"

Taking advantage of every bit of cover and concealment the terrain offered, they pulled to within five hundred yards of the trenches. Hawkins was ready to break into the open and start his run when James yelled down for him to stop.

When the dune buggy slammed to a halt, James clicked in his com link. "David," he said, "I've got a bunch of people heading toward us with their hands up. It looks like they're trying to give it up."

"Aw, shit!" Hawkins exploded. He'd been concentrating so hard on driving that he'd missed seeing them. "What are we gonna do with those dickheads? This ain't the regular army or the UN."

"Round 'em up, but be careful," McCarter replied. "I'll ask the Farm what they want us to do with them."

"Have you heard from Striker?" Hawkins asked.

McCarter paused a second before answering. "Not yet."

PUSHING HER HEADSET back on her head, Barbara Price turned to Hal Brognola. "The Iron Guard's starting to surrender, about a dozen of them, and David wants to know what you want to do with them."

Brognola bit his lip in frustration. He wasn't by

nature a bloodthirsty man. He wasn't in this business to kill anyone and he'd be quite glad never to have to preside over another Stony Man operation again. The harsh realities of the world, however, meant that he wouldn't be out of work any time soon. And part of this work was counting bodies.

In of itself, that wasn't all that difficult a job. Just as long as they were all enemy bodies. Counting prisoners, though, was a bitch.

The Stony Man commandos were a strike team. They didn't have a battalion of MPs waiting in the wings to take over when some moron decided that he'd had enough and threw down his gun. And there was no barbed wire compound in a secure rear area guarded by machine guns to make sure that these guys stayed nice. Men who'd changed their minds once when things got too hot, might very well change them back again when things didn't look that bad.

When Price shot him a look, he shrugged. "Tell them to do what's required."

"That's not an answer, Hal, and you know it."

"You know what I mean."

"I need it for the record," she said.

Which was a nice way of saying that it was his rear on the line this time along with the guys in the field. Which, of course, was how it should be. It was the only way he could share some of the consequences of the action teams, and he was proud to do it.

"Okay—" he straightened in his chair "—Barbara, tell David that the action teams are to take prisoners only if it doesn't impede the conduct of their mission. Completion of the mission has absolute priority."

That was straight out of a classified MACV-SOG operations order from a cross border raid in Vietnam he'd come across in the archives. If it had been good enough back then, it should cover the situation now. It also gave the guys cover in case they did have to waste a few Iron Guard who might have a second change of heart.

"Yes, sir," he thought he heard her say. But, since he'd never heard her use the *s* word before, his ears had to have been playing tricks on him.

"If you like, I'll confirm that through the President, Barbara."

"That's okay. You said it and that's good enough for me."

Pulling her comset back down, she passed Brognola's orders on to Romania.

THE GROUP OF IRON GUARDS approaching the dune buggy with their hands in the air numbered an even dozen. Even through the NVGs, Hawkins saw that they were young, and they looked scared. That was a dangerous combination, and he needed to defuse this thing as soon as he could. He didn't speak much Russian and zero Romanian, but his ALOCS suit and the assault rifle in his hand would speak loudly enough for him.

Sliding out of his seat, he held up his left hand in the universal sign to halt and they did.

"Okay, guys," he said, trying to sound friendly, "let's just take it easy, okay? You'll be okay."

Damned near everyone in the world knew what "okay" meant and hopefully the ubiquitous Yankee word would have reached this far into the Balkans.

"Does anyone speak English?" Hawkins asked.

A young man stepped forward. "I speak some."

"Well, now, that's good. I need you to translate for me. Tell your teammates that you're all safe now. You'll be searched and released. When you're released, you're to walk south as quickly as you can and keep walking for at least two miles—about five kilometers I guess. Anyone who turns back this way, even for a quick look, will be immediately killed. We have snipers on the ridgelines who will watch over you until you reach the end of the valley."

When the words were translated, the Iron Guardsmen had no trouble believing that slight exaggeration. Many of their officers and NCOs had been struck down by bullets they hadn't heard fired.

"When my men search you, do not move. Stand still and you will not be hurt." Hawkins slung his assault rifle over his shoulder and loosened his pistol in his holster.

With James and the big Fifty guarding his back, Hawkins quickly patted down the first of his charges. Up close, he could smell their fear and knew that signaled the danger he was in. Frightened men did things impulsively.

After clearing his man, he turned him toward the south and patted him on the back. "Go." He kept his voice low as he gave a gentle shove. "It's okay. Start walking."

The words were translated, and the freed prisoner took a few cautious steps. When he wasn't gunned down he took off running. The other prisoners anxiously watched him go until he was lost in the darkness. Excited chatter swept through them when they realized that they, too, might live through the night. Some smiled through their tears. Viktor Bladislav's dreams of Serbian glory didn't mean much to men who just wanted to live.

AFTER CLIMBING A FEW FEET into the opening above the tunnel, Bolan and Encizo found iron grab bars set into the stones as steps. From there, it was an easy climb. At what should have been the third floor, they saw a three-by-three iron door set into the stonework.

Bolan paused and pushed on the door. It resisted for a moment before slowly opening on rusted hinges onto a huge fireplace. The room he could see beyond was empty, but showed signs of having been occupied recently. He cautiously exited the fireplace and quickly crossed to the room's door and shot the lock.

"David," Bolan whispered over the com link.

"The walls must still be blocking us," he told Encizo when the Cuban joined him. "We'll head for the basement anyway."

Cracking the room's door open onto a hallway, Bolan saw that it was clear and motioned Encizo to follow him. At the end of the hall, they found a stone stairway leading down and took it. They were on a dimly lit landing on the next floor when the clatter of boots echoing on stone steps sent them hiding in the shadows. Encizo shot two fingers out and wiped them across his upper arm.

Bolan nodded, confirming two men and the need for silent kills.

The Beretta 93-R's sound suppressor was attached and the selector switch thumbed down to single shot. The Executioner was ready and signaled that he'd take the man farther away. Encizo's over-and-under combo wasn't silenced, so he drew his fighting knife from his boot top.

If they waited for the two men to pass their hiding place so they could take them from behind, they risked being seen. This would be an in-your-face takedown.

Bolan snapped his fingers out in a countdown, one…two…three, before taking his man from where he stood with a silenced 9 mm round to the head.

Encizo stepped out in front of his man, his knife arching from the low position plunging in right under the rib cage and angled upward for the heart. The guard's eyes squinted with the momentary pain before going blank. The shout he tried to make died in his throat.

The commandos held still for a moment to make sure that those two had been alone before stuffing the bodies in their former hiding place.

Encizo glanced down the stairs and Bolan nodded.

THE FIRST GROUP of Iron Guard leaving their trenches with their hands up was all Viktor Bladislav had needed to see. Treacherous bastards every one of them. He was fated to be surrounded by traitors instead of true Serbs fighting for their freedom.

Drawing his sword, he turned to his new operations officer who had his back turned while speaking on the radio. Raising the sword over his head, he chopped down, cleaving the man's head in two.

The young radioman screamed when the major's

blood splattered on him, so Bladislav killed him, as well.

Taking the radio from the corpse at his feet, he keyed the handset. "This is Bladislav," he transmitted on his command frequency. "Pull back to the inner wall. We will regroup there and continue the fight."

As he watched, the Iron Guard left their positions and started streaming in through the main gate. What he didn't see was that for every two men who obeyed his orders, another one of them slipped away in the darkness.

WITH THE IRON GUARD deserting their trenches, the Stony Man commandos had to change their tactics from drive-by attacks to storming a walled fortress to finish this up.

"You want me to drop a few 128s in the middle of that place?" Gadgets Schwarz asked when McCarter ordered them to close in. "You know, to cover you on the way in?"

"No! If one of them lands where they're storing that bloody virus we'll all die," McCarter snapped.

"Good point."

"Carl," McCarter called, "swing over here and pick up me and Gadgets. We need to get in there before they get their act together."

"How about picking me up, too, guys?" Gary Manning called from his last sniper's nest. "At least get me in closer so I can clear the walls for you.''

"I'll get you," Lyons answered.

A YOUNG LIEUTENANT, Bladislav's newest second in command and his third for the evening, snapped to attention and saluted as he reported to his general.

"Thirty-three of the Iron Guard are still with you, General," the lieutenant said proudly. "They have vowed on their father's graves to fight the Yankees to the death.''

"Very good," Bladislav replied. "Tell them that their sacrifices will be remembered. Make sure that you get each man's name and give it to me.''

"Yes, sir.''

"Tell them that I expect the Yankees to try to storm the castle, but they must be turned back. The future of Greater Serbia depends on what we do here tonight. Tell them that when the sun rises in the morning, our proud flag must still be flying.''

The young officer was worried more about his being able to breathe without bleeding in the morning, but he would mention the flag to his men.

"I will be sure tell them that, General.''

Bladislav laid his hand on the hilt of his sword. "Make sure that you do.''

The lieutenant saluted. "Yes, General.''

Bladislav watched him go and hoped that it

wouldn't become necessary to kill him, too. He seemed like a true Serbian patriot.

"OKAY," McCARTER SAID once all of the Stony Man warriors had cleared the now empty trenches and gathered on each side of the open main gate, "here's the drill. I want only a driver and a gunner on each vehicle when we go in. Everyone else will go in on foot. Their hearts don't seem to be in dying here for Bladislav, so I think if we keep pressing them, but give them a way out, they'll fold."

"And if they don't wanna play softball once they're behind the walls?" Hawkins asked.

"We go in hard."

"Man, I was afraid you were gonna say that."

The vehicles were their only heavy firepower, but Hawkins really would have rather been alone on his feet with just his rifle for protection. Driving through that massive main gate of the outer walls was too much like putting a spotlight on a sign on top of his head reading Please Shoot Me.

Taking a deep breath, Hawkins dropped the clutch when the Briton signaled. He had just pulled up to the open gate when James screamed "RPG!" and ripped off a punishing burst from his .50-caliber. The heavy slugs chewed into the stonework and the would-be RPG gunner. His riddled body fell from between the battlements.

Lyons had the Hummer alongside in a flash and McCarter jumped out, the vehicle's external speaker activated. "Men of the Iron Guard," he said, his passable Russian echoing from the stone walls, "we have no quarrel with you. You have been betrayed by a madman. There is no reason for you to die here. We want Bladislav, but if you put down your weapons, you can go free."

For a long moment, there was no movement on the walls. Then, one man threw his AK down from the walls. It was followed by several others.

THE BRITON'S AMPLIFIED words echoed inside the castle as well, and the young officer who Viktor Bladislav had appointed to be his operations officer heard them. A day earlier, he would have been proud to serve beside the great man. But that had been before the general had gone mad and turned on his own.

A quick glance showed him that he was both relatively alone as well as close to a sally port leading outside. The general was momentarily occupied waving his sword while he gave orders to a group of nervous Iron Guardsmen.

Acting on impulse more than anything else, the officer dashed for the half-open sally port. It was only thirty yards, but he expected to feel a bullet slamming into his back with every step. When he cleared the door, he lit out for the outer wall in a sprint.

One of the Iron Guardsmen on the inner wall spotted the lieutenant slipping away in the dark. He elbowed his comrade and shrugged. The other man nodded, and they, too, left their positions to make a break for freedom.

# CHAPTER TWENTY-EIGHT

*Transylvania*

When the hammering of Calvin James's Fifty sounded inside the castle, Encizo and Bolan dropped caution and raced the rest of the way down the stone stairwell. The lab, if it was in this pile of stone, would probably be in the basement. After a final turn, the stairs ended at a modern steel door set into the ancient rock wall. Encizo stood ready while Bolan tried the door and found it unlocked.

Easing it open, the soldier saw a modern, well lit, but almost deserted scientific facility. Seven men in white lab coats cowered in one corner of the room, their hands held above their heads. A quick look around showed that the scientists were alone.

Bolan stepped into the lab with Encizo close behind. "Out!" he shouted in Russian. "Go!"

Hesitantly, the men started for the elevator at the other end of the basement.

"Run!" Bolan roared.

The Russians ran.

"All that just to find this," Encizo said as he looked around the newly deserted lab. "Now what do we do with it?"

"Go out front," Bolan replied, "and get a couple of the guys down here to secure this place. Make sure they don't mess with anything, just guard it."

"Where're you going?"

The Executioner smiled grimly. "I'm going to talk to the general."


WHEN THE MAIN GATE to the castle's inner wall slowly opened, Calvin James trained his Fifty on it. A lone man walked out weaponless with his hands in the air.

"Come forward," McCarter said, beckoning.

The man started forward and several others appeared behind him. That few soon became two dozen men standing in the glare of the headlights from the two Stony Man vehicles. "Keep your hands up while my men search you," McCarter said in basic Russian. "When they are done with you, you will be free to go. Move straight out of the fortress and keep on going."

Leaving James and Blancanales on two vehicle-mounted weapons, the others fanned out and started patting down the enemy. As soon as they cleared a man, they sent him on his way.

"You guys got those bozos under control?" the commandos heard Encizo's voice over their com links.

"We've got it." McCarter looked up and saw Encizo in the castle gate. "What'd you need?"

"We located the lab in the basement and we need to secure it ASAP. Can you spare me a couple of warm bodies?"

"T.J., Cal," McCarter called out.

"We're on it," Hawkins replied as he stepped back and swung around his assault rifle. "Let's go, Rafe."

"Where's Striker?" McCarter asked.

"He's rat hunting," Encizo replied as he ducked back inside.

Ex-General Viktor Bladislav hurried through the stone corridors of his castle to his office alone. Marina had betrayed him, Germaine had betrayed him, Zoran Dinkic had betrayed him and now the rest of his Iron Guard had done the same. He was alone as he had been at the start of his struggle to redeem and glorify the Serbian people.

He was alone, but he was still alive and as long as he was, he would have vengeance on those who had betrayed him, Serbs and Westerners alike. He was still lord of a massive European operation that brought him millions of U.S. dollars a year, and that power base would launch him again on his quest. The master plan for his empire was in his office, and he had to retrieve it along with the radio he needed to call his chopper to come and pick him up.

He'd leave for the mountains and the chopper would pick him up there. A few hours' flight would have him back in Milan or one of his other offices. He'd have to rebuild his staff before he could assert himself again, and he was already running a list of names of subordinates through his mind.

Bladislav snapped back to his surroundings when a figure in black suddenly appeared out of the shadows in front of him. "Viktor Bladislav," the figure said.

The general's hand snaked down to the hilt of his sword. He had seen these figures around the castle before, usually out of the corner of his eyes. He had heard the tales of the night stalkers of old and rightfully feared them. He knew that they had preyed on the Turks during the wars of his ancestors, but were said to kill Christians as well. It was also said that they couldn't be stopped by mere bullets.

The sword at his side had been blessed by a

saint, and its holy steel would defend him even from a vampire.

Drawing the blade, he held it hilt upright and kissed the cross formed by the guard.

"I fear no man!" he shouted as he raised the sword over his head.

A massive blow to the chest pushed him back and the sword fell from his hands. He barely had time to form a question in his mind before it went black.

Bolan stepped forward, his Desert Eagle still trained on the Serb. There was no need for an insurance shot, the .44-caliber slug had torn out his heart.

"And look where it got you," Bolan said as he kicked the sword out of the way.

THE LAST OF THE Iron Guardsmen were marching out the fortress gate when Bolan appeared in the castle's open door. "David," he called out, "we're clear. Bladislav's history. Let's go. What's the word on nuking this place to destroy that damned virus?"

"I'll check on that," McCarter said as he keyed his sat com link. "We didn't come all this way to just walk off and leave it unguarded."

THE STONY MAN Annex crew was all smiles, but Hal Brognola had an odd expression on his face when he put down the hot-line phone. "There will be no nuclear sterilizing strike."

Barbara Price couldn't believe her ears. "What's he going to do about that place, then? If I remember correctly, there's a stockpile of mutated smallpox stored there."

"There is." Brognola shrugged. "He's got an entire biowar material team complete with a battalion of paratroopers standing by to go in and take care of it."

"But what about Romania's national sovereignty and all that diplomatic bullshit we hear about all the time?"

Brognola shrugged. "Apparently the Romanians are on board with it now that Bladislav's out of the picture."

"So it's over."

He nodded.

"Right," she snorted. "I've heard that one before. They carry it all away and put it somewhere real safe. I mean, everyone wants bioweapon stocks kept under strict control so half of the population doesn't get wiped out."

Brognola frowned. "Won't that take care of it?"

"Until the damned stuff just happens to show up in the hands of some other megalomanic terrorist."

There was nothing Brognola could answer to that.

At least a CDC team would be able to develop a vaccine, hopefully in time to save some of the crew of the *Bunker Hill*. He took comfort in that. At least it was something.

# DEATH LANDS®

## Hellbenders

*Available in March 2004
at your favorite retail outlet.*

Emerging from a gateway into a redoubt filled with preDark technology, Ryan and his band hope to unlock some of the secrets of post-nuclear America. But the fortified redoubt is under the control of a half-mad former sec man hell-bent on vengeance, who orders Ryan and the others to jump-start his private war against two local barons. Under the harsh and pitiless glare of the rad-blasted desert sun, the companions fight to see another day, whatever it brings....

---